market street

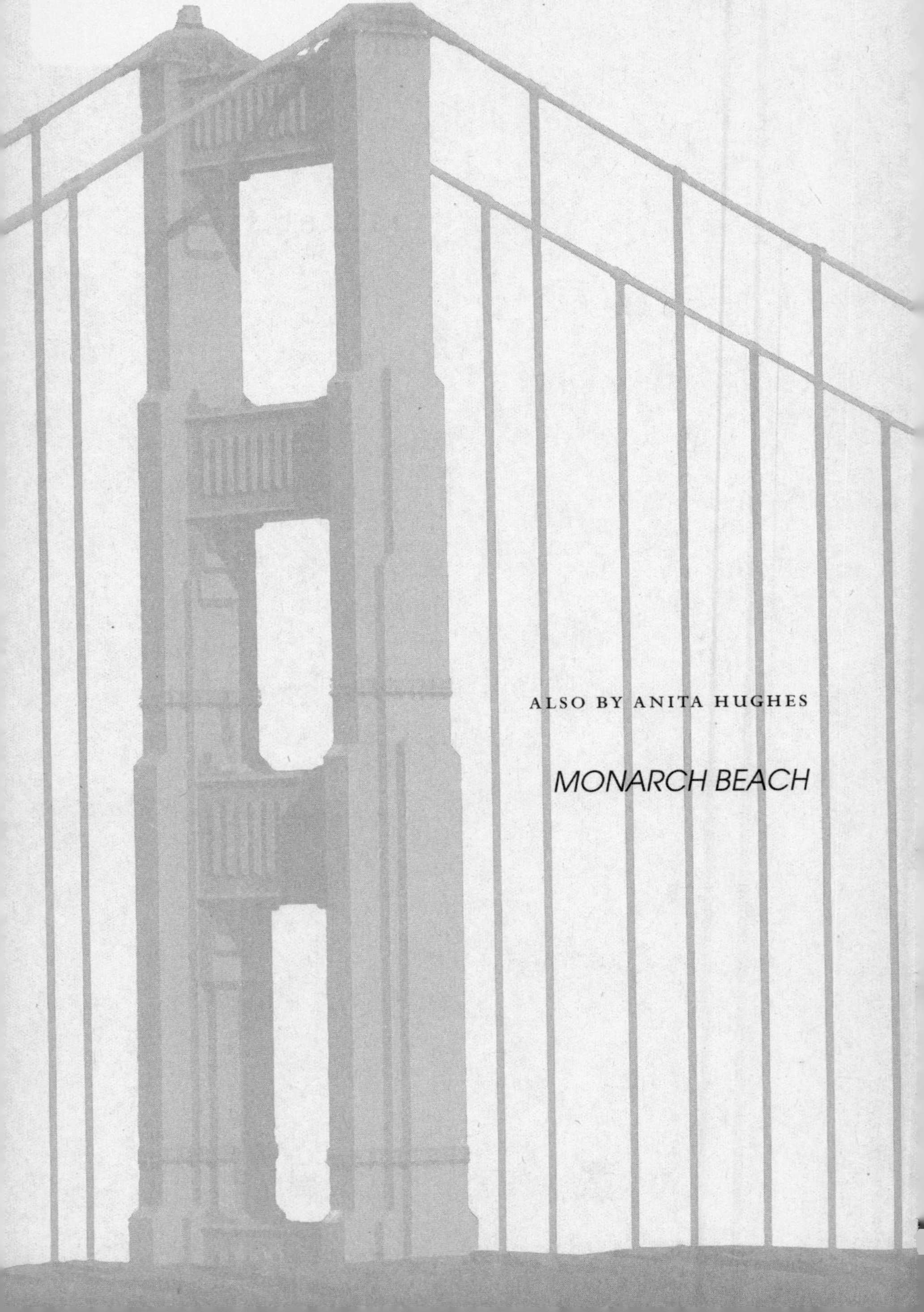

ALSO BY ANITA HUGHES

MONARCH BEACH

market street

ANITA HUGHES

 ST. MARTIN'S GRIFFIN NEW YORK

MARKET STREET. Copyright © 2013 by Anita Hughes. All rights reserved. Printed in the United States of America. For information, address St. Martin's Press, 175 Fifth Avenue, New York, N.Y. 10010.

www.stmartins.com

Design by Meryl Sussman Levavi

Library of Congress Cataloging-in-Publication Data

Hughes, Anita, 1963–
    Market Street / Anita Hughes.—First Edition.
        pages cm
    ISBN 978-0-312-64333-1 (trade pbk.)
    ISBN 978-1-250-02039-0 (e-book)
    1 Women—California—San Francisco—Fiction.   2. Heiresses—Fiction.
3. Female friendship—Fiction.   4. Self-realization in women—Fiction.
I. Title.
    PS3608.U356755M37 2013
    813'.6—dc23

                                                          2013002660

St. Martin's Griffin books may be purchased for educational, business, or promotional use. For information on bulk purchases, please contact Macmillan Corporate and Premium Sales Department at 1-800-221-7945 extension 5442 or write specialmarkets@macmillan.com.

First Edition: March 2013

10 9 8 7 6 5 4 3 2 1

To Vera and Rudi

market street

1.

Cassie tore the edge off her croissant and looked out the Fenton's department store's floor-to-ceiling windows at the street below. Christmas was over, the post-Christmas sales were limping to a close, and men and women walked with their coats wrapped around them. The giant tree in Union Square had been carted away. The dazzling window displays in Gucci and Chanel of Cinderella slippers studded with real diamonds to wear to holiday parties and little black dresses accessorized with stacks of multi-colored bracelets had been replaced with sensible January displays: rain boots, umbrellas, and floor-length winter coats. Even Burberry's window looked bleak. The sweet reindeer wearing a plaid sweater and socks had been exchanged for a faceless mannequin wrapped in scarves like a mummy.

"People in San Francisco don't know how to do winter," Cassie said, dipping her croissant into a white Limoges coffee cup. "They think California in January should be blue skies and seventy degrees."

"We could go to Mexico till March. Stay at Betsy's condo

and sip sangria through pink plastic straws." Alexis picked a petit four from the silver tray on the table and bit into it tentatively. She blotted her lips on the white linen napkin and stirred cream into her demitasse.

"Some people have jobs," Cassie replied, "or at least their husbands work. You don't just jet off to Mexico because the Christmas ornaments are gone."

"Carter would never miss me. He's too busy trimming trees, or whatever he does from six in the morning till midnight. We haven't eaten dinner together since Thanksgiving, and that was only because his mother insisted we join the family in Pacific Heights. You know old Betsy's on her second husband since Carter and I got married. I don't know how she keeps the place cards straight." Alexis tapped her long French-manicured nails on the edge of the coffee cup.

"Your husband runs a hedge fund; he doesn't trim trees." Cassie collapsed in a fit of giggles. She dusted croissant flakes from her pants and glanced around to see if the society matrons sitting at the adjoining tables were listening.

"Trees, hedges, it's all the same to Carter. Money is the only kind of paper he knows. He does compensate well. I got some lovely baubles for Christmas." Alexis rolled her eyes.

"You don't have to pretend with me. We've known each other since kindergarten and even then you made rings out of Cheerios. Be happy Carter buys you jewelry."

"He does have great taste. He gave me the most beautiful sapphire necklace, with tiny diamonds like snowflakes. I just sometimes feel like a courtesan instead of a wife. Fling a necklace or a bracelet at me and bring me out to impress the midwestern clients who want to invest in pork futures," Alexis replied, twisting her diamond wedding band around her finger.

"Carter loves you, it's just his way of showing it. Most wives would be envious," Cassie replied.

"I take it Aidan didn't shower you with jewels?" Alexis raised her perfectly arched eyebrows.

"Fuzzy socks, a cashmere scarf, gardening gloves, and packets of exotic vegetable seeds: fennel, purple spinach, and okra." Cassie counted presents on her fingers.

Alexis picked up another petit four, eyed the layered chocolate, and put it back on the plate. "I've exceeded my caloric limit for the day. Lettuce and soy sauce for dinner tonight."

"You're the only person I know who loses weight over the holidays. I gained three pounds smelling the pumpkin pie." Cassie pushed the plate of mini desserts toward Alexis.

"Only because I swam forty laps before every holiday party and spent thirty minutes in the steam room each night," Alexis said, adjusting her skirt. She wore an emerald green miniskirt and a white angora wool sweater. Her blond hair was scooped into a high ponytail and tied with a green velvet ribbon.

"Oh, to have your own indoor swimming pool and sauna." Cassie finished her coffee and put her napkin on the table.

"You could have all that. As I recall you did have all that. You're the one who married the Communist professor."

"Aidan is not a Communist. He's a professor of ethics, which means he doesn't believe in excess. We live well, just not in a three-story mansion in Presidio Heights with an elevator."

"If you'd gone to UCLA with me instead of Berkeley we would have found you a nice movie star to marry. I remember the day you packed your car and headed over the Bay Bridge. I thought, why is Cassandra Fenton, heiress to San Francisco's oldest, most exclusive department store, going to school in Bezerkely? I was right, you know." Alexis eyed her friend objectively. "Your Tod's are as old as my college diploma and your Michael Kors jacket is vintage. Except it's only had one owner: you."

"I've never had your flair. You could shop at Target and come out dressed for dinner at Chez Panisse. I've always been happier wearing gardening gloves than opera gloves. I am happy, Alexis, and so are you." Cassie played with the cuff of her shirt, twisting off a few stray threads.

"What would we talk about if we didn't complain about our husbands?" Alexis shrugged, sifting through her purse for a tube of lip gloss.

"The homeless on Market Street, the lack of fresh water in Africa?" Cassie suggested.

"We could always talk about shoes." Alexis stood up and pulled her skirt over her thighs. "Let's stop downstairs and see if there are any Jimmy Choos left on the sale rack."

Cassie followed Alexis to the escalator and surveyed the elegant floor displays as they descended to the third floor. The fourth level had always been her favorite; her mother used to treat her to high tea in the café on weekdays after school. Cassie thought every third-grader practiced their cursive on a linen tablecloth while sipping hot chocolate served by uniformed waitresses. Her mother would leave her in the café while she prowled the other departments, making sure cashmere sweaters were stacked in neat piles and salesgirls holding bottles of Chanel No. 5 were positioned in the aisles.

"Cassie, how nice to see you." A tall man wearing a navy suit took Cassie's hand as the escalator deposited them on the third floor. "You just missed your mother. She had to rush off to a restaurant opening. Emerald on Post Street. The *Chronicle* says it's going to be the next dining destination in the city."

"My mother's always rushing around." Cassie smiled. "I saw her on the way up. Do you remember my friend Alexis?"

The man put on rimless glasses and looked closely at the two women. "Of course. The last time I saw you, you were being trailed by half a dozen bridesmaids collecting cosmetics samples."

"I'm an old married woman now"—Alexis grinned—"with spending power."

"In that case, let me direct you to our newest jewelry line. I'm told all the thirtysomethings are wearing it." The man extended his arm and navigated Alexis through the aisles full of shoppers to a large glass case at the front of the store.

Cassie and Alexis gazed in the glass like small children admiring Halloween candy. Rows of pendants, bracelets, and rings were displayed on a bed of crushed orange velvet. Cassie ignored the bracelets—they would be covered with potting soil within a day—but the pendants caught her attention: bright-colored stones on short filigree chains. She put her hand to her neck as if imagining she was wearing one.

"These are right up your alley." Alexis tapped her nail on the glass. "That one would go so well with your eyes, Cassie. Try it on."

"Okay, just for fun." Cassie nodded. "Derek, could I see that one?"

Derek unlocked the case with an oversized gold key and placed the pendant in Cassie's hand. "Your mother found these on a buying trip to Buenos Aires. They are *the* accessory on the polo fields this season."

Alexis watched Cassie click the pendant around her neck. The stone was a turquoise amethyst and made Cassie's eyes look like a powder blue sky.

"Take it home," Alexis insisted. "Tell Aidan you did your

own post-Christmas shopping so he wouldn't feel guilty for getting you fuzzy socks."

"He didn't only get me fuzzy socks. But it is really pretty." Cassie leaned closer to the mirror.

"He can't complain about excess since it's not a diamond or a ruby. And you'd be supporting the Latin American economy. He'll be pleased." Alexis took a few bracelets out of the case and slipped them on her wrist.

"I don't need it," Cassie said uncertainly. She wasn't very interested in clothes and usually pulled whatever was clean and pressed out of her closet, but she loved colorful jewelry. When she was a teenager her mother brought home bags of necklaces, earrings, and broaches, and Cassie was allowed to pick what she wanted. She still kept them in heart-shaped jewelry boxes and would snap in a hair clip or put on dangly earrings when she drove into the city for lunch.

"Would you two girls mind watching the display for a moment? I just saw Mrs. Benson go up the escalator. She's one of our best customers but she's almost deaf and she tends to scare the salespeople." Derek put the gold key on the glass.

"We'll do anything if you call us girls." Alexis smiled, putting the bracelets back in the case and scooping up a selection of colored rings.

"I can't believe you're flirting with Derek. He's almost a hundred. He used to hold my hand when my mother sent me to sit on Santa Claus's lap. I thought Santa had spiders under his beard and I'm terrified of spiders." Cassie unsnapped the pendant and laid it on the crushed velvet.

"Excuse me, I need to make a return." A girl approached the counter clutching a plain brown shopping bag. She had short blond hair cut in feathery layers around her face and big brown eyes like the dolls Cassie collected when she was a child. She wore a T-shirt emblazoned with Chinese letters and an army green bomber jacket.

"We don't work here." Alexis shook her head, stepping back from the counter.

"The store manager just went upstairs. I can try to find another salesperson for you; they're all busy taking returns. Post-Christmas hazard." Cassie smiled, seeing the girl's face fall. She clutched her shopping bag tighter. Her nails were painted neon pink and she wore a macramé bracelet.

"Crap. My roommate gave me a ride. She's double-parked outside, probably going to get a ticket. The meter maids were circling like vultures around a carcass. I don't know when I'll make it down here again. I never shop in Union Square, let alone Fenton's." The girl drawled the name of the department store as if it was a foreign language.

"We don't work here, but Cassie owns the place. I bet she can process a return for you." Alexis nodded at Cassie.

"My mother owns it." Cassie blushed. She felt like people had been saying that since she was seven years old, when her mother would dress her up in a Chanel suit and black patent-leather Mary Janes and guide her through the departments introducing her to her best customers.

"Please, my roommate will kill me if she gets a ticket. It's her mother's car and she doesn't even know we borrowed it." The girl opened the bag and took out a red satin box imprinted with the trademark Fenton signature.

"Oh, one of these lovely pendants." Alexis picked up the box. "Why would you want to return it? These are going to be a must-have."

"To be honest I could use the money. It was a present and I figured anything in a Fenton's box must be pricey. No offense." The girl looked at Cassie and clapped her hand over her mouth. "It's really nice but I'm a student. I could use a bit of cash."

"Do you have a receipt?" Cassie asked awkwardly. She pulled her long bangs over her ears the way she did when she was nervous. She had tried manning different counters in the afternoons during high school—cosmetics, handbags, Godiva chocolates—but she had never felt comfortable taking other people's money. "You're giving them a bit of their dreams," her mother would coach her, but Cassie always felt the dreams came with a high price tag. She wondered how women could justify paying so much for elaborate gold boxes containing four pieces of chocolate.

"It was a present," the girl repeated, "but maybe you have the credit card on file. The name was Blake, Aidan Blake." The girl kept glancing around, as if one of the uniformed meter maids was going to appear and arrest her for double parking.

"Excuse me," Cassie said.

"Aidan Blake, Professor Aidan Blake actually, but I doubt it says that on the credit card. I guess physicians put 'Doctor' in front of their names but it would seem a bit silly for a professor to, wouldn't it?" The girl looked from Cassie to Alexis as if she was very interested in their opinion.

"Where did you get this?" Cassie held the box at arm's length as if it was a stick of dynamite.

"I told you it was a present. Do you think I stole it or something?" The girl stepped back from the counter. "I may not look like a Fenton's customer but I'm not a thief. It was a Christmas present, from a friend," she finished, her round cheeks turning a light shade of pink.

"How do you know this friend?" Alexis demanded, glancing at Cassie, whose face had turned white.

"We don't give cash refunds, only store credit," Cassie said automatically. She gripped the side of the display case, pressing her knuckles against the glass. Every nerve in her body tingled, as if someone set off a fire alarm only she could hear.

"You two treat customers pretty funny." The girl frowned. "I thought Fenton's was all about customer service. I've seen the ads online: 'Don't just walk the red carpet; take it home with you. At Fenton's every customer is a star.' Hardly." The girl pushed the box into the shopping bag. "Store credit isn't going to do much. What am I going to buy? A two-hundred-dollar pair of seamless stockings? A Marc Jacobs hairbrush? I'll probably never come to Union Square again; I'm obviously not welcome."

"Wait." Cassie exhaled, feeling as though something heavy was sitting on her chest. "I'll give you cash. Here, give me the box."

"Okay." The girl stopped, eyeing Cassie suspiciously. "I want a full refund. I bet it was expensive."

Cassie opened the cash register and extracted three fifty-dollar bills. "Take these." She slid them over the counter.

The girl's eyes opened wide. She picked up the bills and crinkled the edges with her fingers. "I don't think it was that much. I mean, shouldn't you look up the credit card or look at the price tags on the other necklaces?"

"Take the money and leave." Alexis walked to the front of the case. She was almost six feet in her four-inch Prada heels and her body was muscled and lean from hours in the pool and on her bicycle. She stood so close to the girl she could see the brown roots at the top of her head.

"I'm leaving." The girl stuffed the money in her jeans pocket and moved away from Alexis. "You're lucky I don't go on Yelp or something. But thanks for the refund, I hope it doesn't all go to the meter maid."

Alexis walked back to Cassie and put her hand on her shoulder. "Breathe," she said quietly.

"I can't." Cassie's voice was like a robot. "I need some fresh air."

"You're not following her." Alexis grabbed Cassie's sleeve. "We need to sit down in private. Let's go to your mother's office."

Cassie followed Alexis to the private elevator in the back of the store, clutching the red Fenton's box that held the pendant. She felt as though her knees would buckle at any moment and she'd crumple to the floor like an anorexic Victoria's Secret model. She closed her eyes as the elevator doors shut, wishing everything would stay black and the elevator would just keep going up and up and up.

"Cassie"—Alexis poked her with one long fingernail— "get a grip. It can't be that bad. You've been married for almost ten years. There has to be an explanation."

"Maybe Aidan gave each student jewelry, instead of grades. Maybe he gave his whole lecture class gifts: polo shirts for the boys and necklaces and earrings for the girls. That would be so like him, don't you think? That sounds just like my husband who believes material things have no relationship to one's happiness, and makes me do his birthday shopping. If it wasn't for me, he'd still buy Isabel a My Little Ponies every year, even though she's sixteen and lives with us half the time." Cassie was almost shouting.

"Cassie, stop." Alexis pushed the elevator button so the doors stayed open. "We need to think this through calmly, and we need a drink. I hope your mother still has that bottle of Scotch under her desk."

Cassie nodded, biting her lip and pulling her bangs until they reached her chin. She looked at herself in the smoky elevator mirror. Her mother always said she had the face of an angel: almond-shaped blue eyes, long dark lashes, a small nose dusted with freckles, and God's imprint, a dimple on the side of her mouth. The reflection staring back at her looked more like Snow White just after she realized she'd eaten the poisoned apple.

Cassie opened the door to her mother's office, smelling a mix of Lemon Pledge and Chanel No. 5. The walls were papered in beige linen, and the wood floor was covered with a thick Oriental rug. Vases holding bunches of lilies graced the coffee table, the end tables, and the fireplace mantel. There was a cherry desk, a Louis XIV chair, and a cream-colored sofa with throw pillows shaped like seashells.

"Your mother has the best taste, even where no one can see it." Alexis admired the silk pillows.

"I'm not in the mood to discuss interior design." Cassie lay facedown on the sofa.

"Maybe she's Aidan's TA and he bought her the pendant to thank her for grading papers." Alexis opened the drawer under the desk and extracted a crystal decanter and two shot glasses.

"That would be such an ethical thing for a professor of ethics to do," Cassie moaned into the cushions.

"Cassie, sit up." Alexis dropped onto the sofa, holding a shot glass in each hand. She kicked off her heels and tucked her stockinged feet under her legs. "Drink this, quickly." She put the glass under Cassie's nose.

Cassie drank the Scotch in one gulp. She felt the alcohol

burn the back of her throat and her eyes stung. She blinked and held her glass out for another shot, promising herself she would not cry.

"That's the girl who wrote love notes to Father Chatham senior year and signed Sister Agnes's name." Alexis nodded approvingly, refilling Cassie's glass.

"Sister Agnes was in love with him." Cassie threw back the second shot. "The whole school knew. Every song in chapel was a love song."

"I think those were called hymns, to God." Alexis grinned. "Honestly, Cassie, I know Aidan looks like a lion, king of the jungle, and all those sophomoric undergrads hang on his every word, but has he ever given you a reason to doubt him?"

"No"—Cassie shook her head, choking back a hiccup—"but he's never given anyone a Fenton's red box. The only things he buys for me from Fenton's are scarves because my skin is so sensitive I break out if it's not true cashmere."

"Fenton's does carry the best scarves, and I should get more. Maybe on the way down we can check and see if they have any new colors." Alexis rubbed her finger along the edge of her glass.

"You can have the ones Aidan bought me for Christmas, if I don't use them to strangle him."

"I know you've been married much longer than me"— Alexis poured herself another shot—"but it could be completely harmless. A silly misunderstanding."

"This isn't one of those old black-and-white movies where the hero gives the heroine a gift and it's intercepted by the wicked stepsister." Cassie leaned back on the pillows.

"A few weeks ago I found a cigar in Carter's blazer pocket. Not that I snoop of course, I'm not that sort of wife"—Alexis put her glass on the rug—"but I felt this long, hard thing in his pocket, like a small penis."

"How is this relevant?" Cassie interrupted.

"I was really angry because I hate the smell of cigars. It stays in the sheets forever." Alexis plumped the pillow with one hand. "He said he didn't know how it got there and I didn't believe him. I withheld sex"—she sucked in her breath—"until he told the truth."

"Carter without his nightly pillaging? He must have climbed the walls." Cassie tried to smile.

"It turned out one of the guys at work put a cigar in everyone's blazer. Invitation to a bachelor party."

"I hope you gave Carter some sex before he went to the bachelor party. Who knows what might have happened?"

"I'm serious, Cassie. All you have is circumstantial evidence. Don't you watch *Law & Order* or *The Good Wife*? Circumstantial evidence is never going to carry a conviction."

Cassie opened the red Fenton's box and stared at the offending pendant. The stone was light brown on a thin gold chain. She turned it over to see if there was a card or a note enclosed.

"How many times have you told me Aidan gets a dozen friend requests a day from students and deletes them all, unread?" Alexis pressed on. "And what about the fresh pizza that showed up at your front door with a note written in haiku? Aidan threw it away even though it was from Gino's."

"You're turning things around. Aidan gave this to that girl." Cassie waved the box in the air like a red flag.

"It might have ended up in her hands a number of ways."

"Like how?" Cassie sat up straight. The shots had made her brain sharper, instead of numbing the pain.

"That's my point. You have to find out how, and you can't jump to conclusions until you do."

"Do you want me to hire a detective, like that guy on *CSI: Miami*?"

"David Caruso? I don't know what all the fuss is about. How can anyone with red hair be sexy? Do you believe in your marriage?" Alexis asked.

"Yes." Cassie nodded, blinking to stop the tears from spilling down her cheeks.

"Then take the box and show it to Aidan, let him explain it."

"What if he can't?" Cassie stared at the box as if a genie would pop out and give her the answer.

"Do you remember our last semester at the Convent when you found me crying in the boiler room eating peanut butter sandwiches?" Alexis asked.

Cassie closed her eyes. She saw Alexis in her plaid school uniform, her skirt grazing her thighs, her white socks pushed down to her ankles, making her legs look as if they belonged on a racehorse. She wore her blond hair in a thick braid to her waist, and had a henna tattoo of a rose on the inside of her wrist.

Cassie in high school had been the poster Catholic schoolgirl: chestnut hair brushed into a wavy ponytail, white collared shirt pressed and buttoned to the top button. But Alexis managed to look like a *Maxim* cover without breaking any major rules: her skirt a fraction too short, her lips smeared with lip gloss with just a hint of color, her blazer pulled a little too tight over her breasts. Half the boys at private schools in the city attended Sacred Heart volleyball games just to see Alexis spike the ball.

"Why are you crying? You smell like peanut butter, you're

going to get detention." Cassie had squeezed between the hot water furnaces and crouched down next to Alexis.

"Why is this school a peanut-free zone?" Alexis brushed breadcrumbs from her uniform. "It's bad enough they don't let you smoke, but peanut butter always makes me feel better. It's comfort food."

"Come home after school and I'll make you a double-decker peanut butter sandwich." Cassie had tried to pull Alexis to her feet.

"I'm not going anywhere." Alexis had shook her head, her eyes welling with new tears.

"What happened?" Cassie had slid down on the ground beside her.

"Carter is going to Stanford. I thought we were going to UCLA together. I had it all mapped out: a year in the dorms, a couple of years living in frat and sorority houses, and then our final year living in a condo near Wilshire Boulevard. But now he's decided to go to the Farm. He probably heard all those New England prep school girls come to California to get laid."

"Or maybe because Stanford is in the thick of where he wants to be: venture capitalists, hedge funds, dot-coms. There isn't an inch of Sand Hill Road where guys fresh out of Stanford aren't making billions." Cassie had nibbled a peanut butter crust.

"He's going to forget me." Alexis's mascara had run down her cheeks. "He's going to go to the Stanford-Berkeley football game and fall in love with some cheerleader. UCLA doesn't even play Stanford, we play USC."

"No cheerleader could hold a candle to you." Cassie had stroked Alexis's hair the way she used to at their preteen sleepovers.

"I just know he's The One." Alexis had squeezed the last peanut butter sandwich between her fingers.

"Last semester Brian Peterson was the one, and before that Pierce Stone, even though he went to boarding school in Vermont and you guys spent a total of four long weekends together."

"Cassie, I don't know what I'm going to do. I don't want to lose him."

"Then tell him," Cassie had said with the wisdom of countless hours in the school library reading *Seventeen* and *Teen Vogue*. "Go over to Carter's house and tell him four years and five hundred miles is not going to come between you. Whatever happens in college, you're going to be waiting for him after graduation."

"Whatever happens in college?" Alexis had repeated, tearing the sandwich into small pieces.

"You're going to UCLA," Cassie had replied. "Land of surfers and bronze movie stars. But if you believe in your relationship, it'll be there."

Alexis had stood up. She had a spot of jelly on her white shirt and a trace of peanut butter on her blazer. "Do you think he'll listen?"

"Carter worships you. Wear that teddy you picked up in the Fillmore last weekend. With heels. He won't say no."

"I only had to wait for Carter to get his degree, his MBA, and his partnership for him to marry me, but what you said was true. I needed to believe in us for the relationship to work." Alexis slipped on her Pradas and put her glass on the desk. "Don't doubt Aidan, ask him."

"Since when did you become a relationship guru?" Cassie snapped the jewelry box shut.

"You don't just get married and think you'll still be spooning on your golden anniversary. You have to work at it. I take massage classes, Cordon Bleu cooking classes, makeup classes, and we do couples yoga."

"Not couples yoga!" Cassie leaned forward, laughing.

"Carter and I had a bit of a rough patch a couple of months ago so I've ramped it up a bit. And it's working. I set my alarm for eleven-fifty at night so I'm awake when he comes home, and we have sex like porn stars."

"I don't think I have the energy for yoga or a midnight rendezvous." Cassie smiled. "But I get it. Like Sister Agnes used to say, 'face your enemy head on, and you have nothing to fear. God will be at your side.'"

"Aidan isn't your enemy. He's been your twin for a decade. I can never peel you away to go shopping because you're glued to his side. You guys even go to the grocery store together. It's nauseating."

"Not the grocery store." Cassie felt a little better. "The Berkeley Co-op. It's more a gathering place, and they have the most amazing vegetables, better than anything I grow in my garden. Last week I picked up a purple eggplant from Japan. I served it on a bed of long-grain organic rice, and it was delicious."

"Enough." Alexis held up her hand. "I don't want to hear about purple eggplant, let alone eat it. That's why you and your professor live in Berkeley, and I live in Presidio Heights. You're made for each other. Don't let some bottle blond coed come between you. Go home, pour a glass of Kenwood Chardonnay, show Aidan the box, and ask him where it came from."

Cassie stood up, testing her legs to see if they were still wobbly. For a moment she relaxed. She had had a delicious tea in the city, saw her best friend for the first time in weeks, and was going home to sit by the fire and nibble on snow peas with her husband. But then her eyes settled on the red Fenton's box and she sucked in her breath as if she'd been slapped.

"Cassie, go on." Alexis followed her eyes. "You can do this."

"You should have your own afternoon talk show." Cassie picked up the box. "Let's go before I lose my nerve."

They took the elevator down to the parking garage. Cassie had parked in a reserved space, next to her mother's smoky blue Jaguar XL.

"Your mother knows how to treat herself." Alexis peeked through the window at the spotted maple dashboard and the cream leather upholstery. There were three purses on the floor of the passenger seat: Louis Vuitton, Prada, and a Fendi clutch, and a couple of pairs of boots on the backseat.

"Are those Chanel ostrich-skin boots?" Alexis pressed her face harder against the glass. "I've only seen them in *Vogue*."

"Stop drooling, you'll fog up the glass." Cassie opened the door of her Prius. "Wish me luck."

Alexis kissed Cassie's cheek. "Maybe I'll ask Carter for a Jaguar for my birthday."

"Thanks for your support." Cassie put the keys in the ignition.

"You have all my love and support. Trust me, it was some silly mistake. You'll drink Chardonnay and eat Japanese eggplant and have the best sex of the holidays." Alexis grinned. "You're Aidan's angel. You're irreplaceable."

2.

Cassie drove across the Bay Bridge listening to Mariah Carey sing "All I Want for Christmas Is You." She thought someone should tell the DJ Christmas was over. The sparkle, the mistletoe, the eggnog was gone and all that remained were leftovers and returns. She glanced at the red Fenton's box on the passenger seat and considered opening her window and tossing it into the bay. But then she'd be facing Aidan empty handed.

She flipped the radio station and heard an old Train song: "Drops of Jupiter." Instinctively she smiled and hummed along. Train had been their favorite band when they were first married. Cassie remembered going to their concert at the Warfield theater and spending the whole night sharing Irish coffees: Aidan's arm draped around her, her face buried in his leather jacket. When the song "Calling All Angels" was played on heavy rotation, Aidan would turn up the radio and boast that he had asked the lead singer to write the lyrics for Cassie.

Cassie's eyes filled with tears, and she wiped them away so she could see the cars in front of her. She rested her elbows on the steering wheel and remembered the day she met Aidan. She walked into his lecture class fifteen minutes late, and he stared at her, his fierce black eyes sizing her up, as if she was interrupting a presidential address.

"And who is this young lady who has the courage or the bad manners to walk into my class three days and fifteen minutes late?" Aidan addressed the lecture hall.

Cassie blushed and took a seat at the back of the class. She had heard about Professor Aidan Blake: he loved to hear himself talk, he wasn't afraid to offend students if it made his lectures more interesting, and he had the sexiest mouth of any professor on campus. Girls signed up for ethics in modern society just to see him pout.

Cassie had made the class a last-minute add. It was her final semester, senior year, and the philosophy of cooking class she wanted was full. Thomas Keller and Alice Waters were creating such a buzz with reduction sauces and seven-course tasting menus that cooking was the new rock 'n' roll. Undergrads lined up for culinary courses and spent their evenings prowling Williams-Sonoma.

Cassie's roommate suggested Professor Blake's ethics class, so she climbed three stories to the top of Newberry Hall and tried to blend in with the desk chairs.

"Cassie Fenton," she replied when it seemed Aidan wouldn't continue his lecture until she answered.

"Miss Fenton, ethics, if you read the course guide, is about the pursuit of good within the confines of society. We do not murder, rape, or steal from our fellow men, and we do not"— he paused to put emphasis on his words—"interrupt a class that is already in progress."

"Would you like me to leave?" Cassie's voice was very small. She wondered if it reached the podium.

"And disrupt the class further? You make an attractive addition to the back row; just make sure you take notes. I've kicked students out for less."

Cassie wished she had signed up for conversational French. But as she listened to Aidan, her pen filling her notebook, she became interested in the lesson: Plato, Aristotle, the pursuit of good, the idea that happiness was attainable. At the Convent, moral code had been laid out in inarguable language while her mother had one God: Fenton's. Aidan put new ideas in her head, and when the lecture was over she put her pen down reluctantly.

"Miss Fenton," Aidan addressed her as she stuffed her backpack. Cassie gazed at Aidan up close and blushed a deeper pink. Her roommate's description hadn't done justice to his black curly hair. Not only was his mouth gorgeous, but his chin was chiseled, and his eyes were the color of raisins. His shoulders belonged on a quarterback and his waist was as small as a dancer's.

"Yes, sir." She swung her backpack over her shoulder and stood up. She wore white capris and a collared Ralph Lauren shirt. She had a J.Crew sweater tied around her waist and her favorite navy Tod's on her feet. Even after four years of college she shopped at Fenton's, and she suddenly felt preppy and overdressed.

"I keep office hours on Tuesdays and Thursdays from two to four, if you need help catching up." He smiled and walked out of the room.

It took more than a month for Cassie to get up the courage to knock on his door during office hours. She sat at his over-sized metal desk, wearing a tie-dyed shirt and denim cutoffs borrowed from her roommate, and tried to ask intelligent questions about the reading. Cassie told herself she was there because she was interested in the material, but whenever she was close to Aidan, she felt like there was a magnet drawing her even closer.

"What does a department store heiress do with her diploma?" Aidan asked one afternoon in late April, when graduation was just weeks away.

"How did you know about Fenton's?" Cassie looked up from her lecture notes.

"Students don't just gossip about professors, they run a pretty thorough commentary about one another." Aidan didn't seem to notice that she was blushing. He wore a black cotton T-shirt, khaki pants, and his signature leather jacket. His teeth were blinding white and his fingernails were smudged with ink.

"I'll probably join my mother at Fenton's." She shrugged.

"Is that what you want to do? Sell overpriced merchandise to women whose closets will swallow it up like a black hole?"

"It's what I should do," Cassie said. She had spent every afternoon of her childhood at Fenton's; the elevator music still played in her head. "It's what I'm expected to do," she repeated, as if trying to convince herself.

"Noble, to take over the family store"—Aidan flipped open his textbook—"but to grow, first you have to be true to yourself. What's your passion?"

Cassie's pen froze midsentence. When she looked up, Aidan was underlining words in the text.

"My passion?"

"What you wake up in the morning thinking about."

Cassie gazed past him, at his framed doctorate on the wall and a print of Monet's *Haystacks*.

"I want to grow organic vegetables," she said. "I love everything to do with cooking and gardening."

"Then that's what you should do with your diploma."

It was a few weeks after graduation, when Cassie saw Aidan in the frozen-food section of the Berkeley Co-op, that she admitted to herself he was part of the reason she decided to spend one more summer in Berkeley.

"Cassie Fenton." His face broke into a smile when he saw her. He was holding hands with a small girl of about seven, with the same dark eyes and black curly hair. She was pointing stubbornly at a box of frozen pizza and stamping her feet like a young bull.

"Hi." Cassie avoided running into an elderly woman with her shopping cart. Her roommate had mentioned Aidan was divorced, but she never said anything about a daughter.

"I thought you would have decamped back to San Francisco and taken up your position on the fourth floor of Fenton's."

"I'm interning for Alice Waters at Chez Panisse for the summer," Cassie replied.

"Well that sounds interesting." Aidan nodded approvingly. "This is my daughter, Isabel. We come to the co-op for fresh, local produce and Isabel wants frozen pizza."

Cassie glanced at Isabel, whose eyes flashed like a gypsy. "You could make pizza, it's really easy."

"That sounds like a terrific compromise. Why don't you come over and show us? Tonight, eight o'clock?"

Cassie hesitated. She wasn't sure if she was being invited to dinner or to perform a cooking demonstration. "I don't want to intrude."

"Isabel and I have lots of time together since her mother

is gone for a month this summer. I'll get a couple of bottles of wine. What should we put on the pizza? Eggplant, yellow peppers, green olives?" His hair was damp as if he'd been running and he wore shorts and a plain white T-shirt.

"Heirloom tomatoes." Cassie avoided looking at Isabel, who was scowling and peeling price tags from bags of vegetables.

"I love heirloom tomatoes." Aidan pulled Isabel away from the frozen foods. "We'll see you at eight."

Aidan's house was at the end of a long gravel drive, behind an impressive plantation-style mansion. Aidan answered the door wearing an apron, shorts, and rugby socks.

"It's the smallest house on Professor Row, but I just got tenure." He shrugged, guiding her through a small living room and an adjoining dining nook. The table was covered in papers, and more papers were piled on the floor and on the chairs. The sideboard had been converted into a bookcase with two bottles of wine serving as bookends.

"It's lovely." Cassie had never been in a professor's house. She didn't know if she expected dark wood and the smell of pipe tobacco, or a modern bachelor pad with black-and-white cubic sofas. Aidan's house was like a toy house: it had the correct number of rooms but in miniature proportions.

"My wife left me a couple of years ago, so it's just me and Isabel every other week." He opened swinging doors to the kitchen.

"I'm sorry," Cassie replied awkwardly.

"She remarried a dot-com guy. His summer cottage is twice the size of this place"—Aidan motioned her to sit on a stool—"but some guys have to make money so their wives can shop at Fenton's."

Cassie blushed. "You shouldn't judge it," she said clearly. "Fenton's provides their customers with great quality and service. It's been in my family for sixty years. It brings pleasure to many people."

Aidan put his hand on Cassie's shoulder. She instinctively flinched; he had never touched her before. "You're right, Fenton's does contribute to society. I asked you over to make pizza, not talk ethics. Would you like an apron?"

Cassie nodded and he pulled an apron from a drawer and tied it carefully around her waist. They stood side by side at the counter, rolling out dough, slicing tomatoes, sautéing mushrooms. He poured them each a glass of wine and asked her to set the table, as if they knew each other intimately and had done this dozens of times before.

"Come out back and see the garden. It's nothing much yet but I'd love to grow some tomatoes and some broccoli," he said when the pizza was in the oven.

Cassie was a little drunk and the night air felt suddenly cold after the cramped kitchen. The fog had settled over the bay and the sky was without stars.

"There's not much to see." She peered off the deck into the black space that held the garden.

Aidan put his hand on her back and pulled her close. He stroked her hair and tipped her face up to his. She could smell wine and olive oil, garlic and Parmesan cheese. "I just wanted to kiss you." He brought his lips down on hers. "I've wanted to kiss you for a long time."

When they went inside, Isabel was sitting on the stool, covering the counter with tomato sauce handprints. Aidan's face turned to stone. He wiped the counter and put the plates in the sink. Finally he turned to Isabel and said in a strained tone, "Isabel, if you want to join our dinner party you will behave like a young lady, not a little barbarian."

Isabel brushed off her father's words and jumped down from the stool. "I turned off the oven, your pizza was burning."

Isabel smoothed her white appliqué skirt and slipped pink clogs on her feet. She sat demurely at the kitchen table, placed her napkin in her lap, and asked her father politely for a glass of water and some garlic bread.

Cassie watched her performance, saw the small gypsy eyes flash as Aidan poured Cassie another glass of wine, and wanted to put her arms around Isabel and hug her. But it was as if the child put a moat around herself, eating her pizza with small delicate bites, wiping her mouth with her napkin, folding her hands in her lap. When Aidan put three bowls of ice cream on the table, Isabel pushed back her chair. "I'm not hungry. May I be excused?"

"Aristotle says to be a good person it is important to have a happy childhood." Aidan finished his ice cream and took a bite of Isabel's. "But she fights me every step of the way. God help me when she becomes a teenager."

"Maybe I should go"—Cassie pushed her bowl away—"so you two can be alone."

Aidan put down his spoon and moved his chair closer to Cassie. He traced her lips with his fingers and picked up her hair and let it fall down her back. "People think ethics is about deprivation but that's incorrect. Aristotle and Plato believed someone who leads a balanced life could achieve the greatest good. Pleasure and friendship are integral to that balance." He rested his hands on her shoulders and kissed her softly on the lips.

"I remember that reading," Cassie replied weakly. He tasted like cinnamon and vanilla bean.

"Let's listen to some music." Aidan took her hand and led her into the living room. He turned on the CD player and sat on the sofa, tucking Cassie under his arm like a bird. They listened to Miles Davis and the Beatles. He found an old Jefferson Starship CD and then played Train and some Cars. He opened another bottle of wine and sang into her hair, drumming his fingers against her skin. When Cassie started dozing off, he pulled her up, locked his arm around her waist, and climbed the stairs to his bedroom.

Isabel's door was closed and it was almost midnight, but Cassie hesitated at the top of the stairs. It was their first date, Aidan was more than a decade older, and he had been her professor just weeks ago. But when Aidan unbuttoned her cotton top and pressed her body into his, she felt an electric force binding them together. He led her to the bed and slid her skirt past her ankles. He stripped off his shirt and shorts and lay gently on top of her. His body was so hard, so commanding, she dropped her legs open and waited, straining, reaching, for him to push inside her. When he came, rocking back and forth, his hands cupped behind her head, she felt her whole body tremble and her eyes fill with tears.

"I should go before Isabel wakes up," she whispered into his back.

"Cassie Fenton, you're an angel that fell into my bed." He pulled her tighter against him. "I want you to stay."

Cassie pulled the Prius down the long driveway and parked in front of Aidan's ancient Toyota. She was glad Isabel's MINI Cooper, a birthday present from Isabel's stepfather, was missing. Isabel at sixteen was like the heroine of a daytime soap opera: raging around the house slamming doors or prone on her bed sobbing, and Cassie couldn't face her today.

She walked straight to the kitchen and put on the kettle, sifting through colored tea cartons for something that promised to soothe and relax. The downstairs was quiet; she could hear the shower running upstairs. Aidan had probably just returned from the gym. She imagined him peeling off his boxers and stepping into the shower, and she suddenly felt like a stranger in her own home.

When Aidan came down the stairs, she was cutting a piece of pecan pie left over from Christmas and was covering it with a puff of whipped cream.

"That looks delicious. Can I have a piece?" He walked over to the counter and kissed her on the cheek. He wore a terry robe and he smelled of avocado shampoo.

Aidan's hair was peppered with gray and his waist had grown thicker over the years, but he still had the presence of a lion. Cassie often watched him correct his students' papers with fierce red strokes. Sometimes he'd crumple them into balls, moaning that no one taught these kids how to write anymore.

"You can have mine; I'm not hungry." She pushed the plate toward him.

"Long lunch with Alexis? Did Carter buy her a private jet for Christmas?" Aidan finished the pie and cut himself another slice.

"Just some really nice jewelry." Cassie felt the words stick in her throat.

"Lucky that Alexis has a long neck or she'd tip over with all the jewelry she owns. Did you tell her your miserable husband only bought you socks and vegetable seeds?" He put his hands on her shoulders and kissed the side of her mouth.

"And a cashmere scarf." Cassie gulped her tea quickly, burning the tip of her tongue.

"I thought we'd stay in tonight. I'll cook pasta with some of your tender shiitake mushrooms. You can inspire me by modeling the scarf and the socks."

"You want me to sing for my supper?" Cassie tried to smile.

"I was thinking more a striptease. Maybe we could play with some whipped cream after dessert." Aidan held up the bottle of whipped cream.

Cassie took a deep breath and took the Fenton's box out of her bag. She snapped it open and placed it on the counter.

"What's that?" Aidan put down the can of whipped cream.

"It's a pendant from Fenton's."

"More presents?" Aidan frowned.

"It was a return from a young girl with short blond hair wearing a bomber jacket. I didn't get her name but she said it was a gift from Professor Aidan Blake." Cassie's whole body trembled.

"I don't know what you're talking about." Aidan looked at her blankly.

"Yes, you do." Cassie's voice rose. "She didn't pull your name out of a hat. Some young girl, some student, received a present from you and I want to know how, when, and why."

Aidan was silent. Cassie thought she could see his mind turning over the problem. "You're an ethics professor," she wanted to scream at him. "You can't lie."

"Molly Payne," he said.

"Why did you give Molly Payne a pendant from Fenton's?"

"I didn't give Molly that pendant," Aidan replied. He opened the fridge and took out pesto sauce, chives, mushrooms, and two large yellow tomatoes.

"Stop what you're doing and look at me." Cassie tried to keep her voice level.

Aidan took olive oil, oregano, basil, and pine nuts from the pantry. He arranged them on the counter and searched for his favorite chopping knife. He wiped the blade and sliced mushrooms, tomatoes, and chives with the concentration of a conductor leading a symphony.

"I gave her a cash refund in case you're interested." Cassie slumped on the stool.

Aidan stopped slicing and poured the vegetables into the pesto sauce. He tasted it with a mixing spoon and added a splash of salt and some pepper.

"Try this, you'll love it." He put the spoon to Cassie's mouth.

"Aidan, please." Cassie pushed the spoon away.

Aidan put the spoon down and wiped his hands on a paper towel. "I bought the pendant for you. I went to Fenton's to get you a cashmere scarf, because you can't live without them. I thought I'd buy something special, something you didn't expect. I picked out the pendant and on the way home I stopped at the Peet's on Shattuck. Molly Payne was sitting at a table crying like a child who just discovered Santa isn't real."

"She's not a child," Cassie interrupted.

"She's a child to me. What is she, twenty-one, twenty-two? Christ, Cassie, what are you thinking?"

"Your students fawn over you like you're the Messiah. I've seen them line up for office hours, carrying home-baked cookies and Starbucks coffees. You're like a Greek god on your podium channeling Plato and Aristotle."

"I'm glad you think that." Aidan put his hand under her chin. "My students think I'm a harsh grader who doesn't cut them any slack."

"How did Molly Payne end up with my Christmas present?" Cassie grabbed the Fenton's box and threw it on the floor.

Aidan's face turned cold like it did when Isabel came home past curfew. He turned back to his sauce, stirring it over the stove, adding garlic and Parmesan cheese.

"Molly's boyfriend left her a week before Christmas. He took the money they had saved to buy each other presents and hopped on a train to Seattle. Molly was crying over the letter he sent her. It was a classic 'Dear Jane,' that he wasn't good enough for her; she shouldn't waste her time on him. And a neat little P.S. saying he was traveling with their friend Kate, and they were going to open an organic bakery together." Aidan stopped stirring.

"Poor thing," Cassie murmured.

"I preach about doing good every day in class, but when do I get the opportunity to do good? You spend half your time at the Edible Schoolyard teaching kids how to grow their own vegetables. Sometimes I'm jealous."

"Jealous?" Cassie repeated.

"You're teaching them something that will serve them always. You're helping form a healthier generation. I'm proud of you, Cassie, but sometimes I'm frustrated standing in front of a bunch of students who want to intern at a Fortune 500 company."

Cassie blushed. She loved working with Alice Waters,

but she was a volunteer. She thought anyone could do what she did: teach kids when to plant certain seeds, how often to water them. Often the kids were more interested in worms and snails than red peppers and yellow asparagus.

"Molly started sobbing that she was going to quit school, that nothing worked out for her. Her boyfriend ran off with her best friend because she baked awesome pumpkin muffins. I reached into my bag and handed her the Fenton's box. I didn't even think about it, I just wanted to help someone." Aidan put his hands on her shoulders. "I'm sorry, I should have told you."

Cassie felt her shoulders relax. She closed her eyes and let Aidan kiss her neck. He put his arms around her and hugged her against his chest.

"It's okay," she said when he released her.

"I'll ask your permission the next time I want to be a good Samaritan." He smiled. "I did get a late Christmas present from another professor in the department, a male professor. A 2002 Pengrove Chardonnay. It will go perfectly with this pesto pasta."

Cassie got the wine out of the fridge and set two glasses on the counter. She sat on the stool and watched Aidan toss a Caesar salad. Watching him prepare dinner was like observing an artist in his studio. He wasn't satisfied unless each plate was a riot of color, smell, and taste.

"I have outdone myself." He put a sprig of spinach on each plate. "If my love will join me at the table, dinner is served."

After dinner they shared a piece of pecan pie and two glasses of Drambuie. Aidan took their brandy glasses in the living room and put a Beatles CD in the disc player.

"It's been thirty years since John Lennon's death but

their music never gets old." He put his arm around Cassie and traced a path from her chin to her breasts.

"All you need is love," Cassie mumbled. Her cheeks were warm from the brandy and the pie left a sweet, cinnamon taste in her mouth.

"All I need is your love." Aidan took Cassie's hand, kissed her fingers, then placed her hand in his lap.

Cassie felt him grow hard inside his robe. He pressed her hand against him, and bent down and kissed her breasts. She leaned back, closing her eyes, feeling her nipples pucker.

"Let's go upstairs," Cassie whispered.

"No, let's do it here." Aidan laid her down on the sofa, tossing the cushions on the rug. He unzipped her pants and lifted her shirt over her head. He threw off his robe and entered her quickly, cradling her head in his hands. They came at the same time, like two teenagers afraid their parents would come home. Aidan gathered her against his chest, breathing deeply into her hair, and fell asleep.

Cassie slept too. When she woke, Aidan was snoring, and she felt stiff and thirsty. She took his arm off her stomach and got up and went into the kitchen. She poured a glass of water and opened the freezer and took out two ice cubes. She saw her phone buzzing on the counter and checked her texts.

"How was the make-up sex?" It was from Alexis, signed with two smiley faces.

Cassie grinned and texted back: "None of your business." Then she went back into the living room and slid onto the sofa beside Aidan.

3.

Cassie pulled up in front of the Edible Schoolyard and tugged on her rubber boots. She loved arriving early, while the students were still in class, chewing on pencils and filling in their workbooks. She walked straight to the shed, selected a spade, and slipped on her gardening gloves.

The ground was wet and the chickens darted out of their coop as if checking for rain. Cassie chatted with the ducks and watched the hummingbirds extract breakfast from the feeder. The purple broccoli was flowering, and the lemon trees bulged with lemons.

"Good morning, Mrs. Blake," a small voice called.

Cassie turned around and saw Heewon Kim, a sixth-grader who recently transferred from an inner-city school in Oakland.

"Aren't you supposed to be in math, fretting over logarithms?" Cassie stopped tossing compost and leaned on her shovel.

"I hate math," Heewon groaned. She was small for her age, with glossy black hair that fell straight to her shoulders.

She wore overalls and old tennis shoes with shredded laces. "I'm not going to use logarithms when I grow up. I want to work in a garden, like you."

"Remember, I volunteer. You need a profession and math might be necessary. You don't want to limit your options." Cassie smiled.

"My teacher said I could check on the chickens," Heewon explained. "I collected six eggs yesterday."

"We can make omelets for lunch." Cassie zipped up her sweater. Thick gray clouds hung low in the sky and the air felt damp. "I want to pull some vegetables before it rains. Will you help me?"

"Yes, please." Heewon nodded as if she had been singled out to receive an award.

"What would go well in an omelet?" Cassie studied the vegetables lined up in neat rows. "How about you pull green onions and mustard greens, and I'll pick heirloom tomatoes and snow peas for a salad."

Cassie and Heewon worked together. Cassie loved the stillness of the garden, the way the students took pride in the fruits and vegetables, as if the schoolyard was their own personal fiefdom. The bell rang and children spilled onto the dirt, jostling one another to claim their favorite spades and shovels.

"Good morning," Cassie said loudly, waiting until they were quiet. "I hear your chickens have been laying eggs. Heewon and I thought we'd collect vegetables to make omelets. What are your favorite omelets?"

A redheaded girl raised her hand. "Ham and cheese."

"A classic." Cassie nodded. "But let's be more creative. We have so much to choose from: mushrooms, cauliflower, spinach, broccoli. Let's make omelets you've never tried before."

"Peanut butter and bacon?" A boy with short brown hair snorted, glancing around to see if his friends appreciated his joke.

"I don't know where you'll find bacon unless you slaughter a pig." Cassie shook her head. "Everyone pick one vegetable and we'll pool our resources. Please hurry, I think it's going to pour."

"Awesome," another boy cheered. "Mud fight!"

Cassie directed the children. The girls gathered beans and peas, squash and zucchini, filling their baskets with pride. The boys shifted from foot to foot in the corner, waiting for others to do the work.

"Paolo, Manny, you don't get lunch unless you help." She handed them each a basket.

"My mother gave me one piece of toast for breakfast," Paolo complained. He had big black eyes and light brown skin. "I grew six inches last year. She doesn't feed me enough!"

"You're not going to faint from doing a little manual labor. You're the tallest boy here so why don't you pick lemons? We'll make lemonade with brown sugar."

When the first raindrops landed on the ground, the children's baskets were full. Cassie ushered them into the industrial-sized kitchen where chopping boards, knives, and large bowls waited on scrubbed counters.

"How do you get these kids to dig in the mud?" One of the teachers stood at the sink, rinsing spinach leaves. "I can't make them open their math books unless pictures of Justin Bieber are hidden inside the cover."

"You can't eat fractions." Cassie pulled off her gloves and washed her hands in the warm water. "That's why gardens and kids go well together: instant gratification. In twenty minutes the beans they pulled will appear in piping-hot omelets."

"You're the Pied Piper." The teacher wiped her hands on her apron. "Will you teach my geometry class this afternoon?"

"Now *that* sounds scary." Cassie filled a pot with water and turned on the stove. She surveyed the room. Clusters of girls chopped carrots and green beans. Heewon stood by herself, squeezing lemons into a ceramic bowl. Paulo and Manny made paper airplanes out of napkins.

"Manny, Paulo, help Heewon with the lemons. Bethany"— she signaled to a tall girl with a neck like a young giraffe— "please help me set the table, our young men left their manners outside."

The room quieted as the students cut into their steaming omelets. They scraped the plates clean, drank tall glasses of lemonade, and asked for refills. Cassie rewarded each child with a homemade brownie she had warmed in the kitchen's double oven. By the time she got in the car she was pleasantly exhausted, longing to stand under a hot shower.

"Darling, is the weather as miserable on your side of the bay?" Cassie's mother called as she pulled out of the parking lot.

"Alexis wanted me to go to Mexico till March. I should have taken her up on it," Cassie said laughing. "I haven't seen the sun since Thanksgiving."

"This apartment is frigid. I keep turning the thermostat up and Maria keeps turning it down." Diana Fenton's voice was low and throaty.

Cassie pictured her mother in the library of her Nob Hill penthouse, standing by the window and looking out over her city. Cassie thought San Francisco belonged to her mother ever since she was five and they moved to the top of the tallest building on Sutter Street. Cassie's father had keeled over from a heart attack on the squash courts. Her mother sold their Pacific Heights home and bought a two-bedroom pent-house with giant balconies and no place for a little girl to play.

Diana coped with the loss of her husband by devoting her-self to Fenton's. Cassie only got her attention by trailing along to Fenton's after school, or parking herself in her mother's library when she needed help with her homework. Diana usu-ally waved her away and said Maria could help her, though Maria's English was limited to words she used at the neigh-borhood shops.

"I'd like you to join me for lunch tomorrow; there's some-thing I want to discuss with you," Diana continued.

Cassie hesitated. "Aidan doesn't start classes for a couple of weeks."

"You can't come into the city because you're babysitting your husband? He's a big boy, Cassie. Noon tomorrow. I'll have Maria make vegetable paella. You can take Aidan home some in a doggy bag." Diana hung up before Cassie could reply.

Cassie pressed the end button and sighed. Aidan and her mother got along by keeping each other at arm's length. There were so many things about Aidan that Diana didn't approve of: his age, the fact that he didn't want more children until Isabel was out of the house, his failure to provide Cassie with the lifestyle she had as a child. Yet Cassie knew her mother admired his wit, his intelligence, and the way he truly loved Cassie.

Cassie nodded to the doorman in her mother's building and took the elevator up to the thirtieth floor. She wore a cream-colored knee-length skirt and a matching cashmere sweater. Cassie examined herself in the elevator mirror, won-dering if she would pass her mother's inspection. She had

spent extra time on her makeup, had applied mascara and lipstick, and had tied her hair in a knot at the nape of her neck.
Diana expected all young women to dress a certain way, and
despite herself Cassie wanted to measure up.

"Darling, I'm so glad you came." Diana opened the door.
She wore wide cashmere slacks with a thick black belt and
black ankle boots. Her blouse was exquisite: turquoise silk
with tiny pearl buttons and large cuffs that hung perfectly at
her wrists. Diana carried an enamel cigarette holder with an
unlit Virginia Slims cigarette.

"Aidan is wrestling with a paper he's submitting to a conference." Cassie kissed her mother's cheek and put her purse
on an ivory end table.

Walking into her mother's apartment was like walking
into a modern art museum. Every inch was designed to elicit
a reaction. Diana redecorated every two years, employing
San Francisco's brightest design star.

The penthouse was in its "white phase." The floors were
imported white marble covered with white wool rugs. The
fourteen-foot windows were hung with white silk curtains,
and the dining table was tinted white glass under a white
pendulum chandelier.

"Darling, sit." Diana led Cassie to the conversation pit:
three artfully arranged love seats under a white canvas in a
white gold frame.

"Mother, I love the flowers." Cassie glanced around the
room. Flowers were everywhere: bunches of lilies in crystal
vases, birds-of-paradise in long glass tubes, yellow roses,
purple daisies, orchids on end tables, side tables, and on the
fireplace mantel.

"Thank you, darling. I love the white but I felt a bit like I
was living in a Swiss clinic. The flowers add drama. Maria

complains about having to refresh the water but what else does she have to do? She's getting lazy."

Cassie smiled. Maria had been with her mother for thirty years and Cassie had never seen her without a dust mop in her hand.

"We'll have lunch in a minute, but I have something exciting to discuss." Diana leaned forward on the love seat. "Next birthday I'll be sixty, God willing. It's time you came to work at Fenton's."

Cassie gazed at her mother. It was hard to believe Diana would be sixty. Her skin was smooth as alabaster, and she had the hands of a debutante. Diana's eyes were pale blue like Cassie's, and she wore her auburn hair in a pageboy cut to her chin.

"I have a full life, Mother. Working at the Edible School-yard and being a professor's wife keeps me busy."

"I adore Alice, she is a dear, dear friend"—Diana waved her cigarette holder in the air—"but you're mucking around in dirt with schoolchildren. It was fine when you were in your twenties but you're thirty-two. It's time to grow up. Fenton's needs you."

Cassie leaned back on the white silk cushion and remembered the last time her mother demanded she work at Fenton's. It was a year after she graduated from Berkeley. Cassie had managed to turn her extra summer into a full year and was still in the first flush of love with Aidan. She kept her studio apartment in North Berkeley because Isabel still coveted Aidan's undivided attention, but they managed to spend long nights together in his king-sized bed.

"You've been playing for a full year now." Diana sat at the desk in her office at Fenton's. "It's time you came to work."

"I'm not sure I want to work at Fenton's," Cassie had replied, hearing Aidan's voice in her head. "Alice is starting an exciting project and I want to be part of it."

"Volunteering is fine." Diana stood up and walked to the window overlooking Union Square. It was spring and the trees were covered in pink buds. Shoppers had shed their winter coats and wore bright colors: lime green dresses, orange pants, canvas loafers instead of knee-high boots. "But Fenton's is your store."

"I love Fenton's, but I'm not really made for it." Cassie averted her eyes from her mother. "I don't have your fashion sense."

"Nonsense." Her mother turned and looked sharply at Cassie. "You're young, your look will mature. The trick is to surround yourself with people who excel at what they do."

After that first conversation with her mother, Cassie had driven over the Bay Bridge and gone straight to Aidan's house. Aidan was in the kitchen, preparing an egg white omelet.

"Sweetheart"—he kissed her on the mouth—"I picked up a 1996 Rutherford sauvignon blanc. Wait till you taste it."

Cassie sat on the stool and watched Aidan crack eggs. Her lower lip trembled. She loved spending Saturdays at the Berkeley Co-op with Aidan, combing the aisles for exotic vegetables. She loved growing spinach and zucchini and giving them to Aidan to use in their dinner.

"My mother wants me to move back to the city and work at Fenton's," she blurted out.

Aidan put down the spatula and wiped his hands on his apron. He led Cassie onto the deck and wrapped his arms around her.

"Tell her you can't do that," he said.

"I tried."

"Tell her you're going to be very busy because we're getting married."

Cassie pulled away and looked at Aidan. He was smiling his white, brilliant smile.

"We are?"

"We are." His black eyes flashed. "In the Redwood Grove on campus, followed by an intimate dinner at Chez Panisse." Aidan got down on one knee and took her hand. "Cassie Fenton, will you marry me?"

"Yes," she murmured.

Aidan stood up and kissed her softly on the mouth. "I hear there's a little bistro serving egg white omelets with a fine Rutherford sauvignon blanc." He drew her into the kitchen. "I think it's time to celebrate."

"Aidan needs me," Cassie replied. "Working at Fenton's is all-consuming. You should know."

"If that's a dig that I didn't give you enough attention as a child, I'm not listening. You had a wonderful childhood: we had front-row seats at the ballet; we ate at all the new restaurants; and you had your pick of clothes from top designers."

"I didn't get to wear them. I was stuck in the Convent uniform every day," Cassie mumbled.

"You loved the Convent, you cried at graduation. You and Alexis are still thick as thieves."

"Mother, I'm not arguing. I'm just don't have time to give Fenton's that kind of attention."

"You don't want to give it your time, but I have an idea I think you will find more interesting than pulling weeds and folding Aidan's T-shirts." Diana tapped her cigarette holder on the glass.

Cassie sighed. "I'm listening."

"I went to the opening of a fabulous new restaurant last week, Le Petit Fou. It's right up your alley: organic everything. I had watercress salad with the dearest little yellow tomatoes. The entrée was organic lamb's shank on a bed of wild rice with truffles that melted like butter. If I closed my eyes I thought I was eating caviar, not mushrooms." Diana walked over to the coffee table and examined a vase of purple irises. "The restaurant was divinely decorated: sea green walls and an orange mosaic floor. The tables were covered with some sort of 'green' tablecloths, made from recycled dollar bills. Can you imagine? We were eating on money." Diana pulled an iris out of the vase.

"Sounds delicious, but what does that have to do with Fenton's?"

"I sat at a table with the young architect who designed the space. His name is James Parrish. Lovely man from Chicago, terribly young. I suppose everyone seems young these days."

"Mother, I'm getting hungry from all this talk about food."

"Wait till I finish. You always were impatient," Diana huffed. "James works for an architecture firm in Chicago that specializes in interior design for restaurants. His mother is from San Francisco, and she flies out regularly to shop at Fenton's. He said she has a whole closet of Fenton's boxes. We started talking about Europe. James spent last summer in England and he raved about Harrods. Then he said the most fascinating thing. He said wouldn't it be brilliant to have a food emporium on the ground floor of Fenton's, like Harrods, but have everything organic and locally grown." Diana paused to let the idea sink in.

"I said not the ground floor of course, Fenton's isn't a supermarket, but the basement has been a dead zone for years. A whole floor dedicated to stationery when no one writes letters anymore."

"A food emporium," Cassie repeated.

"Fresh fish caught in the bay, oysters, crab when it's in season. Counters of vegetables you only find in the farmers market, those cheeses they make in Sonoma that smell so bad they taste good. Wines from Napa Valley, Ghirardelli chocolates, sourdough bread, sauces made by Michael Mina and Thomas Keller. Everything locally produced. And maybe a long counter with stools so you could sample bread and cheese, cut fruit, sliced vegetables. Not a true café because we'd keep the one on the fourth floor. It would have more the feel of a food bazaar, with the salespeople wearing aprons and white caps."

Cassie closed her eyes and saw large baskets of vegetables, glass cases filled with goat cheese and baguettes, stands brimming with chocolate-covered strawberries.

"The design of course is key. It has to be something exceptional, a reason itself to go down the escalator. James drew some sketches. Look." Diana walked over to an antique desk and picked up a leather binder. She placed it on the coffee table and took out four sheets of paper.

Cassie leaned forward and looked at the designs. James had drawn a space with a checkered floor, yellow walls, and display cases of all different colors. Pots and pans hung from the ceiling, and every counter was filled with vegetables, fruits, loaves of bread, and wedges of cheese.

"It looks like a Roman orgy," Cassie said.

"Exactly!" Diana beamed. "Produce spilling into the aisles, wine bottles lined up like soldiers, oranges and lemons forming pyramids. And I want wonderful smells. Fresh croissants, just-baked apple pie, stinky cheese."

"It's interesting," Cassie conceded.

"It's revolutionary! I don't know why I didn't think of it before. Of course all the interior design would be 'green.'" Diana paced across the marble floor. "James works mainly in Chicago but he doesn't have another project lined up for a few months. He said he'd consider taking it on."

"It would cost a fortune," Cassie said doubtfully.

"Reinvention is the key in marketing and I've fallen behind. Of course Fenton's gets the old guard, and the thirty-somethings who need Ferragamo shoes and Chanel bags. But that's the beauty of young ideas and young energy: James was inspirational."

"Why are you pacing, Mother?"

"Because I've been up all night thinking about this. I need you to run it."

"Me?"

"You're young, you know all the women who would shop there. Think if we can convince the girls in the Junior League and the Young Friends of the Opera to buy their produce and cheeses from Fenton's."

"I'm not a member of those organizations." Cassie shook her head.

"But you went to school with them. And you'd be the perfect buyer. You can find local growers who produce twenty different kinds of lettuce. You can stock asparagus tips, artichoke hearts, avocados, pomegranates. No other store would offer a greater selection."

Cassie looked out the window at the skyline. She could see Coit Tower and the red cable cars crisscrossing the streets like figures on a Monopoly board. Her mother's excitement was contagious. She imagined herself presiding over the food counter, handling heirloom tomatoes the size of cantaloupes.

She pictured herself encouraging customers to purchase the sweetest snow peas, to stay away from peaches when they weren't in season, to buy locally grown strawberries instead.

"It would be a huge undertaking." Cassie fiddled with her wedding ring. "I don't have the time."

"You don't know how satisfying it is to wrap something in a Fenton's box, and know when the customer takes it home it will give her and her family pleasure. You'd be making a difference in kitchens all around San Francisco. Don't you think Aidan would find that worthwhile?"

"It's not about Aidan." Cassie blushed.

"It's always about Aidan. He's like a black bear, growling at everything you do."

"Aidan told me just a couple of days ago how proud he is of my volunteer work." Cassie sniffed.

"Volunteering doesn't compete with Professor Aidan Blake's sense of grandeur." Diana sat on the love seat opposite Cassie.

"Cheap shot, Mother," Cassie replied.

"Darling, let's not talk about Aidan. A food emporium might be terrifically successful, and I can't think of anyone more suited for the job."

Cassie took a deep breath. "I'm starving. You invited me to lunch. I smelled Maria's paella when I walked in."

"I'll tell Maria we're ready for lunch on one condition." Diana stood up.

"What?" Cassie asked.

"You have dinner with James and me next week and hear his vision."

Cassie glanced at her mother. She resembled a modern Katharine Hepburn, all angles and hard edges. "Either you are a very good saleswoman or I'm so hungry I can't think straight. I'll have dinner with you and James."

"Excellent. Tuesday at eight o'clock at Boulevard. I already made the reservation."

"Of course you did." Cassie smiled, following her mother into the dining room.

When Cassie left her mother's building, carrying a Burberry lunch box of Maria's paella, a familiar Range Rover was idling at the sidewalk.

"I'm not stalking you." Alexis rolled down the passenger window. "I called your house and Aidan said you were having lunch with your mother. I need a favor."

Cassie peered into the car. Alexis wore oversized Oliver Peoples sunglasses and a Miu Miu purple shirtdress.

"What kind of favor?"

"Hop in and I'll tell you." Alexis opened the car door.

Cassie climbed into the passenger seat, moving a stack of books to the floor. "Do you read all these?" Cassie flipped through Jane Green, Jennifer Weiner, Lauren Weisberger, and the latest Shopaholic.

"I belong to four book clubs. We don't actually read the books, we use them as coasters for our wineglasses." Alexis laughed.

"Where are we going?" Cassie remembered when Alexis would drive her home from school, and they'd cross the Golden Gate Bridge on a whim, or go down to Fisherman's Wharf and eat ice cream with the tourists.

"Thursdays is couples yoga and Carter is in Dallas. Will you be my yoga partner?"

"You're hijacking me to attend couples yoga?"

"I can't go alone to couples yoga," Alexis protested. "The class will think my marriage is in trouble."

"They might think your marriage is in more trouble if you bring me." Cassie grabbed the dashboard as Alexis took a sharp turn onto Chestnut Street.

"Please, yoga really centers me. I don't want to miss it."

"I don't have yoga clothes." Cassie pointed to her pleated skirt and wool sweater.

"I brought an extra leotard, just in case."

"I've wasted most of the day, I guess I could be Zen for an hour. As long as they don't make me stand on my head because it gives me a headache. Can we go to Just Desserts after and have those amazing custard Danishes?"

"What good is yoga if you follow it with custard Danish?" Alexis shook her head.

"I meditate better if I'm imagining custard," Cassie replied.

"How did it go with Aidan before the make-up sex?" Alexis asked over cups of steaming chai tea. They sat at a window table at Just Desserts, watching the joggers run around the Marina Green.

Cassie peeled off a layer of Danish. She was flushed and sweaty from the yoga. The instructor was a German woman who had glided around the room pressing in stomachs and straightening backs.

"That wasn't yoga, that was boot camp." Cassie poured hot milk into her tea.

"You'll appreciate it if you take a few more classes. Gerta is a disciplined teacher, but she gets great results," Alexis replied.

"If you want your body to be shaped permanently like a

pretzel. I'm going to stick with early morning walks to the Rose Garden." Cassie added two spoonfuls of honey.

"You're avoiding my question. How is the professor?"

"Aidan was only trying to do good," Cassie mumbled. The Molly episode still hurt, like a pin stuck in the hem of a dress.

"I thought charity began at home." Alexis ate a thin slice of Danish.

"He bought the pendant for me for Christmas. He ran into Molly at Peet's on his way home. She was all broken up because her boyfriend ran off with her best friend, so he just gave her the box."

"Handed her a Fenton's box in the middle of Peet's?" Alexis raised her eyebrows.

"He said he preaches about doing good in his lectures, but never gets the opportunity to put his words into action." Cassie shrugged.

"He could volunteer at the soup kitchen, or adopt a stray kitten." Alexis pushed her Danish aside.

"No kittens, thank you. I still have to feed and clean up after Isabel." Cassie dipped her finger in the custard. "I think he meant spontaneous good. Helping someone without being asked, just because the situation presents itself."

"Are you going to keep the pendant?" Alexis asked.

"I don't think so," Cassie said. The box had been sitting in her closet all week. Somehow she couldn't bring herself to open it. "The color doesn't do much for my eyes."

"Then exchange it for something fabulous, like another cashmere scarf. One of the new patterns."

"You get one, and I'll borrow it." Cassie ate the center of the Danish. The custard was light and sweet.

"I'm sick of shopping." Alexis put down her teacup. "I know that sounds spoilt but I've been shopping since we got married. First it was for a wedding gown and bridesmaids' dresses, then bikinis and sarongs for the honeymoon. Then a whole year of shopping to furnish the house. Christmas presents for Carter's clients, hostess gifts for their wives. I'm shopped out."

"Don't let my mother hear you say that. Women should never get tired of shopping." Cassie laughed.

"How was Lady Diana at lunch?" Alexis asked.

Cassie smiled. Alexis referred to Diana as the "The Duchess" during high school because she dressed as if she was attending a royal tea. Alexis said she never saw Diana without a silk scarf tied around her neck, or without her gold Cartier dangling from her wrist.

"Mother wants me to work at Fenton's. She met a young architect who had this brilliant idea of turning the basement of Fenton's into a food emporium, with locally grown produce. Vegetables, fruits, local cheeses, bread, wine. She wants me to run it."

"Is he cute?" Alexis leaned forward.

"Is who cute?" Cassie frowned.

"The young architect."

"You're married, remember." Cassie shook her head.

"I'm kidding, I'd never cheat on Carter. I just see Carter so rarely; sometimes I forget what he looks like. Every girl needs a little eye candy."

"I have no idea. He's from Chicago. I'm having dinner with him and my mother next week," Cassie replied.

"So you are considering it." Alexis looked at Cassie. "What would Aidan say?"

"I don't know if I'm considering it, though it is interesting. Can you imagine driving to local growers and finding their best produce? Discovering white eggplant, Chinese broccoli, cheese made with chives and garlic. Then displaying it all in a beautiful space." Cassie's eyes sparkled.

"Broccoli doesn't excite me, but I think it would be a gas to work at Fenton's. I'm dying to work; I sit at home and watch my nails grow."

"Why don't you get a job?" Cassie asked.

"I was a dance major. I don't think the San Francisco Ballet is hiring hedge-fund wives for the corps de ballet. We don't want to have a baby yet. I read if you have a baby too early in the marriage you'll never be a 'fun young couple' flying to Europe, trying new restaurants, attending the theater. The problem is Carter travels nonstop on business. When he's here he entertains clients at night, or he's so tired he falls asleep before I can fix a pre-dinner martini."

"You could open a little boutique on Sacramento Street. You have the best style," Cassie suggested.

"Every wife in Presidio Heights has a boutique on Sacramento Street. I can't walk a block without one of my friends waving hello from their bath boutique, or their antique furniture salon, or their high-end consignment store. It's like a never-ending Tupperware party."

"Yoga instructor?" Cassie grinned.

"I'd have to hold in my stomach all day." Alexis blotted her mouth with her napkin and re-applied pearl pink lip gloss. "Carter has his eye on a summer home in Napa. It's on an acre of vineyard. He wants to gut it and furnish it in 'early Californian.' That will keep me busy for a year and by then it'll be time to shop for bassinets and booties." Alexis looked at her watch. "I should go. He's on the six o'clock into SFO and I need to pick up a dozen oysters."

"Don't you think you spoil him?" Cassie put her napkin on her plate.

"Oysters are a natural aphrodisiac. Carter's been gone for five days, at least we can have great 'welcome home' sex. I'll drive you back to your car."

Cassie drove into the parking lot of the Berkeley Co-op. She walked into the co-op and looked around with new eyes. She noticed how the green vegetables were grouped together, and the front of the store was piled with citrus fruits. One corner was devoted to varieties of lettuce: endive, bok choy, arugula, mesclun. A wooden table held pots of mustard with handwritten labels. Cassie sampled a horseradish Dijon on a stone wheat cracker.

"Are you looking for something special?" the clerk asked. He had a scruffy goatee and wore a green T-shirt that said, "Order Whirled Peas."

"My husband loves to make soup. Which are the tastiest vegetables in season?" Cassie asked.

The clerk scratched his chin. "Our buyer just scored some turnips from a farm in Stockton. With the right herbs, they make a delicious base."

"I'll take a bag. Do you have any chard? And brussels sprouts. My husband can make brussels sprouts taste like candy." She loaded her shopping basket with produce.

Cassie stood at the checkout. The paper bags also said "Order Whirled Peas" under a picture of two doves. The clerk put a sample of organic fruit loaf in her bag and suggested she try a jar of kiwi jelly. Cassie walked back to the car, her arms filled with produce, thinking about her mother's idea. A food emporium, having a job involving the things she loved, was suddenly tempting.

*   *   *

Aidan was hunched over his laptop when Cassie walked into the house. He had a pencil tucked behind one ear and a box of dark chocolate truffles on the table beside him.

"You came home at just the right time. I'm out of truffles and getting nowhere with this paper. Maybe you could create a diversion." Aidan kissed Cassie and lifted a grocery bag from her arms.

"I bought ingredients for soup. But I don't know how exciting that is after a box of truffles." Cassie carried the other bag into the kitchen.

"I was thinking of a horizontal type of diversion. In bed, with a bottle of warm brandy. I can't get the thermostat up high enough." Aidan placed the bag on the counter and put his hands around Cassie's waist.

"Didn't you say Isabel would be home for dinner tonight?" Cassie laid her purchases on the counter: a bunch of turnips, a head of purple cauliflower, a tree of brussels sprouts.

"All the more reason to climb into bed now. She said she has something to tell us, which means she's failing a class or has a new boyfriend. Fucking you will make me a better listener." Aidan kissed Cassie's neck.

"Can we make the soup first?" Cassie took butter out of the fridge. "The co-op had sourdough bread fresh out of the oven."

Aidan kissed the top of her head. "Soup before sex? That sounds very bourgeois."

"Just tonight." Cassie smiled. "The clerk gave me a recipe he said was delicious."

"Okay, but you have to sit here while I slave at the stove. I'm having trouble relating Aristotle's tenets on treating your fellow man to the Facebook age."

Cassie watched Aidan slice turnips. Driving across the bridge she had rehearsed how she would broach the subject of the food emporium, but suddenly she was nervous. She looked at Aidan's hands, imagining how later they would travel over her body, touch her in places that made her ache with desire. Cassie took a deep breath.

"My mother sent me home with Maria's paella and I bought you a slice of red velvet cheesecake from Just Desserts."

"How did you end up at Just Desserts?" Aidan smeared a thin film of olive oil inside the soup pot.

"Alexis coerced me into doing couples yoga with her, so we rewarded ourselves at Just Desserts."

"Powwows with my favorite two women on the same day? Did they bring an Aidan doll and stick pins in it?" Aidan frowned.

Cassie blushed. "My mother likes you as much as she likes anyone who doesn't spend every minute shopping at Fenton's. You and Alexis just need to spend more time together. We should have dinner with her and Carter."

"At their mosaic dining-room table imported in pieces from Italy? Going to their wedding was enough. I was the only man in the room not wearing an Armani tux, including the waiters." Aidan opened a bottle of red wine and poured himself a glass. "And Carter only drinks French wine. What kind of guy drinks wine from the Loire Valley when he lives an hour from Napa?"

"Actually Alexis said Carter's thinking of buying a summer home on a vineyard."

"Of course, then he'll drink his own 'private' label." Aidan poured a glass for Cassie.

"I agree with you about buying locally." Cassie sipped the wine. "My mother actually had an interesting idea."

"I'm listening." Aidan threw turnip, baby onions, and chopped kale into the pot.

"She met an architect who specializes in the interior design of restaurants. He just did a new restaurant in the city that is all 'green.' He suggested we turn the basement of Fenton's into a food emporium, featuring locally grown produce, cheese, bread, wines."

"The Fenton's crowd doesn't strike me as particularly 'green.' Don't they all drive Range Rovers and hop on planes the way most people hop on buses?" Aidan added basil and oregano to the soup.

"My mother wants to attract a younger clientele. The young moms whose kids are learning to be environmentally responsible. They recycle in the classroom and want their school lunches to be packed in reusable containers." Cassie took a large sip of wine.

"I guess it could work, though I don't see them trading their alligator boots for Keds." Aidan shrugged.

"We'd have a counter where you could sample the produce, maybe even a chef who would demonstrate recipes using different vegetables," Cassie said, excitement creeping into her voice.

"You keep saying 'we.' " Aidan put down his wineglass.

"My mother thinks I'd be the perfect person to be in charge," Cassie replied.

"In charge of a food emporium? That sounds pretty demanding." Aidan frowned. He put down his knife and sat on the stool next to Cassie.

"Mother has wanted me to work at Fenton's for so long. She'll be sixty on her next birthday." Cassie smelled Aidan's aftershave. His navy shirt was unbuttoned and she could see the gray hair on his chest.

"Fenton's isn't a child. It's a department store," Aidan said quietly.

"What do you mean?" Cassie glanced at Aidan. Usually when Aidan sat so close to her, she could think of nothing but sex. She stood up and walked to the pantry.

"Diana talks like Fenton's is a baby that you have to take charge of when she retires. It doesn't have to stay in the family, it's not your responsibility." Aidan's eyes flashed.

Cassie tried to keep her voice steady. "What if I want it to be my responsibility?"

"Our marriage is your responsibility. Running this house, caring for Isabel when she's here. Working at Fenton's is a seven-days-a-week commitment." Aidan took the loaf of bread from the pantry and cut it in thick slices. He stabbed a stick of butter and spread it on the bread.

"I could do both. It doesn't have to be seven days a week."

"How often was your mother home when you were a child? Didn't you have dinner in her office, peanut butter sandwiches packed by Maria and eaten on Diana's Louis XIV rug? How many times have you told me you did your homework in Fenton's café?" Aidan swallowed a slice of bread and washed it down with red wine.

"I love Fenton's, I just don't have the eye for fashion. But a whole floor of fruits and vegetables!"

"You have that at the Edible Schoolyard. I don't want you spending all your time in the city."

"Isabel's sixteen. She's hardly here. . . ." Cassie kept her eyes on her glass of wine.

"I'm here. I need you. Christ, Cassie. I'm not the young genius professor anymore. This paper is very important to me. If it doesn't get accepted at the conference it will reflect badly on the whole department." Aidan put his hands on Cassie's shoulders.

"I'd like to think about it," Cassie said stubbornly.

"I'd like to put this soup on simmer, take our wineglasses upstairs, and show you how much I need you." Aidan kissed Cassie gently on the lips.

Aidan put his hands behind Cassie's head and pulled her against his chest. He caressed her back and then he lifted her skirt and slipped his fingers under her panties. Cassie's knees buckled and she felt herself opening up, her body tensing, and wanting him inside her.

"Come on," Aidan whispered in her hair, "I've missed you all day."

Aidan took her hand and led her upstairs. He closed the bedroom door and pulled Cassie's sweater over her head. He unbuttoned his shirt and slipped off his shorts. His legs were covered in dark hair; his calves were strong and muscled from years of running. He kissed her again, his arms wrapped around her, guiding them onto the bed. Aidan kept his eyes on Cassie's face as he entered her, moving like an athlete, wanting to fill her up, not stopping until she shattered against him.

Cassie and Aidan walked downstairs dressed in terry robes as Isabel slammed the front door. Isabel at sixteen was like a fashion model that stepped off a runway straight into the kitchen. Everything about her was intense and exaggerated. She was the only person Cassie knew who could pull off the clothes designers splashed across the fashion pages. Baby-doll dresses with fishnet stockings and four-inch heels. Cargo pants with lace halter tops and ankle boots. Isabel's mother gave her an allowance bigger than Cassie and Aidan's house payment, and Isabel spent it all on clothes.

"Your mother shouldn't let you out of the house dressed like that," Aidan observed tightly. Isabel wore a wool dress barely covering her thighs and knee-high boots with suede tassels. Her hair fell to her waist in glossy black waves and she wore a minimum amount of makeup: thick black mascara and sheer lip gloss.

"Come on, Dad, I need to express myself. You're the one who says it's important to embrace who you are." Isabel tossed her bag onto the counter and buttered a slice of sourdough.

"You could embrace who you are more quietly, by wearing a longer skirt," Aidan muttered.

"Look at you two, you've already finished off half a bottle of wine and it's only six o'clock." Isabel held up the wine bottle.

"Put that down and set the table," Aidan said tersely. He put the bottle of wine in the fridge and filled three glasses with water and ice.

"Honestly, you're supposed to be my cool Berkeley parent. Mom is getting so uptight these days; she walks around in tennis skirts and bobby socks." Isabel rolled her eyes.

Cassie watched the exchange between Aidan and Isabel silently. The warm flush of sex was wearing off and her head hurt from the red wine. She wanted to curl up in Aidan's lap in the living room and listen to Prince or U2.

"Discipline is a virtue. The second semester of your junior year is the most important of your high school career." Aidan placed a bowl of carrots and hummus on the table.

"Like I don't have that drummed into me twenty-four-seven. Between Mom and the guidance counselor, you'd think if I don't find a cure for cancer I shouldn't show up for school. Your generation isn't making life for our generation easy." Isabel put her elbows on the table.

"And take your elbows off the table," Aidan replied.

"I was wondering if you're going to be around this summer," Isabel said casually as they ate their soup.

"I'm teaching a summer course on Socrates and Plato. Guaranteed to entice incoming freshmen that'd rather be surfing in Santa Cruz." Aidan sprinkled a large spoonful of grated cheese in his bowl.

"Mom and the dreaded Peter are taking a six-week cruise around the Arctic Circle, Scandinavia, and Norway, and other impossibly boring places." Isabel dunked a bread crust into her soup.

"I may not be fond of your mother's husband but he clothes and feeds you pretty nicely. Not to mention bought you the little sports car in my driveway. Don't call him 'dreaded,'" Aidan replied.

Cassie concentrated on her soup. The turnip had been even sweeter than she expected and Aidan had added just the right amount of spices. She thought about some of the other vegetables the co-op clerk had suggested: yellow squash, zucchini, shiitake mushrooms. Tomorrow she'd go back and get some more recipes and try a vegetable crepe or an egg white omelet.

"Those cruises are fine if you're over forty and want to play shuffleboard and learn swing dancing. Mom wants me to go with them and I'd rather be stranded at a Justin Bieber concert." Isabel looked at her father.

"You're asking if you can stay with us." Aidan put down his spoon.

"Yes, if you plan on being around. Mom won't let me stay at the house by myself," Isabel mumbled.

"Of course you can stay, but you have to live by our rules: a reasonable curfew and some sort of productive labor during the day. You can get a job or help Cassie at the Edible Schoolyard."

"I'm not ruining my nails in all that dirt." Isabel inspected her bloodred fingernails.

"The Edible Schoolyard doesn't do much during the summer," Cassie said. She felt a big lump in her throat. She thought about the meeting with her mother and the architect. She wanted to say she wasn't sure what she'd be doing this summer but she knew it was important they present a united front.

"Then any kind of job, at Peet's or the yogurt store. I don't want you sitting around texting your friends," Aidan replied.

"It's summer before senior year," Isabel muttered. "Doesn't anyone remember you're supposed to have fun in high school? Cassie, you didn't go to high school that long ago." Isabel looked sideways at Cassie.

"I worked at Fenton's every summer." Cassie got up and put her soup bowl in the sink.

"Then we're all in agreement." Aidan smiled. "We're happy to have you stay with us. I'll call your mother and let her know."

After dinner Isabel grabbed a Häagen-Dazs bar from the freezer and announced she had to meet her calculus study group. She kissed her father on the cheek, grabbed her bag, and flew out the front door. Aidan put two bowls of ice cream and the slice of red velvet cheesecake on the kitchen table and handed Cassie a spoon.

"Remember when Isabel would sit with us after dinner and eat a bowl of vanilla ice cream?" Aidan asked.

"No," Cassie said. "I remember her running up to her room and slamming the door while we ate her bowl of ice cream."

"That's why I'm getting soft in the middle. I've been eating Isabel's dessert for sixteen years. She's not getting any easier." Aidan ate a bite of cheesecake.

"She's sixteen." Cassie shrugged. "When Alexis was sixteen she dated identical twin brothers. Her parents never knew. She said she liked getting double the attention, and double the presents. Sixteen-year-old girls like to push the envelope."

"Except you." Aidan grinned. "You were the model Catholic schoolgirl."

"I just didn't fall in love," Cassie mumbled.

"That's why I got lucky." Aidan kissed her on the lips. "I'm guessing Isabel has a new boyfriend she doesn't want to leave unattended. Even a cruise to the Arctic is more attractive than staying home unless there's a boy involved."

"You're probably right." Cassie got up and put the dishes in the sink. She was suddenly tired. It seemed like ages ago she had lunch with her mother and took the yoga class with Alexis.

"I'm glad you'll be home to keep an eye on her." Aidan stood beside her and filled the sink with soap.

Cassie wanted to reply, but she kept silent and watched the dishes disappear under the bubbles.

4.

I t was turning into the wettest January the Bay Area had experienced in years. The Berkeley hills were emerald green, the sky was heavy with rain clouds, and the streets were muddy and windblown. Cassie hadn't worked at the Edible Schoolyard for a week. She picked up fresh produce from the co-op each morning and spent her afternoons in the kitchen trying different recipes. She pictured herself presiding over a gleaming marble counter, handing out samples of asparagus crepes, mushroom tarts, and spinach soufflés on red plates inscribed with Fenton's signature.

They hadn't discussed the food emporium again. Aidan was caught up in the first week of classes. On Tuesday morning, Cassie served Aidan whole-wheat toast, soft-boiled eggs, and organic coffee.

"I'm having dinner with my mother at Boulevard tonight," she said, filling a jug with cream.

"It's going to pour." Aidan looked out the window. He wore a ribbed sweater, thick cords, and his black leather jacket. His hair was damp from an early morning workout, and he had a shaving nick on his chin.

"I'll be careful. I might be a bit late." Cassie stirred cream into her coffee.

Aidan scraped the last bite of his egg, grabbed a stack of papers, and kissed the top of her head. "I'm knee-deep in research at the library. I'll meet you in bed."

Cassie stood in front of her closet, wondering what to wear. She debated between a Burberry dress bought years ago for Fenton's Christmas party, and a brown turtleneck and mid-length skirt. She thought the Burberry was dated; her mother could discern its vintage in a minute. She pulled the turtleneck over her head and brushed her hair so it fell in thick waves to her shoulders.

Cassie looked at the Fenton's box on her dressing table. She opened the box and put the pendant against her throat, turning in front of the mirror. She placed the pendant back in the box, and chose a Tiffany heart necklace. She rubbed on some lip gloss and walked downstairs.

Cassie arrived at the restaurant late. The Bay Bridge traffic moved like a snail and parking near Boulevard was impossible. She finally gave up and handed her keys to the valet. She saw her mother through the window, dressed in all white like a snow queen. Diana wore a cashmere cardigan over a quilted skirt and white boots with steel tips. A silk scarf was knotted around her neck, and she tapped her cigarette holder against the bar.

Diana waved at Cassie. "There you are, darling, we were beginning to worry." Cassie handed her London Fog to the maître d' and straightened her skirt. The man standing opposite her mother was about thirty-five, with wavy brown hair and green eyes. He wore a blue button-down shirt, pleated slacks, and a wool blazer. He shook Cassie's hand and made room for her at the bar.

"This is James Parrish. He's been filling me in on his preliminary work on the food emporium." Diana beamed.

"Your mother tells me you're involved with Alice Waters's projects. She's one of my gurus." James smiled. He had a smattering of freckles on his cheeks and a dimple on his chin. He stuffed his hands in his pockets and shifted from foot to foot.

"Let's get our table." Diana swooped up her martini glass. "I can't hear a thing over this din, and I don't want to miss a word."

They sat at a window booth and Cassie sipped white wine. The gold-trimmed menu written in spidery cursive was intimidating.

"The lamb comes in a reduction sauce. And the clay pots of whipped potatoes and garlic butter are one-of-a-kind." James leaned across the table and pointed to Cassie's menu.

"How do you know their menu so well?" Cassie asked.

"San Francisco is an amazing town for a foodie. I could eat out every night: Bix, The Waterfront, One Market. People here are passionate about dining. That's why I think the food emporium will be a success." James leaned back against the booth.

"You have to hear James's ideas for the design. Did you know he works for the top interior design firm in Chicago?" Diana ran her fingers down the menu, stopping on poached salmon with cut green beans.

"My mother grew up in San Francisco, so I've always had a soft spot for the city. She used to sing Tony Bennett songs while she cooked dinner." James broke a breadstick in half and dipped it in olive oil.

"We're very lucky to steal James away from Chicago for a few months." Diana stirred her drink with her olive.

James blushed and Cassie frowned and shook her head. "Mother, I'm not sure I can commit to running the venture full-time."

Diana stopped stirring and stabbed the olive with a toothpick.

"Cassie, you have to! James's designs are in *Gourmet Magazine, Architectural Digest, Restaurant Monthly*. Every page shouts boy genius! He's going to rocket Fenton's into the twenty-first century."

"Mother, you're talking about James as if he's not here." Cassie kept her eyes on her wineglass.

"Cassie is married to an ethics professor," Diana said dryly. "He doesn't believe in commerce and he doesn't like Cassie to leave the house. He wants her waiting at home with a casserole on the stove and slippers by the fireplace."

"I'm right here, Mother," Cassie said. She was beginning to regret that she came. It was raining even harder outside; the wind blew umbrellas into the street. She wished she were lying in bed with Aidan, gray down comforter pulled up to her chin.

Diana finished her martini and signaled the waiter for another. "James, show Cassie your sketches."

James moved aside the bread plates and put four storyboards on the table. They were more detailed versions of his earlier sketches: shoppers carrying red Fenton's bags of fruits and vegetables, glossy red stools at small round tables, crystal vases holding long red roses.

"Red will be the predominant color: red ceramic bowls

of cherries, plums, apples. Giant sketches of tomatoes and red peppers in red lacquer frames. The floors are quite beautiful, they just need a bit of polish, and the ceiling is the perfect height for hanging pots and pans." James talked with his hands, making sweeping gestures over the artwork.

"Brilliant." Diana sipped her second martini. "Neiman's will be green with envy, Gump's will be furious they didn't think of it first. We'll be the talk of San Francisco."

"It's beautiful." Cassie nodded.

James sat back against the booth and smiled like a schoolboy. "I'm glad you like it," he said to Cassie.

The lamb arrived on a white porcelain plate. Each slice melted in Cassie's mouth. Scooping the potatoes from the earthen pot and eating them with a forkful of lamb, Cassie felt two steps closer to heaven.

Her mother switched from martinis to a Chateau St. Jean Pinot Noir and regaled James with a history of Fenton's.

"My father was stationed in Italy during World War II and fell in love with fashion. No one cut a dress, made a shoe, created a bag like an Italian. After the war, he convinced his father to loan him money to open a department store on Union Square." Diana sniffed the rim of her wineglass.

"Fenton's was an immediate success. Women were tired of wartime fashion: drab dresses designed to wear in a factory, coats made to keep warm without an ounce of sex appeal. My father filled the racks with ball gowns, silk scarves, and stiletto heels. I went to work with him every Saturday since I was five years old. He let me use the cash register and ring up the customers." Diana paused and ate a bite of salmon.

"I married Gray, Cassie's father, and the three of us ran

the store together. Then my father died of cancer and it was just Gray and I. One afternoon Gray dropped dead on the squash court. That's when I started bringing Cassie to work. I wanted her to feel the pulse of Fenton's, because one day the store would be hers." Diana put down her fork and looked at Cassie.

"I don't have your eye for fashion," Cassie mumbled.

"Maybe not, but you have an innate love of fruits and vegetables." Diana drank her wine. "Cassie was born with a gardening shovel in her hand."

"My mother said her earliest memory is of shopping at Fenton's at Christmas," James interjected. "She was sure Santa Claus and the elves lived on the top floor because the merchandise was stunning."

"We're fortunate to have instilled that kind of loyalty," Diana replied thoughtfully. "The food emporium will win over a new generation. Food is the new fashion."

Cassie ate the last slice of lamb. She put her napkin on her plate and glanced at James's storyboards leaning against the table.

"Wouldn't it be cool to showcase a local grower each week? I know a Japanese family in Stockton with an asparagus farm. They deliver asparagus to the Berkeley Co-op in bundles tied with bamboo," Cassie said quickly.

"And we could package samples in red boxes. Not the kind of boxes that get soggy and fall apart the minute you put them in your bag, but more like Tupperware containers made especially for Fenton's." Cassie stopped to catch her breath.

"I think those are brilliant ideas." Diana smiled at Cassie. "Let's order dessert."

James suggested the poached pear in apricot brandy

liquor. He placed his storyboards on the table and they pored over them again: adding a bench where customers could rest, putting in a circular display in the center of the floor. Cassie felt her cheeks flush from the warm pear, the brandy, the excitement of seeing the emporium come to life. When she looked outside and saw taxis honking, she realized she had forgotten it was raining.

"I should go. It's going to take hours to get home." Cassie pushed her plate away.

"James, these sketches are perfect. You can start ordering materials." Diana took her gold American Express card from her wallet.

"Mother, I need to talk to Aidan," Cassie interrupted.

"Darling, this is going to be brilliant. And you're a natural. At one dinner you thought of half a dozen things that will thrill customers."

"Your mother is right." James nodded. "Your ideas are inspiring."

Cassie blushed. "Aidan is writing a really important paper, and he needs my support. Isabel is going to stay with us for a month this summer."

"James"—Diana tapped her American Express card on the table—"tell Cassie about the food hall at Harrods."

"The architecture is Beaux Arts style, all gold finishes and intricate ironwork. The floors are black-and-white marble, and the most amazing chandeliers hang from the ceiling. The cheese hall has more than three hundred varieties of cheese, and the meat hall serves wild boar and Cornish hens. The candy hall is like Christmas every day with giant jars of jelly beans, caramels, lollipops, and candy canes." James's green eyes sparkled.

"Cassie." Diana handed the waiter her American Express card.

Cassie looked from her mother to James to the storyboards on the table. "I'll talk to Aidan." She stood up and asked the maître d' for her coat.

Driving across the bridge in the rain, Cassie listened to the wipers cutting across the windshield. Her head swam with images of Harrods: rows of jams and jellies, shelves of spices. She pictured James's sketches of glass cases full of truffles and fridges stuffed with cheese.

When she pulled into the driveway the house was dark. Aidan's car was in the garage; the front seat was littered with textbooks, a laptop, and empty coffee cups. Cassie smiled. She'd clear it out for him as a surprise. She'd cook his favorite breakfast: whole-wheat pancakes with fresh orange juice. She'd pack lunch so he didn't have to stand in line at the campus food court. She crept into the house, hung her London Fog in the closet, and climbed upstairs.

Aidan slept on his stomach, his arms splayed across the bed like a swimmer doing the butterfly. Cassie undressed and climbed in beside him. She draped his arm over her chest, hoping he'd wake so she could tell him about the sculpted mermaids in the Harrods fish hall, about her idea for red Fenton's airtight containers. He snored softly, his foot twitched, but he didn't stir. Cassie closed her eyes and pulled the down comforter up to her chin.

5.

Alexis called the next morning. "How was dinner at Boulevard?"

Cassie stood by the kitchen window, watching her garden become a river of mud. Aidan had left for an early meeting, grabbing a pancake and the turkey sandwich she packed in Maria's lunch box.

"Rack of lamb, potatoes, and poached pears for dessert." Cassie sipped the remains of Aidan's coffee.

"I wasn't talking about the food. Give me the dish, did your mother turn it on thick?"

Cassie laughed. "You know her too well. Very thick, and James showed me his designs."

"And?" Cassie pictured Alexis perched on the ostrich-skin stool in her chrome kitchen, sipping a cup of chai tea.

"They were fantastic"—Cassie breathed—"and he described the Harrods food hall. It sounds amazing, Alexis, like a fairy-tale castle filled with food."

"Are you going to do it?"

"I don't know." Cassie sighed. "I need to talk to Aidan."

"You should, I spent all day in Fenton's yesterday. I am in love with the new Ella Moss sweaters, and your mother stocks the most fabulous Prada flats. I bought three pairs: orange, cream, and black," Alexis replied.

"I'll tell her, she'll be pleased." Cassie put the coffee cup in the sink.

"Today I'm doing Neiman's. It's raining too hard to do anything but shop. I figured I'd spend one hour per floor. With an hour lunch break, that's an eight-hour workday," Alexis said.

"Sounds like a hard job." Cassie laughed.

"Was he cute?" Alexis changed the subject.

"Was who cute?" Cassie put away berries, syrup, and whipped cream.

"The architect. I told you I want the dish."

"He looked like Clark Kent." Cassie put the orange juice in the fridge.

"Oooh, I love the nerdy, bookish type. Does he wear those round, rimless glasses?"

"I can't remember. Shouldn't you be focusing on Carter and your couples yoga classes?" Cassie sat at the kitchen table. The rain was falling sideways against the glass. The flowers in the window box were plastered against the soil.

"Carter is in Luxembourg, researching a new telecommunications company." Alexis sighed. "Tonight we're going to try Skype sex. I bought a black lace teddy."

"I don't need the visual." Cassie grimaced.

"Come with me to Neiman's today, you can't play in the garden in the rain."

"I'm going to make pizza for Aidan," Cassie said, suddenly deciding she'd go to the co-op and buy fresh ingredients for mozzarella pizza.

"Do the food emporium, Cassie. Your talents are wasted on Aidan."

"You sound like my mother." Cassie grabbed a pen and scribbled down a shopping list.

Cassie folded her raincoat over the shopping cart and consulted her list. Heirloom tomatoes, round and firm and just a little bit sweet, were the key to delicious pizza. She put oregano and fresh basil in the cart, and added anchovies and a ball of mozzarella cheese.

The tomatoes were displayed on a table at the back of the co-op. Cassie picked out two red tomatoes and weighed them on the metal scale.

"The yellow tomatoes are sweeter." A girl stood behind her, holding a bag of yellow tomatoes.

"Thanks, I'll try one."

The girl had feathery blond hair and big brown eyes. "The co-op has the best heirlooms." She placed her tomatoes on the scale. "I eat them with salt and oregano."

"I'm making pizza." Cassie frowned. The girl looked vaguely familiar, like she'd seen her at the co-op before. She wore a bomber jacket and army green rain boots.

"I eat pizza every other day. The waiter at Gino's gives me buy-one-get-one-free coupons." The girl looked closely at Cassie. "Hey, I know you. You're the woman who owns Fenton's."

Cassie blushed. "My mother owns Fenton's."

"I returned that pendant after Christmas and you gave me a refund." The girl stood very close to Cassie. She had long blond eyelashes.

"I remember." Cassie froze. She gripped the handle of her shopping cart.

"It was nice of you to give me cash instead of store credit."
The girl smiled. She had full red lips and straight white teeth.
"I bought myself a microwave so I can heat up chicken rice
bowls. I was vegetarian for a while; my boyfriend made
me feel guilty for eating meat. We lived on tofu for months. I
mean, tofu is okay if you drench it in soy sauce"——the girl ate
a grapefruit sample and handed one to Cassie——"but I grew
up on a farm in the Midwest. We ate eggs for breakfast and
chicken or lamb for dinner."

Cassie wished the girl would stop talking and go away.
She wanted to maneuver her cart to another aisle, but it was
clogged with shoppers sampling produce.

"My parents weren't happy I was dating a vegetarian. They
weren't pleased that I came to Berkeley to go to school; they
thought everyone wore tie-dyed T-shirts and had dreadlocks.
I told them the sixties was decades ago, and that Berkeley is
one of the top universities in the country." The girl tried
cucumber and hummus, a cup of salsa, and a few baked pita
chips. "I love the co-op, you can have lunch without buying a
thing. Try the chips, they're really good."

"No, thank you." Cassie shook her head.

"The professors are so nice, they really seem to care.
When my boyfriend broke up with me, my ethics professor
gave me a present. I was sitting at Peet's sobbing, and he just
walked up to me and handed me that Fenton's box. He's kind
of old but he has the most amazing black eyes."

Cassie felt her knees buckle. She tightened her grip on
the shopping cart.

"It was sweet, I was so upset I considered going home.
But I thought, fuck it, I'm going to forget Jack——that was my
boyfriend——and get on with it. I bought an organic chicken
and ate the whole thing." The girl brushed the hair from her

eyes. "And then I went to Fenton's to return the pendant and you were so nice, I called my mother and said California is full of nice people. I just picked the wrong guy. Jack wasn't even from California; I think he was from Michigan." The girl paused, sucking on a slice of orange.

"I baked pumpkin muffins for the professor to thank him. Jack said I made the best pumpkin muffins. He lied about that too. He ran off with my best friend to open a bakery. He took all the money we saved and went to Oregon."

Cassie didn't know where to look. The girl just kept talking and talking. She tried to push the cart but the girl leaned against it, as if they were chatting at a cocktail party.

"I mean who wants to go to Oregon anyway? It rains like three hundred days a year. Anyway, I'm so over him. I made the professor pumpkin muffins and I bought a red lace bra and panties from the lingerie store on Bancroft." The girl paused and popped a zucchini stick in her mouth. "No matter how old they are, men can't resist lace."

Cassie leaned forward against the shopping cart. She could hear her heart hammering in her chest. When she looked up the girl's face was close to hers and she was frowning.

"Are you okay? You look like you're going to faint. Maybe you're getting the flu. It's all this rain. I take tons of vitamin C, and vitamin D. Can I get you a glass of water?"

Cassie opened her mouth but she couldn't form any words. She grabbed her bag and ran out of the store. She stood at the car door, rifling through her purse for her keys. She turned the bag upside down on the wet cement, scattering lip gloss, credit cards, Kleenex, cell phone. She found her keys, swept everything in the bag, and climbed into the car. The rain drummed on the windshield and she half expected to see the girl's face pressed against the glass, asking if she was okay. She laid her head on the steering wheel, closed her eyes, and started to cry.

Cassie stumbled into the house and shut the door. She wanted to run upstairs, turn on the shower, and dissolve into the steam. But she couldn't get farther than the laundry room. She grabbed a towel from the top of the pile, pulled out the kitchen chair, and waited.

Now it was almost dark outside. Her clothes were damp and there was a puddle of water on the kitchen floor. She checked her cell phone; it was past five o'clock. Aidan could be home any time.

Her mother left a message and Alexis sent texts detailing her Neiman's shopping adventure. "Found the most divine ruby earrings." "Cashmere gloves on sale! Picked you up a pair." "In the café, eating coq au vin." Cassie read the texts, deleted them, and wrapped the towel tighter around her shoulders.

Her head ached, her throat hurt, her forehead was on fire. She wanted to rest her head on the kitchen table, but every time she closed her eyes she saw Molly Payne in a lace bra and panties, offering Aidan a pumpkin muffin.

Aidan walked in the back door and put his lunch box on the table. "Cassie, why are you sitting in the dark? You're all wet." He kissed the top of her head. "Christ, you're burning up! You should be upstairs in bed."

Cassie opened her eyes wider and looked at him. He looked the same: hair damp and curly from the rain, wet splotches on his leather jacket, shaving nick on his chin.

"Molly Payne," Cassie said.

"Who?" Aidan sat down at the table.

"Your student, Molly Payne." Cassie's head felt so heavy it was an effort to talk.

"What about her?"

"I saw her at the co-op. I was going to make pizza tonight."

"You're in no condition to cook. Go up to bed. I'll bring tea and brandy." Aidan stood up and turned on the stove.

"How were her pumpkin muffins?"

"Cassie, you're not making sense. C'mon, I'll take you upstairs."

It was when he touched her that she snapped. "Molly Payne made you pumpkin muffins"—she was almost yelling—"and she bought a red lace bra and panties to seduce you."

"I don't know what you're talking about." Aidan grabbed Cassie's arm.

"Let go of me." She pulled away. "You know exactly what I'm talking about. Where did you fuck her? On the sofa in your office?"

"I'll pour some brandy."

"I don't want any brandy." Cassie was shivering again. Her hands shook, her lips chattered, her knees knocked together.

"I do." Aidan took the brandy from the pantry and filled his glass.

"Tell me what happened," Cassie said, trying to keep her body still, "or I'm going to come to your class tomorrow and find out myself."

Aidan drank the brandy and refilled his glass. He looked at Cassie carefully. He took off his jacket, sat down, and clasped his hands together.

"I'm not proud," he said quietly, "but I'm human."

"Would you stop playing the ethics professor?" Cassie

interrupted. "I don't want to hear about Aristotle and human weakness. I want to know if you fucked Molly Payne."

The silence was broken by the rain beating against the glass. Cassie waited for Aidan to tell her it never went that far, that she got it all wrong.

"Just once"—he put his head in his hands—"and I'm so sorry. It will never happen again."

Cassie opened her mouth but nothing came out. She looked at Aidan. His lips were set in a thin line, his eyes focused on his glass. She tried again.

"Tell me."

"Molly left a plate of muffins on my desk the first day of classes, with a note thanking me for the pendant. She waited for me after the lecture, said she wanted my help with the paper she was writing." Aidan poured another shot of brandy. "I explained I don't hold office hours the first week of classes. She asked if I could squeeze in a few minutes at Peet's, on my way home. It's nice to see a student care about the class."

Cassie wanted to scream that Molly only cared about fucking the professor, about erasing the pain of being jilted.

"Molly was sitting at a table near the window. She'd ordered me a peppermint latte. She said her paper was on her desktop and she couldn't get her printer to work. She asked if I could come to her apartment."

Cassie gripped the edge of the kitchen table. She watched her knuckles turn blue.

"I said no, I couldn't go to a student's apartment. She said please, just for a minute. She'd just grab a latte for her roommate." Aidan looked at Cassie, his eyes were wet. "I figured if her roommate was there it was no big deal. We walked two blocks. Her roommate was just going to work."

Cassie didn't look at Aidan. She studied the pile of mail on the kitchen table.

"I sat at her computer and read the paper. It was a small room but it wasn't her bedroom. There was a futon and a wooden coffee table and a galley kitchen with a microwave on the counter." Aidan reached out and touched Cassie's hand. "Molly said she'd heat up some muffins. I thought she was in the kitchen but she was standing behind me. She'd stripped off her clothes."

"Stop." Cassie took her hand away. "I don't want to know."

"I was like Pavlov's dog, you've got to believe me." Aidan grabbed her hand and squeezed it hard. "Christ, Cassie, she was almost naked, she was kissing me, sitting in my lap before I could move. She dragged me onto the futon, I don't even remember taking off my pants."

"Get out," Cassie whispered.

"I said I wasn't proud, fuck, Cassie, I've been beating myself up all week. I've never done anything like this before. I love you, do you understand? I love you." He was almost shouting.

"Aidan, just stop."

"We've been married ten years and I've never strayed. I'm not going to let this come between us."

"You screwed her, Aidan, you fucked your student." Cassie's voice was hoarse. She was sweating and freezing at the same time.

"Cassie, I know I made a colossal mistake. Let me carry you upstairs and put you to bed. We'll talk about it tomorrow. Please, I'm begging you." Aidan grabbed her wrists and pulled her toward him.

Cassie's head throbbed. It would be so easy to let Aidan put her to bed. She could drink a shot of brandy, take some

Tylenol, wait until the fever subsided and she had time to think.

She pulled her hands away and knocked Aidan's lunch box onto the floor. A half-eaten sandwich flew out. Cassie bent down to pick it up. She stuffed wheat bread, turkey, and wilted lettuce back in the box. She scrunched up a piece of plastic wrap and a cupcake doily. She put the lunch box on the table and grabbed her purse.

"I'm going to stay with Alexis for a while." She stood up. Her legs were wobbly and black spots exploded like flash-bulbs in front of her eyes.

"It's pouring and you've got a fever. I'm not going to let you drive over the bridge." Aidan blocked the kitchen door.

Cassie felt her head clear. "I'm not your student, I'm not your daughter, and I don't know if I'm still your wife," she said the words slowly. "I'll text you when I get there."

6.

Cassie started hallucinating as she circled Alexis's block. Driving across the bridge, she kept her eyes glued to the lights of the car in front of her. She gripped the steering wheel so tightly, she thought she'd rip the leather. She turned on the radio and listened to KFOG as she climbed the hills into Presidio Heights.

The rain became a constant drizzle instead of a downpour, and she found a parking space a block from Alexis's house. She locked the car and walked down the street. Suddenly every house—three-story brick mansions behind iron gates crawling with ivy—looked the same.

Cassie couldn't remember which corner Alexis's house was on. She walked up a stone pathway, rang the doorbell, and waited. A girl with short blond hair answered the door. Cassie blinked. When she opened her eyes, the girl was wearing a red lace bra and panties. Cassie turned and ran down the path to the street.

Cassie tried the house at the next corner. Alexis answered

the door wearing a velour sweat suit and UGG slippers. She carried a tiny white puppy swaddled in a blue blanket.

"Cassie, you're soaking wet."

Cassie looked down at her clothes. She was still wearing the running pants and long-sleeved T-shirt she had put on in the morning. She vaguely remembered folding her raincoat over the shopping cart at the co-op. She must have left her rain boots in the kitchen because she had moccasins on her feet.

"Can I come in?" Cassie asked.

"Of course you can come in. Why didn't you call? What are you doing, where's Aidan?" Alexis dragged Cassie inside.

The inside of Alexis's house looked like the grand salon at the Ritz. The living room had marble floors and thick wool rugs. A grand piano filled one corner and crystal chandeliers hung from the ceiling. The walls were painted a glossy eggshell and the curtains were French silk.

"Sit down, I'll get some tea." Alexis moved a stack of magazines from a long velvet sofa.

"I don't want tea."

"Cassie, you look terrible. Your cheeks are bright red."

"I think I have a fever." Cassie felt her forehead. The light in the room was very bright and everything seemed to be covered by a yellow filter.

Alexis put the puppy on the sofa and touched Cassie's head. "You're on fire. I'll call a doctor."

"I don't need a doctor." Cassie shook her head. "But I'd like to lie down."

"Let's go upstairs. I'll have Pia bring some Tylenol."

Alexis led her into a bedroom with white carpet and a canopied bed. She opened the armoire and took out a silk robe and red slippers. She turned down the covers and helped Cassie take off her pants and shirt.

"Get some sleep; we'll talk in the morning." Alexis turned off the bedside light.

Cassie remembered someone else saying the same thing. She thought it was Aidan, but she couldn't be sure. She wanted to answer Alexis but she lay back against the silk pillowcase and fell asleep.

When Cassie woke it was dark outside. She listened for the rain, but it had stopped. Her throat was so dry she could barely swallow. Her eyes focused on an antique clock on the bedside table. The hands read eight o'clock. She tried to sit up, but her head was too heavy. She closed her eyes and slept.

"Cassie, have some juice. You haven't eaten in two days." Alexis sat in a lacquered red chair next to Cassie's bed. She held a glass of orange juice on a silver tray. The puppy was curled in her lap, making small snuffling noises.

Cassie opened her eyes and looked around the room. There was a mahogany desk by the window and framed Chinese writing on the walls. A red ottoman sat at the foot of the bed, and gold pillows were piled on the floor.

"Let me guess, you call this the red room," Cassie said.

"You haven't talked in two days and the first thing you do is criticize my design." Alexis handed Cassie the orange juice. "Carter had an extended stay in Beijing last summer. He wanted to re-create the ambience." Alexis waited until Cassie drank the juice. "I've been really worried. You had a fever of a hundred and four."

Cassie tried to sit up. Her head still felt heavy and her eyes had trouble staying open.

"Slow down." Alexis took the glass back. "One baby step at a time."

"Thanks for letting me stay. I hope Carter doesn't mind me intruding on your love nest."

"Carter is still in Luxembourg, followed by Venice, Berlin, and Zurich. The only ones in the love nest are me and Poodles." Alexis held up the tiny white puppy.

"That's a very small poodle." Cassie frowned.

"He's a shih tzu, I just named him Poodles. Carter gave him to me as a going away present." Alexis kissed the dog on the nose. "Aidan's been calling every hour. Your mother keeps calling too. What's going on? You don't just appear at my door in the middle of a monsoon for tea and biscuits." Alexis nuzzled the puppy against her sweater.

"Aidan fucked the student."

Alexis's face crumpled. "He wouldn't do that."

"I ran into Molly at the co-op. She said she bought lace underwear with the refund she got for the pendant. I confronted Aidan and he admitted it. She lured him to her apartment to read a paper she was writing. They fucked on the futon," Cassie replied.

Alexis stood up and paced around the room. She clutched the puppy so tightly he made choking noises.

"Aidan's a goddamn ethics professor. He still looks like a sex god but he wouldn't cheat on you. You're his angel."

"He said it was a reflex reaction, like Pavlov's dog. He said it would never happen again."

"Does that mean if he sees a topless woman on the beach he goes up to her and sucks her nipple?" Alexis collapsed on the chair. "Aidan." She shook her head. "I don't believe it."

"What did you tell him when he called?" Cassie asked weakly.

"He wanted to drive over and take you home. I told him the doctor said you weren't to be moved. I made that up, but I figured there was something going on. If you wanted to be home you would have stayed home."

"Thanks." Cassie smiled.

"He's been calling hourly. I told him the doctor thought it was Asian bird flu and you were quarantined," Alexis continued proudly.

"I'm impressed."

Alexis plumped Cassie's pillows. "Now we have to figure out what to do next."

"Next?" Cassie tried to keep her eyes open.

"Whether you're going to give him a second chance or cut his balls off and make them into a necklace," Alexis replied.

"I don't know what I'm going to do." Cassie shuddered.

"You're going to stay here. I'll call Aidan and tell him you're out of the woods, but you need complete rest for a week." Alexis scooped up the puppy and walked to the door. "And I'll call your mother too. She keeps saying she needs you at Fenton's."

"Oh, God," Cassie mumbled.

"Cassie, they can get by without you for a few days. Get some sleep."

When Cassie woke again the room was dark and she felt hot. She pushed off the covers, expecting Aidan to mumble that he was cold, but there was silence. She sat up and looked around the room. Everything was red, like the end of a kaleidoscope.

Alexis opened the door, carrying a bowl of soup and a plate of saltines.

"Now that the fever is gone, we're going to feed you." She set the tray on the bed.

"I don't know what day it is," Cassie mumbled.

"Thursday night. I had Pia make your favorite soup, chicken tortellini."

"How do you know that's my favorite?" Cassie sat up.

"Aidan has been calling with detailed instructions of your favorite soup and how you like your eggs. He wanted to cook the soup and bring it himself but I told him the whole house was quarantined. Asian bird flu can't be taken lightly." Alexis put a spoonful of soup to Cassie's lips.

"I'm glad my best friend is such a good liar." Cassie swallowed the soup. It burned her mouth and got stuck in her throat.

"Fibbing is different than lying." Alexis put the bowl on the tray. "You can't go through Sacred Heart without learning to fib."

"Remember when Molly came into Fenton's and you said the whole thing meant nothing? That I had to believe in my marriage?" Cassie asked.

"Ah, ha." Alexis tried the soup. "This is good. I hope Pia wrote down the recipe."

"This isn't the time to talk about Aidan's cooking skills." Cassie swallowed another spoonful of soup. She closed her eyes and saw Aidan at the stove, slicing tomatoes and mushrooms and throwing them into the pot.

"I'm listening." Alexis brushed saltine crumbs from her lap.

"Every time I think of Aidan I see Molly Payne wearing red lingerie." Cassie's lips trembled.

"But you won't always picture that. Think of the ten years you've spent together. Skiing in Tahoe, wine tasting in

Napa. Remember when you guys went to Mexico, and you celebrated New Year's in a hot tub overlooking the Pacific Ocean?"

"Two years ago Aidan took me to Rome and we ate a different kind of pasta every night. We sat in the piazza and drank espressos till midnight." Cassie nibbled a saltine.

"Does it really get erased by one fuck?" Alexis put the tray on the bedside table. She stood up and walked around the room. "I'm not advocating cheating. If Carter screwed around I'd probably pack his bags and throw them on the street. But you and Aidan have a history, and you're so good together."

"I know." Cassie felt a little stronger. Flashbulbs stopped popping before her eyes. "That's what makes it so hard. I love him, Alexis, but can you love someone who hurt you so badly?"

"The only point in Aidan's favor"—Alexis smoothed her blond ponytail—"is he hasn't lied. He fucked up but he copped to it."

"So?"

"Think about it. He gave Molly the pendant for innocent reasons. Stupid, but innocent. Her boyfriend dumps her. Aidan hands her this Fenton's box, makes her happy. And he didn't go to her apartment to fuck her. He thought her roommate was there. I can't see Aidan in a ménage à trois, he's not that kind of guy."

"What are you getting at?" Cassie leaned forward.

"Fucking up and admitting it is one thing. Lying is another. If a guy can lie he can screw around forever. Secret cell phones, bogus e-mail accounts, credit cards in different names for clandestine weekend trysts."

"Let me guess, *The Ellen Show*?" Cassie smiled.

"Honestly, you should hear what some guys do. But Aidan's clean in that department."

"He had sex with another woman." Cassie lay back against the pillows. Suddenly she felt hot and shivery.

Alexis sat down and touched Cassie's hand. "I just don't want you to do anything quickly."

"I need to talk to him." Cassie sighed.

"How about if I tell Aidan to come here on Saturday. I'll take Poodles for a walk, give you two some time alone," Alexis suggested.

"How about I walk Poodles and you talk to him?" Cassie smiled. "You understand this stuff better than I do."

"We'll watch *Dr. Phil* together tomorrow afternoon." Alexis picked up the silver tray. "You'll do fine."

7.

On Saturday morning, Cassie put on the red Chinese silk robe hanging in the armoire and ventured downstairs. Her hair sat limply on her shoulders, her cheeks were pale, and her stomach was completely flat. The smell of blueberry pancakes wafted up the stairs, and suddenly Cassie had a craving for maple syrup and whipped cream.

Pia stood at the chrome counter and poured pancake batter onto the griddle. She turned to Cassie and smiled, motioning for her to sit at the kitchen table. Alexis's kitchen was the opposite of the regally elegant living room. Every surface was chrome, polished so you could see your reflection. There were matching chrome dishwashers under the sink, and a chrome fridge with a built-in juice bar.

"Good morning, Mrs. Blake," Pia said in her Norwegian accent. "Would you like orange juice or coffee?"

"Coffee please," Cassie replied. Pia had the kind of Scandinavian beauty that made most women leery of hiring her. She was six feet tall with white blond hair and creamy skin no cosmetic could reproduce. It was a testament to Alexis's supreme self-confidence that she hired her on the first interview when she discovered Pia knew how to make a bed military style and could iron Carter's shirts without creasing a collar.

"Hey, you made it downstairs." Alexis held Poodles in her arms. She wore a pink Juicy sweat suit and knee-high black UGGS. "It's freezing outside, but at least it's sunny."

"I feel like Miss Havisham in *Great Expectations*." Cassie sipped her coffee.

"Never read it." Alexis shook her head. "You do look really pale. Here, try some of these." Alexis walked over to the pantry and put an assortment of bottles on the kitchen table.

"What are these?" Cassie asked.

Alexis read the labels. "Codfish oil, vitamin C, vitamin A, chewable calcium, and wheatgrass to rejuvenate your digestive system."

"I think I'll stick with pancakes." Cassie grimaced.

"You want to look amazing when Aidan arrives." Alexis swallowed two vitamin C tablets. "What are you going to wear?"

"This robe and slippers? I don't have any other clothes." Cassie shrugged.

Alexis looked at Cassie critically. "Only Hugh Hefner can wear a robe and be taken seriously. Aidan has to know you're hurt but not broken. After breakfast, we'll find you something in my closet."

"You're three inches taller than me and your waist is two inches smaller."

"I've got a bunch of miniskirts that will fit perfectly. And you look like you lost ten pounds. A woman should write the 'Adultery Diet.' It would be an instant bestseller." Alexis poured herself a cup of coffee.

"I'd rather keep on the extra pounds." Cassie sighed. She

hadn't talked to Aidan in days and she realized she was desperate to hear his voice. She thought about what he was doing right now: working out at the gym, showering, eating egg whites on toast.

"We'll make you look like Jessica Alba." Alexis attacked half of a grapefruit.

"How are we going to do that?" Cassie rolled her eyes.

"I've been taking makeup lessons with Damien White. Give me a few hours and I can turn you into Angelina Jolie."

Cassie studied her reflection in the chrome fridge. "I'll settle for Drew Barrymore. She always has that wounded-but-sexy thing going."

Alexis studied Cassie's face. "I can do Drew Barrymore in twenty minutes."

Cassie followed Alexis into the master bedroom suite, which occupied half of the second floor. Double French doors led into a private foyer with a framed Matisse over the mantel. The bedroom had a circular bed with an enormous white headboard. White curtains trimmed with fox fur covered the windows, and there was a sable throw on the love seat.

"You've redecorated." Cassie ran her hand over the mink bedspread.

"Carter spent a month in Moscow last winter. He wanted the bedroom to resemble the Winter Palace. He has one of Czar Nicholas's footstools in his closet, and a Fabergé egg in the bathroom." Alexis led Cassie through a short hallway.

"Don't you feel guilty about all the fur?" Cassie asked tentatively.

"It's faux fur." Alexis opened the door to her walk-in. "Carter would kill me, he likes things to be authentic. But how could I hug my adorable Poodles knowing that animals have been killed to make my bedspread?"

Cassie stepped into Alexis's closet and took a deep breath. She had never seen so many clothes in a small space. There were rows of blouses, drawers of cashmere sweaters, baskets of lacy underwear, a whole wall of shoes and boots.

"If I walk in deep enough do I end up in Narnia?" Cassie turned around.

"I told you I don't have anything to do but shop. Maybe I should get another puppy to keep Poodles company, or I could start a dog-walking business. The only problem is dogs Poodles's size don't like to actually walk, they want to be carried. And I miss him, Cassie. I propped our wedding photo on Carter's pillow and I talk to it before I go to bed. Honestly, sometimes I think I'm going crazy." Alexis collapsed onto a velvet ottoman.

"When Carter gets back from Yugoslavia or wherever he is, tell him you want a job." Cassie fingered a silk shirt with pearl buttons.

"Carter's ego is bigger than his bank account. He doesn't want his wife in the workforce; he thinks it makes his penis smaller."

"I'll settle for a husband with a small penis, as long as he keeps it in his pants." Cassie touched gabardine slacks in a pink-and-black check.

"What do you think, miniskirt and boots for the retro 'I'm too hip to give a fuck' look or cashmere twin set with pearls for the 'I'm too good for you, I'm a former deb' message?" Alexis held up a pink-and-white mini and white Moon Boots and a cashmere pleated skirt and matching sweater.

"How about jeans and a T-shirt that says 'You broke my heart'?" Cassie slumped down on the ottoman.

"Aidan is coming to see you with his tail between his legs. You hold the power, dress accordingly," Alexis admonished her. "How about this Stella McCartney dress with Tory Burch pumps?"

"Dress designed by the daughter of Aidan's favorite Beatle. Shoes by New York socialite who started her own fashion empire." Cassie held the dress up in front of the mirror.

"By George, I think she's got it." Alexis grinned. "And we'll tease your hair into a Jennifer Lopez tousle."

"What is a Jennifer Lopez tousle?" Cassie tried on the burgundy pumps with the round gold buckles.

"I learned it in my hair design class; you're going to love it."

The doorbell rang as Alexis put the finishing touches to Cassie's makeup. Cassie studied herself in the full-length mirror. The dress was navy with burgundy trim. The wide leather belt made her waist look small and the thick black mascara made her lashes seem wet. Alexis brushed a light bronzer on her cheeks "so you don't look like you're dying of consumption," and pinned her hair with a diamond Tiffany clip. "Diamonds are a girl's best friend," she said, examining her handiwork. "What do you think?"

"I think I'd rather be in my garden wearing gardening gloves and a co-op T-shirt." Cassie adjusted the diamond hair clip.

"How about a shot of brandy for courage?"

"I still feel as if my head's about to crack open."

"You look gorgeous. Better than Jennifer Aniston after she dumped John Mayer. Where do you want to meet Aidan?"

"Not the living room, I'd feel like Queen Elizabeth. And not the library, too Donald Trump." Cassie frowned.

"How about the conservatory?" Alexis sprayed Cassie with a bottle of Obsession.

"I didn't know you had a conservatory."

"Carter had it built after he returned from Vienna. It gets lovely light in the afternoon."

Cassie sat down on the ottoman. "Aidan's my husband and I feel like I'm going in front of the firing squad."

"Remember, he's the one who committed the crime." Alexis pulled her to her feet. "And no bringing him up to the second floor. I don't want him getting you horizontal until you know that's what you want."

"You mean no fucking." Cassie grinned.

"You're a fast learner."

Cassie waited in the conservatory. It had a bay window overlooking the garden, and a white baby grand piano with a framed photo of Alexis and Carter in Gstaad. She heard the door open but she didn't turn around. Aidan put his hand on her shoulder and sat down on the piano stool beside her.

"I've missed you." He pulled her against his chest. She could hear his heart beating and taste coffee and cinnamon on his breath.

"I've missed you too." She got up and sat down on the armchair by the window.

"I brought you a present." Aidan handed Cassie a brown paper bag. He wore tan slacks, a brown turtleneck, and loafers.

"What is it?" Cassie took out Maria's Burberry lunch box.

"I made a sun-dried tomato panini with a special pesto sauce."

"Thanks." Cassie put the lunch box on the side table. "I'm not really hungry."

"Christ, Cassie"—Aidan stood above her—"I was so worried you were sick and Alexis wouldn't let me near you. This has gone on long enough. You need to come home."

"I don't know if I'm ready to come home," Cassie replied.

"Do you want me to beg?" he said angrily. "I will never meet a student outside of office hours again. I fucked up, Cassie, I know I fucked up." Tears sprang to his eyes.

Cassie gulped. The only times she had seen Aidan cry were when he and Isabel fought. When Isabel was a little girl she'd storm up to her room and Aidan would hunch over the kitchen table, eyes filling with tears. Cassie would sit in his lap, wrap her arms around him, and tell him he was a great dad.

"I know you do." Cassie nodded.

"I haven't lied to you and I won't lie to you, ever." Aidan walked to the window. "I've almost finished my paper. If it gets accepted, we can go to the conference together. It's in Florence in April. We can take day trips to Venice and Rome. Remember the pine nut pasta with pesto sauce we ate in Rome?"

"Yes."

"I made the same pesto sauce for the panini. Try it." Aidan picked up the lunch box and snapped it open.

Cassie smelled tomatoes and garlic, oregano and onions. She took a small bite of the toasted bread. "I'm really not hungry." She put it back in the lunch box.

"Then let's go home and I'll feed you soup till you get better. I'll get the purple asparagus you love and make cream asparagus and mushroom."

"You haven't let me say anything," Cassie interrupted, twisting her wedding ring on her finger.

"Sorry, old habit." Aidan sat on the piano stool. "I'm listening."

Cassie took a deep breath. "You don't know what it's like to have the image of you and Molly running through my head. It's like a movie I can't switch off. I want to love you, but the image doesn't just go away."

"Cassie, you have to love me," Aidan pleaded. "I need you to love me."

Cassie wanted to get up and sit next to him on the piano. She wanted him to play "Let It Be" or "The Long and Winding Road" or any other Beatles song they listened to while curled up on the sofa at night. She stood up and knocked over the lunch box. Panini and lettuce spilled on the floor. She bent down and stuffed bread and tomatoes back in the lunch box.

"Come here," Aidan said, "I know an old Billy Joel song."

"No." Cassie sat down on the armchair. "I'm not ready, Aidan. I'm sorry."

"What do you mean you're not ready?"

"I'm going to stay with Alexis for a few weeks."

"A few weeks? Christ, Cassie. What do you want me to do?" Aidan jumped up.

"I want you to wait," Cassie said slowly.

Aidan rubbed his hands through his hair. He jammed his hands in his pockets and paced around the room. He walked back to the window, leaned down, and kissed Cassie softly on the lips. "Okay, I'll wait."

Alexis walked into the conservatory and placed Poodles in Cassie's lap. "I just saw Aidan leave. He looked like Johnny Depp in *Edward Scissorhands*."

"He wanted me to come home." Cassie stroked the puppy's fur.

"And your answer was?"

"That I need more time. Could I stay here for a while?"

"Of course you can! Carter won't be home for two weeks. You can have the Scarlett O'Hara suite on the third floor." Alexis sat down on the piano stool.

"You could always turn this house into a theme park if you need extra income." Cassie grinned.

"Give me the scoop. Did Aidan get down on his knees and grovel?"

"He said he was really, really sorry." Cassie nodded slowly. "If his paper gets accepted to the conference he wants us to go to Italy together."

"Make-up travel is even better than make-up sex. He'll take you to the most romantic places and feed you grapes and caviar." Alexis walked over to the window. "Mmm, what's that smell?"

"Aidan made me a sun-dried tomato panini." Cassie pointed to the lunch box on the side table.

"It smells divine, can I have a bite? I'm starving. I did a two-mile run while Aidan was here."

"It fell on the floor."

"I don't care. Pia keeps these floors clean as the White House." Alexis opened the lunch box and picked up the sandwich.

"I knocked over the lunch box by accident and the sandwich fell out. I remembered the night I drove here: Aidan came home; I was sitting in the kitchen. He put the lunch box on the table. I made him lunch that day: roasted turkey sandwich on wheat bread. When I bent down to pick it up, there was a cupcake doily in the lunch box."

"I don't get it." Alexis shook her head.

"I didn't put a cupcake in his lunch box."

"Oh, come on." Alexis put the sandwich down. "An empty cupcake wrapper is hardly a matchbox from Motel Six. One of the other professors could have had a birthday, or he could have bought something at a bake sale on campus."

"That's my point." Cassie handed the puppy to Alexis. "I

can't interrogate Aidan about every little thing, but I can't doubt him either."

"I'm still not seeing this clearly." Alexis kissed the tip of Poodles's nose.

"If Aidan had a cupcake wrapper in his lunch box before he fucked Molly I would have just thrown it away. Now I can't stop thinking about it. Did Molly bake him cupcakes? Did another student give it to him? I can't live with him unless I completely trust him."

Alexis hugged Poodles. "Maybe I'm lucky Carter travels so much. I can't watch his every move. What are you going to do?"

"Stay here for a while. Maybe with a little time and space I'll be able to look at Aidan and not wonder what he's been up to." Cassie's eyes filled with tears.

"I'm sorry, Cassie."

"I'll catch up on my reading." Cassie brushed the tears away. "Maybe I'll reread *Anna Karenina* or *Madame Bovary*."

"Reading about women who didn't have Internet access or cell phones isn't very helpful." Alexis fed Poodles a corner of the bread. "Their lives aren't relevant."

"Right now I'd like to go upstairs and lie down." Cassie stood up.

"You have another visitor," Alexis said sheepishly.

"Who?"

"Your mother called and I let slip that Aidan was here. She figured the quarantine was over and wanted to see you right away. You know I'm afraid of your mother. She's in the library."

"If she finds out what Aidan did, she'll ship me off to Vegas and sign the divorce papers herself." Cassie put her head in her hands.

"Tell her your house flooded and you're staying here while they fix the roof."

Cassie looked up and smiled. "You really are a good liar."

"Fibber," Alexis corrected her, "and always for the right reasons."

Diana sat in the high-backed leather desk chair, tapping her cigarette holder on the desk. She wore a cowl-necked wool sweater with an ostrich-skin belt cinched at the waist. Her hair was brushed smoothly to her chin and she had a silk scarf tied at her throat.

"Alexis has an interesting decorator. I feel like I'm in a Dickens novel." Diana glanced at the rows of leather-bound books lining the bookshelves. The floor was covered with an Oriental rug and an ivory elephant stood by the fireplace.

"She has a little too much time on her hands," Cassie said. Looking at her mother, who was all pent-up energy and drive, Cassie suddenly felt exhausted. She wanted to go upstairs, drink hot tea, and climb into bed.

"You look dreadfully pale and there are huge circles under your eyes." Diana eyed Cassie critically.

"I haven't been on vacation, I had a fever for five days."

"I don't understand why you're here."

"Our roof leaked in the storm. Aidan and I thought it would be better if I recuperated somewhere dry." Cassie studied the pattern on the Oriental rug.

"You should have come and stayed with me," Diana replied huffily. She stood up and walked to the bookshelf. She wore three-inch ivory heels with delicate satin bows.

"You turned my room into a music room when I went to college."

"You could have stayed in the guest room. When are you going back to Berkeley?" Diana asked.

"I love your shoes." Cassie tried to change the subject. "New designer?"

"James is working faster than I expected. I want you to start buying food for the emporium."

"I thought you came here to see if I was feeling better." Cassie felt light-headed. She debated pouring a shot of brandy from the decanter on the sideboard.

"Of course, you shouldn't come into the store till you're rested. But you could contact growers by phone, make appointments. James has already ripped out the whole basement. He's ordered the counters and food cases. You should see the artwork he commissioned: people carrying baskets of cherries, sacks of oranges, milling around a village square. It's like a modern Bruegel, it's fabulous."

Cassie hesitated. "I don't know, Mother, I'm really weak."

"I hope this isn't about Aidan. You can't spend your life being his geisha. He can't complain you're spending too much time in the city if you're staying here anyway." Diana poured herself a shot of brandy.

Cassie closed her eyes. Aidan hadn't consulted her before he gave Molly Payne her Christmas present. He hadn't asked her if it was okay to visit a student's apartment. He hadn't required her permission to have sex with Molly on her futon.

"Okay, I'll do it." Cassie opened her eyes. "I won't promise that I'm taking the position permanently. But while I'm staying here, I'll give it a try."

"I'm so pleased," Diana said genuinely. She poured another shot of brandy and handed Cassie the glass. "I propose a toast: to a new era for Fenton's."

Cassie clinked crystal shot glasses. She swallowed the brandy. It burned her throat and hit the empty space in her stomach.

8.

Cassie sat in the living room of the Scarlett O'Hara suite, sifting through a pile of boxes. Her mother sent her four pairs of wool pants, six cashmere sweaters in different colors, and a selection of dresses from Michael Kors, Stella McCartney, and Ella Moss.

"Mother, I have clothes. I was going to send Pia over to Berkeley to pick them up." Cassie picked up the phone when the red Fenton's boxes arrived at Alexis's front door.

"Your clothes are dated. You have to set an example when you walk around Fenton's. Women want to buy what you're wearing," her mother replied. "I'm late for a meeting with a calligrapher. The announcements for the opening of the emporium look brilliant. I wish you'd hurry and come into the store."

"Soon, Mother." Cassie hung up. She tried on pleated navy pants and a pale pink sweater. She brushed her hair and tied it back with a pink ribbon.

She knew she should go to Fenton's. Leaving Alexis's house, except to take Poodles for a walk, was proving difficult. She felt a pain in her chest when she saw a girl with feathery blond hair, or a man who wore a leather jacket like Aidan's. It was easier to stay upstairs.

Alexis knocked on the door. "Aidan sent another care package."

"Should I call him and tell him I can't eat a gallon of soup every day?" Cassie shook her head.

Aidan had been delivering thermoses of soup with notes written on yellow Post-its. "Clam chowder and no one to share it with." "Split pea with snap peas from your garden." Half a counter in Alexis's kitchen was filled with thermoses and Tupperware containers.

"He sent pizza." Alexis handed her the cardboard box.

Cassie opened the box and took out the card. " 'I tried to make our favorite pizza but I'm missing the most important ingredient: you. I'll wait as long as I have to.' "

"I think Aidan's been watching daytime soap operas." Alexis took out a slice of pizza. "This is pretty good. Your husband is quite the chef."

Cassie turned back to the piles of clothes so Alexis couldn't see her crying.

"You're crying again, aren't you?" Alexis finished the piece of pizza. "Come on, we have to get you out of here. I'm taking you to Fenton's today."

"I can drive myself." Cassie wiped her eyes.

"I don't trust you. You'll drive around the block and sneak back upstairs to read *Anna Karenina*. I'm taking Poodles to 'puppy and me yoga' anyway, we'll drop you off."

Cassie felt better the minute she walked through Fenton's double glass doors. The front of the store smelled like Sarah Jessica Parker's perfume Lovely. White lilies announcing a

January white sale were placed on counters, on top of display ads, behind cash registers. Women jostled one another to grab one-thousand-count Egyptian cotton sheets and terry bath towels.

She had forgotten the thrill of being in the midst of so much activity. The buzz in the air was intoxicating. Cassie found herself stroking a white silk robe, though she had no intention of buying one.

"Good afternoon, Cassie. It's wonderful to see you." Derek wore a black suit and a crisp white shirt. He had a white lily pinned to his suit pocket.

"Hi, Derek. I came to see my mother."

"She went to lunch at Waterfront with the sales rep for Estée Lauder." Derek held Cassie's hand to his lips.

"Oh." Cassie frowned. "Maybe I'll come back tomorrow."

"Your mother told me you're going to head the food emporium. She's been telling everyone you're going to inject the store with new life." Derek kept her hand in his. "Why don't you go downstairs and see how it's coming along?"

Cassie took the escalator down to the basement. Workers were everywhere: hammering, painting, carrying industrial-sized fridges. James was standing in the middle of the space, staring at a marble bust of a Greek god.

"I didn't know you wore glasses," she said, and immediately wished she hadn't. James blushed a deep red and took the glasses off to rub his eyes.

"I don't wear them for business meetings because they make me look like I'm twelve years old. But contacts make my eyes water." He smiled.

Cassie turned to the statue. "Let me guess. Dionysius, god of excess?" The marble figure was in a semi-reclining position, nibbling a bunch of grapes and holding a marble goblet.

"I prefer to think of him as god of wine and food. I want the customer to have the feeling of abundance and decadence," James replied earnestly. "What do you think?"

"It's too bad there isn't a female god who represents those things. But I guess Hera was always in the kitchen with a needle and thread." Cassie walked around the statue.

"You studied Greek mythology?"

"I attended the Convent of the Sacred Heart. The classics were an important part of the curriculum," Cassie replied.

"At St. Ignatius we sang hymns every morning. In senior year there was a required trip to the Vatican." James dusted the bust with a white cloth.

"I traveled to Italy a couple of years ago," Cassie said.

"I haven't been back since a post-college backpacking trip. Next time I want to stay in a hotel, not on the floor of a youth hostel." James motioned for her to follow him.

One section held a brick pizza oven, a panini press, and a large fondue pot. A floor-to-ceiling wine rack took up another wall, and a corner of the store was built out to resemble an English library.

"I'm going to put a fireplace in here and fill the bookshelves with jams and jellies. I thought we could have toasters on the tables so shoppers could toast their own bread." James moved his hands when he talked.

"How about scones with clotted cream? I always envied the British their afternoon tea because it's an excuse to eat jam and whipped cream before dinner." Cassie walked over to the bookshelf.

"I like that." James pulled up the cuff of his shirt and looked at his watch. "I haven't stopped for lunch. Will you join me in the café upstairs? I can tell you my ideas for lighting and artwork."

Cassie rode beside him on the escalator to the fourth floor. James wore a yellow collared shirt and khaki pants. His hair was brushed to one side and smoothed down with gel.

"You're very good at what you do," Cassie said as they waited for a table.

James blushed and smiled at the same time. "I love that people have the confidence to turn over a space and let me create something magical. Your mother is so passionate, it's contagious."

Cassie laughed and followed the waiter to a table by the window. "She's like a gale-force wind. You can't be running the other way or you'll be blown over."

"I think our mothers are similar. Mine is a corporate attorney." James pulled out Cassie's chair. "It's probably why I picked a fiancée from the South: someone who knew how to relax and drink peach daiquiris."

"You're engaged?" Cassie consulted the menu. It was the first time she had eaten out since she was sick and the choices looked too filling: gnocchi in Alfredo sauce, steak tenderloin with roasted potatoes. She glanced out the window at Union Square and suddenly felt exhausted. She wanted to be in bed with a bowl of Aidan's chicken tortellini soup and a stack of plain saltines.

James adjusted his glasses and stared at the menu. "We've been together since Northwestern. Emily is from Atlanta and she's an interior designer in Chicago."

Cassie ran her fingers over the entrée selections. The French onion soup looked the easiest to swallow. She seemed to have a permanent lump in her throat that made it impossible to eat steak or chicken.

"We planned a summer wedding at her parents' home in Atlanta. A giant tent, dance floor over the pool. Swans floating on a man-made lake." James took off his glasses and rubbed his eyes. "But we hit a bump in the road at Thanksgiving."

"What happened?" Cassie asked.

"I got the job designing Emerald in September. It was a big deal for me: once you start designing in different cities you get a national reputation." He paused and took a sip of water. "I asked Emily to join me but she was in the middle of a project. In the beginning I'd go home every weekend or she'd come here and we'd play tourist." James stopped and signaled the waiter.

"I met her in Atlanta for Thanksgiving; her parents host a huge dinner. I had to get back here, so Emily stayed on for a few days," James continued after the waiter took their order.

"A few days later I saw some Thanksgiving weekend photos posted on her Facebook page. There was a whole album of her and Percy Bingham. They went to elementary school together. He's head of an accounting firm in Atlanta, belongs to the same tennis club as her father."

"Oh," Cassie mumbled.

"She called me frantically apologizing. Said someone else posted them, they were just kidding around like when they were children. I don't think Percy had his hand up her shirt and his tongue down her throat in the first grade."

"I'm so sorry." Cassie sipped a glass of water.

"We've patched things up, but it's not easy to gain back the trust. I check her Facebook page every day. I watch her cell phone bill to see if she calls any numbers in Atlanta. She keeps telling me she loves me, that it will never happen again, but I can't erase the image of Percy sucking her face."

"You're still getting married?" Cassie scraped butter on a piece of Melba toast.

"The wedding is not till August." James smiled. "Hopefully by then the image will have faded. Sometimes I feel like a fool, but Emily has a lot of wonderful qualities. Long-distance romances are hard and I blame myself for taking this job. I hope when we live in the same city things will return to normal."

Cassie let the waiter put the bowl of French onion soup in front of her. The smell of onions made her stomach turn. She pushed the plate away and nibbled another piece of toast.

"If you don't like the soup, you can share my salmon," James offered.

"No, thank you. I'm just not hungry these days." Cassie shrugged.

"Your mother told me you were sick. You're staying in the city while you recover." James ate another bite of salmon.

"My husband had sex with his student." The words came out before she could stop them. "Her boyfriend jilted her. Molly asked Aidan to come to her apartment to read a paper and they did it on the futon." Cassie stared out the window.

"I'm sorry." James put down his fork.

"I shouldn't be telling you. Please don't say anything to my mother. Aidan has never been her favorite person. I haven't been out in public since it happened, and I just feel . . ." She stopped. Her hands were shaking and her lips trembled.

"Like everybody knows," James finished. "When I went back to Chicago at Christmas I thought the whole town read Emily's Facebook page."

"That's it." Cassie nodded. "All these women have perfect lives and they see through me like an X-ray."

"You didn't do anything. You're the same person."

Cassie smiled. "I'm trying to be the same person. I keep

thinking I'll run into Molly, which is silly. She lives in Berkeley and she's not the type to shop in Union Square. But she's like Hamlet's ghost, hovering over my shoulder."

"Are you going back to your husband?" James cut a piece of salmon.

"I want to go back to him, I miss him." Cassie dipped her spoon in the soup. "We've been married for ten years. He has a sixteen-year-old daughter I've helped raise, not always a pleasurable experience." Cassie laughed.

"But you don't know if you can trust him?"

"I don't know if I can trust myself to trust him." Cassie frowned. "Even if he is a choirboy now, I'll wonder why he's home late, or who he sees at the gym. I found a cupcake doily in his lunch box and I went crazy."

"You're protecting yourself from getting hurt again." James ate a bite of salmon.

"I want things to go back to the way they were." Cassie nibbled Melba toast. "Nothing tastes good. I used to love French onion soup."

"The solution is to eat dessert first." James grinned. "Why don't I ask the waiter to bring Fenton's lemon custard soufflé?"

Cassie pushed the soup bowl away. "I'm sorry to ruin our business lunch. Tell me about the art you commissioned. My mother said it's fabulous."

"I found an artist in Sonoma, he uses the side of a barn as a canvas." James signaled the waiter. "He paints murals of outdoor markets. I'm driving up there on Monday. Why don't you come with me? I could use another set of eyes."

"Could we visit a dairy I've been talking to?" Cassie watched the waiter replace her bowl of soup with a fluffy yellow soufflé.

"Of course, and there's an antique store I'd like to visit.

I'll pack a picnic." When James smiled he looked like a school-boy.

"You're right." Cassie ate a spoonful of soufflé. It tasted sweet and slipped down her throat. "It's much easier to eat dessert."

Alexis was standing in front of the Fresh counter on the first floor, spritzing her wrist with perfume. She waved as Cassie and James descended the escalator. "We just finished yoga and I thought I'd see if you're ready to go home. Derek is sweet enough to hold Poodles while I sample these delicious new scents." Alexis wore orange tights and a purple leotard. She had taupe ballet slippers on her feet and her hair was pulled into a ponytail.

"Only you could walk into Fenton's half-naked and look better than any other woman in the store." Cassie grinned. She studied herself in the makeup mirror. Her eyes were puffy and her cheeks were pale but she felt a little better. The lemon soufflé had been the first thing that tasted good all week.

Alexis took Poodles from Derek. "We should go home, Poodles needs his nap. Unless you'd like to stay." Alexis looked pointedly at James.

"I'm sorry, I didn't introduce you." Cassie blushed. "This is James Parrish, the interior designer."

"I heard you're a boy genius." Alexis smiled.

"Hardly a genius," James replied. He turned to Cassie. "I better get back to work. Shall we say ten o'clock on Monday? I'll pick you up."

"That would be great." Cassie nodded, avoiding Alexis's questioning gaze.

* * *

"You didn't tell me he wears glasses," Alexis said as they drove home.

"I didn't remember." Cassie gripped the dashboard as Alexis took a sharp turn onto Sacramento Street.

"He reminds me of Hugh Grant in *Four Weddings and a Funeral,* before he got soft and middle-aged." Alexis pulled into the garage. "Getting out was good for you. You have a little color in your cheeks."

"Thanks." Cassie nodded. "The emporium is coming to life."

"Did I hear you planning a date with James?" Alexis asked casually, scooping up Poodles and opening the car door.

"A business trip. We're going to drive up to Sonoma and look at some art." Cassie slammed her door. "I'm married, Alexis, and James has a beautiful southern fiancée."

"I'm just saying"—Alexis opened the door to the kitchen—"you have a little color in your cheeks."

Cassie climbed up to the third floor and collapsed on the bed. She missed her own bedroom, her view of the garden, her sock drawer with socks of every length and fabric. She wanted to slip on fuzzy slipper socks and climb under her down comforter.

It had been fun to go to Fenton's, to see the emporium take shape, but suddenly she felt like there was a weight flattening her chest. She picked up her cell phone and saw six missed calls from Aidan. She dialed his number and was about to hit SEND when the phone rang.

"Where have you been?" Aidan asked before she could say hello. "I've been calling all afternoon."

"I left my phone here. I was at Fenton's."

"You have a whole closet of clothes here," Aidan said tightly.

"I'm going to help with the food emporium while I'm staying with Alexis," Cassie replied awkwardly.

"So your mother can point out how terrible your husband is? You don't have time for the emporium, Cassie. We talked about that."

"I have time at the moment," Cassie replied. "And I haven't told my mother about the affair."

"It wasn't an affair. It was one mistake." Aidan's voice was low and firm. "I want you to come home. I can't open a bottle of red wine because you're not here to help me finish it."

"I want to come home." Cassie lay down on the bed. "Just not yet."

"Why don't I come into the city for dinner tomorrow night? We can try one of those restaurants your mother raves about. I'll wear a suit."

"I wouldn't want to make you wear a suit." Cassie laughed. "I'm not really up for eating out yet. Maybe next week."

"Okay, next week." Aidan paused. "I love you."

"I love you." Cassie hit END. She curled her body around the embroidered pillows. She just said no to a date with her husband, when there was nowhere else she'd rather be than in their bed, feeling the weight of his body against her.

9.

Alexis stood at the dining-room window, peeking through the silk curtains. She balanced a porcelain coffee cup in one hand and Poodles in the other. She wore navy leggings, a knee-length sweater, and gray UGG slippers.

"You're like an UGGs catalog. How many pairs do you own?" Cassie walked up behind her. She had spent a half hour in front of the mirror, dressing for the trip to Sonoma. She finally settled on a pair of pencil-thin black slacks, a yellow sweater, and a pair of Alexis's black leather boots.

"One of Carter's clients is an investor. I have more UGGs than an Australian cowboy." Alexis put her coffee cup on the sideboard.

"I hope you don't mind, I borrowed your leather boots. My mother only sent me Prada and Gucci. I don't think that'll work in Sonoma."

"Today's the big date." Alexis turned around. "You look very stylish."

"It's not a date. And I'm dressing for the potential vendors we'll be meeting." Cassie scowled.

"Then you look businesslike and stylish." Alexis grinned. "I'm proud of you. You're going to make the emporium a fabulous success."

"Mother wants the grand opening to be April thirtieth. She thinks everyone moves as fast as she does. What are you doing at the window?"

"Looking to see what kind of car James drives. You can tell a lot about a guy by his choice in automobile." Alexis ducked behind the curtain. "Silver Audi, I approve. Doesn't feel like he has to drive a BMW to be manly. Doesn't think he has to buy Japanese to be intelligent."

"You sound like you're in high school." Cassie shook her head.

"If my husband was home more I could think about other things: running up to Tahoe for a weekend's skiing, sharing fondue at Fleur de Lis, making love in our own bed. I'm tired of Skype sex, it's so one-sided." Alexis walked to the foyer and stood at the front door. "Maybe I'll e-mail Aidan and ask him to send over the recipes for his soups. I could hunker down with Pia and make soups all winter."

"You've never mixed anything in your kitchen except coffee and cream." Cassie giggled.

"Be good." Alexis watched Cassie walk down the stone path. "I'll wait up."

James jumped out of the car and opened Cassie's door. He wore navy slacks and a white button-down shirt under a Shetland wool sweater. His hair was parted to the side and flopped over one eye.

"I brought a picnic." James peered out the car window. The sky was dark and clouds hung low over the bay. "Soft cheese, fresh baguettes, and rice pudding. All foods that don't require chewing."

Cassie blushed. "I hope it doesn't rain." Suddenly she was embarrassed she'd told him about Aidan's transgression.

James saw her cheeks redden and tried to change the subject. "Alexis has quite a house. Like an English manor in an Evelyn Waugh novel."

"Alexis's husband runs a hedge fund. He just broke the nine-figure barrier. He's traveling in some European country that has the square footage of a postage stamp and half of California's gross product. Alexis is pretty lonely."

"Why doesn't she get a job?" James maneuvered the car onto the Golden Gate Bridge.

Cassie looked back and saw the outline of San Francisco, the tops of buildings hidden by fog.

"Carter's not too keen on the idea. I told Alexis she should join a charity, but she doesn't want to be bossed around by a bunch of aging debutantes. She does a lot of yoga."

"Emily loves to cook. She makes a lot of southern dishes: pan-fried chicken, corn bread, peach cobblers. Somehow she manages to stay rail thin; she inherited a fast metabolism," James replied.

"My husband spends a lot of time in the kitchen. He makes the best soups," Cassie said. Suddenly she didn't want to talk. She watched the hills and redwood trees of Marin turn into the countryside of Sonoma.

"I'm sorry," James said when the silence stretched on. "I didn't mean to talk about your husband."

"It's my fault. I want to concentrate on the emporium but I can't get Aidan out of my head." Cassie shrugged.

"Hamlet's ghost." James grinned. "I brought a bottle of Chardonnay for our picnic. That will help blur the images."

"We have an appointment at Bridges Dairy Farm at eleven." Cassie took out a pen and notepad from her purse. "It's a family-owned dairy in east Sonoma."

Cassie watched the vineyards slip by outside the window: miles and miles of green and purple grapes. She turned to James. "How did you end up as an interior designer?"

"My parents live in a high-rise in Chicago. My father's an architect. He wanted me to be an architect; my mother wanted me to be an attorney. Growing up, I spent weekends and summers on my grandparents' farm." James maneuvered the car off the main road, down an unpaved lane.

"When my parents started fighting over my career, I told them I wanted to move to the farm." James laughed. "That set off a family war. I finally agreed to go to college and I discovered I loved designing buildings: not the hard exteriors, but the warm insides. I loved creating spaces that made people happy. Designing restaurants seemed natural. People are happiest when they're eating and drinking." He pulled up in front of a white farmhouse.

James jumped out of the car and opened Cassie's door. The outside air was frigid. Cassie wished she'd brought a thick coat and a pair of gloves. There was a picture of a cow on the front door and a black-and-white doorbell.

A blond man answered the door and a petite woman with blue eyes stood next to him. A girl with blond pigtails jumped behind them, as if she was waiting for a clown at a birthday party.

"Come in." The man ushered them inside. "This is my wife, Selma, and our daughter, Jenny."

"Would you like to see the cows?" the girl asked. She was

about ten years old, with a snub nose and a face full of freckles.

"Not quite yet." James grinned. "I bet the cows are the stars around here."

"Our cows won five gold medals at the county fair." Jenny nodded proudly. "Would you like a glass of milk and some chocolate chip cookies? I made them myself."

Jenny disappeared into the kitchen and Cassie and James sat in the living room opposite a bay window overlooking the cow pasture.

"We own over twenty acres." Selma followed her gaze. "We have two hundred cows, and they're free to graze in the pastures. We don't use antibiotics and all their feed is organic."

"It sounds like just what we're looking for at Fenton's." Cassie smiled.

"We're very excited about our new line of products." John squeezed his wife's hand. "We produce churned butter with sea salt imported from France. And we just started a line of yogurt with cream on top that sold very well at the farmers market."

"Try the milk. It's from Ollie, my favorite cow," Jenny interrupted, placing a tray and two glasses on the coffee table.

"Did you milk her yourself?" James took a cookie and dipped it in the glass of milk.

"My dad says I'm not old enough. Ollie is my best friend. Would you like to meet her?"

"I'd love to meet Ollie." James stood up and brushed cookie crumbs from his slacks. "Some of my best friends growing up were cows."

James followed Jenny to the barn and Cassie pored over brochures and marketing plans with John and Selma. She liked the design of their butter containers: ceramic pots with black-and-white labels and a cow's hoofprint on the bottom.

"And I love the idea of selling your milk in reusable glass bottles." Cassie put down her pen. "We'll have a whole fridge of milk in colored bottles. And we'll put a display of the butter pots next to the bread oven. Customers can sample fresh baked bread with churned butter."

Cassie heard the kitchen door slam and Jenny walked in, followed by James smiling sheepishly.

"Your shirt is all wet." Cassie frowned.

"Ollie and I were getting along so well, I thought I'd see if I remembered how to milk her." James took the tea towel Selma produced and sponged his shirt. "I remembered where to put the stool but I forgot to warm my hands." He smiled at John and Selma. "Ollie got pretty upset and sprayed milk everywhere."

Cassie stood up and put her hand out to John and Selma. "We'll be thrilled to sell your products at Fenton's."

"Can we have cake to celebrate?" Jenny looked at her parents.

"We have a few more appointments." Cassie smiled. "But you'll have to come to Fenton's with your parents. I'll share a piece of chocolate cake with you."

"In San Francisco?" Jenny jumped up and down.

"We can take the elevator to the top of the St. Francis. Then you can see the whole city," Cassie said.

James and Cassie climbed into the car and James backed down the lane.

"I hope I didn't embarrass you," he said when he turned onto the main road.

"I've never seen a man wearing a Brooks Brothers shirt soaked in cow's milk." Cassie giggled.

"Cows have an innate sense about people. Ollie could tell I was an amateur." James turned to Cassie. "It's nice to see you smile."

"That was my first business deal." Cassie took her note-pad out of her purse.

"Congratulations." He squeezed Cassie's hand. "You're going to make the emporium a huge success."

Cassie put her hands in her lap and kept her eyes on the window. Farmers drove tractors over fields of lettuce. Cassie saw apple orchards and roadside stands selling baskets of cherries.

James broke the silence. "I'd like to see the artist next. He's a bit eccentric. He doesn't have any furniture. I hope you don't mind sitting on hay."

Cassie pulled her gaze from the window. For a minute she wished she were driving with Aidan in his ancient Toyota. She wanted to smell the familiar scent of his shampoo and feel his leather jacket rubbing against her arm.

James pulled up in front of a red barn with a giant mural painted on its side.

"What an amazing painting," Cassie said, looking out the window.

"Isn't it? I drove by one afternoon and I had to stop. It reminds me of Bruegel. All those paintings he made of village life." James paused. "I'm babbling. I minored in art history at Northwestern."

"You have a lot of talents." Cassie opened the car door. "Dairyman, art historian."

"Emily and I are members of the Art Institute in Chicago.

Maybe we could visit the Legion of Honor. They have a ret-rospective of van Gogh."

"I should spend all my time at the emporium, if I'm go-ing to be ready for Mother's grand opening."

"You're right," James replied awkwardly. "We both better work like mad. Your mother wants everything yesterday."

Suddenly Cassie felt very cold. She rubbed her hands to-gether, remembering how Aidan would blow on her hands until she was warm.

"Are you okay?" James turned around. "You look pale."

"I wish I had worn gloves." Cassie felt tears spring to her eyes. "I forgot how cold it gets in the country."

James knocked on the door but no one answered. "Let's go in." He opened the door and motioned Cassie to follow him.

Cassie breathed in sharply. The barn was huge, with square skylights cut into the ceiling. Every surface was cov-ered in murals: the walls, the ceiling, even the floor was painted in bright colors.

She stood in the middle of the barn, turning slowly so she didn't miss anything. Every scene was full of people. Women shared platters of fruits and pastries. Children kicked a ball in a village square; men played chess on outdoor chess tables.

"I love it," she said. "I feel like I'm standing in a group of women, listening to their conversation."

"Exactly." James joined Cassie in the middle of the barn. "I imagined a whole wall of murals in the emporium. When you go down the escalator you already feel the space is full of people shopping and eating and drinking."

A stocky man wearing an apron entered the room. He had gray hair and short fingers covered in paint.

"Gregory, this is Cassie Blake, the owner of Fenton's."

"My mother is the owner." Cassie blushed. "I just work there."

"It is an honor to meet you, Miss Blake." Gregory kissed her hand. "I've finished your pieces, they're in the loft. But first we must have lunch. I've been working since six o'clock."

"We have to make a few more stops." James shifted his feet.

"Nonsense." Gregory shook his head. "I must eat and it would be impolite to eat in front of you. My neighbor gave me two bottles of an excellent sauvignon blanc. Miss Blake, please allow me to make a chair for you."

Cassie sat cross-legged on the bale, looking at the feast Gregory had prepared. There was a long French roll, a tub of goat cheese, and three steaming bowls of vegetable stew.

"I never understood the starving artist." Gregory poured three glasses of wine. "How can you paint if your stomach is growling? To a long business partnership with the beautiful owner of Fenton's."

Cassie smiled. Gregory's enthusiasm was catching. She ate stew and cheese and bread and washed it down with wine. She listened to James and Gregory discuss art and felt a warm glow spread over her.

"Your paintings are wonderful." Cassie sipped her second glass. The wine had a slightly fruity taste.

"Wait till you see the pieces for Fenton's. But first we must have dessert." He pulled himself up and disappeared into the kitchen.

Gregory returned with an apple pie and a pitcher of whipped cream. "I'd starve if I lived in the city." He cut three wedges and scooped whipped cream on each plate. "My neighbors leave food at my door: salads, pies, sometimes whole chickens."

After lunch, James and Gregory spent a long time discussing art. Cassie leaned against the wall, feeling warm and content. She followed the men up to the loft and looked at the canvases for Fenton's. She imagined the murals in the emporium, and felt excitement bubbling inside her like champagne.

"You must come to Fenton's when the paintings are installed." Cassie smiled as they got ready to leave.

"I'm not very keen on cars and buses, but for you I will make an exception." Gregory kissed her hand. "Take the rest of the apple pie, I have more in the kitchen."

Cassie hugged the apple pie as they ran to the car. Suddenly it was pouring sheets of rain. The ground turned instantly to mud.

James backed down the lane onto the main road. Cassie tucked her feet under her and watched the vineyards disappear into the mist. James put on a Green Day CD and sang quietly, drumming his fingers on the steering wheel.

"Don't tell me you're a musician as well." Cassie grinned.

"I was in a band in college," James admitted. "We played a few fraternity parties and broke up the day after graduation."

"Anything else to add to your résumé? Magician, horse whisperer?"

"Cuckolded fiancé," James joked, keeping his eyes on the road. "I had fun today."

"So did I." Cassie sat up straighter. They crossed the Golden Gate Bridge into the city. Cars flashed their fog lights and pedestrians ran with newspapers over their heads.

"Maybe you should wait till it lets up, I don't want you to get soaked," James said as he pulled up in front of Alexis's house.

Cassie could see her breath on the windshield. "In San Francisco it can rain like this for hours."

"Let me get the picnic blanket. You can wear it over your head." James jumped out before Cassie could stop him. He opened her door and slipped the blanket over her shoulders.

"I'll return it to the store." Cassie could already feel the rain soaking through her skin.

"See you tomorrow." James leaned forward and kissed her on the lips. He stood for a moment, and then climbed in the car and drove away.

Alexis walked into the kitchen as Cassie was pouring a cup of tea. The blanket was draped over a chair, making a puddle on the stone floor.

"You're dripping on my Italian granite." Alexis picked up the blanket.

"I'm sorry, it was raining so hard James gave it to me to get inside. I'll throw it in the laundry."

"He has excellent manners. I watched him open your car door when you left." Alexis went to the pantry and brought out peanut butter, jam, and a loaf of wheat bread.

"I had lunch." Cassie warmed her hands on her teacup. She had taken off her sweater and wore a UCLA sweatshirt she found in the laundry.

"I'm eating comfort food." Alexis made herself a peanut butter sandwich. "I swam fifty laps this morning and I did a three-mile run in the house, carrying Poodles. I hate this rain. Maybe I'll go with you to Fenton's tomorrow and buy some new lingerie for Carter."

"When is he coming home?" Cassie sat at the kitchen table.

"No clue, he's at some Eastern European financial summit

where they confiscate your cell phone." Alexis poured herself a glass of milk. "Sometimes I think I should fold myself
up in his carry-on, but I wouldn't be welcome. The Eastern
Europeans think women belong in the kitchen making stru-
del. Tell me about your day."

"We visited an artist who kissed my hand and told me I
was beautiful," Cassie said. "He made us a picnic in his barn.
We drank a bottle of wine and ate fresh apple pie and whipped
cream."

"I'm jealous." Alexis licked the corner of the bread. "I
counted how many stairs there are from the second to the
third floor. You look like you're about to cry, Cassie. What
happened?"

"When I was getting out of the car it was raining really
hard." Cassie took a deep breath. "James got the blanket out
of the trunk and wrapped it around me. Then he kissed me."

"He kissed you?"

"Just for a second, we were both soaked. He got in the
car and drove away."

"Did you want him to kiss you?"

"Of course I didn't want him to." Cassie jumped up. "I'm
married, Alexis. And James is engaged."

"I just think James is really cute. With the owl glasses
and the floppy brown hair. It might be nice if you had a little
diversion."

"You mean get back at Aidan by having an affair?" Cassie's
eyes flickered. "Aidan made one mistake."

"You can have a little fun." Alexis dunked the sandwich
in her milk.

"Cheating on your husband isn't fun!" Cassie stormed
over to the counter. "Lying in bed with Aidan is fun, watch-

ing him make soup is fun. Drinking red wine together and moaning about Isabel is fun."

"Where are you going?" Alexis put her sandwich on the plate.

"I'm going to call my husband"—Cassie fished her phone out of her purse—"and ask him out to dinner."

10.

Cassie closed her laptop and looked at her watch. It was almost noon and she hadn't eaten breakfast. She walked from the library to the kitchen and opened the fridge. She felt like making a big salad with the sweet red peppers she found at the grocery near Alexis's house.

Cassie was pleased with the progress she was making. She had secured another dozen suppliers and received Alice Waters's promise she would attend the grand opening. With Alice on board, she was sure she could get Michael Mina and Bradley Ogden to participate. Her mother would be thrilled.

Aidan called every night before she went to bed: short phone calls that were awkward at first, but now she looked forward to them all day. She didn't tell him much about the emporium, but they laughed about Alexis's yoga addiction and Isabel's latest demands. Aidan grumbled he turned the sheets gray in the laundry, and told her what he made for dinner. On Saturday he was taking her to dinner at Green's, an impossible reservation to get, that he somehow secured without the three-month wait.

"The captain of industry takes a break." Alexis stood by the window. She wore long johns and red UGG slippers. Her cheeks were pale and she had circles under her eyes.

"I'm making a salad. I found a delicious herb vinaigrette at a shop on Fillmore. I think I'm going to stock it at the emporium." Cassie wore a beige Michael Kors dress and navy tights. She had been swimming in Alexis's pool every night and her muscles felt taut.

"Not hungry." Alexis shrugged. "What's new in the world of commerce?"

"I snagged Alice for the grand opening. Can you imagine if I get Thomas Keller? I heard he has a Havanese dog that only eats steak. I'm going to send him a doggy bag of prime rib." Cassie put spinach and arugula on the counter. She rinsed a tomato and glanced at Alexis. "You don't look very good. Has the yoga Nazi been tough on you?"

"Carter called this morning. Apparently big things are happening in Prague and Budapest. He's going to extend his trip another month." Alexis sat at the table. "I love Carter for crisscrossing the planet creating the yellow brick road, but sometimes I want him home so badly it's a physical pain. I should have gotten pregnant. If I had a mini Carter I wouldn't be so lonely. You waltz off to Fenton's every day and I plan Poodles's dinner menus."

"You could join a charity. You have so much to give."

"Those charities are never about giving. They're a competition to see who wears the most expensive gown to the AIDS ball or the diabetes dinner. I'm so desperate I called Carter's mother to see if she needs help with the ballet gala. At least I'm interested in dance."

"That sounds promising." Cassie drizzled dressing into a wooden salad bowl.

"She'll be critiquing my every move. Carter is a big player now. I have to wear the correct number of carats in my ears when I go out in public."

Cassie's phone vibrated on the counter. She looked at the caller ID and frowned. "It's my mother. She's in Palm Beach, at the Breakers. She says she can't stock the right resort wear unless she spends some time at a resort." Cassie picked up the phone and balanced it under her chin. "No, I'm not at the store, Mother, I'm working at home." Cassie made a face at Alexis. "That's terrible, poor Derek." She sprinkled grated cheese in the salad bowl. "No, you don't have to come home." Cassie gazed at Alexis. "I know someone who can cover for him. She's an old school friend." Cassie carried the salad bowl to the kitchen table. "Yes, she has experience in fashion. She was a personal shopper for Gordon Getty's wife." Cassie moved the phone to her other ear. "Yes, I'll call her right now. Don't worry, Mother, enjoy the Breakers."

Cassie pressed END and pulled out the kitchen chair. She ladled salad onto two plates and passed one to Alexis.

"Why are you looking at me like that?" Alexis asked.

"Derek hurt his back and is confined to bed for six weeks." Cassie poured herself a glass of lemonade from the Limoges pitcher on the table. "The assistant manager is on maternity leave and Mother's not scheduled to be back for two weeks."

"Cassie, you didn't." Alexis shook her head.

"You would be a fabulous store manager. You know more about fashion than Anna Wintour." Cassie's eyes sparkled.

"You told your mother I was a personal shopper for Ann Getty?"

"You and Ann did that Macy's charity fashion show together. You told me you picked out everyone's outfit. You're a natural." Cassie grinned.

"Standing in Fenton's all day, surrounded by Pucci scarves and Prada boots?" Alexis nibbled a spinach leaf.

"Sometimes the customers can be exhausting, but it beats turning your body into a pretzel." Cassie speared tomato wedges with her fork.

"It sounds absolutely fabulous." Alexis pushed her chair back. "Do you think your mother would give me a discount? I'd love to stock up on spring Manolos. I saw them online and they have the sweetest cork heels."

"Alexis, you don't need a discount." Cassie giggled. "You're married to a gazillionaire."

"But if I get a discount, I have to buy them. It would be fiscally imprudent not to." Alexis studied her reflection in the fridge door.

"You're already talking like a saleswoman." Cassie blotted her mouth with a napkin. "Go upstairs and put on one of your drop-dead outfits and we'll drive in together."

Alexis handed the keys to her Range Rover to the valet and stood on the sidewalk straightening her skirt. She wore a yellow wool skirt with a zipper up the back and a black angora sweater. Her feet were squeezed into four-inch-heel Christian Louboutins and she balanced a pillbox hat on her head.

"You don't give the car to the valet when you work here." Cassie got out the passenger side. "It'll cost you a fortune."

"I'm setting an example for our customers. If they all valet park, Fenton's will make more money." Alexis scooped Poodles up and placed him in a Louis Vuitton handbag. "Besides, I'm not ruining these heels on the parking garage cement. The soles are encrusted with real diamonds."

"I feel like Cinderella's stepsister." Cassie studied her

reflection in Fenton's window. She smoothed her hair and smeared on an extra coat of lip gloss.

"Shit, Cassie." Alexis clutched Cassie's arm as the doorman ushered them inside. "I never realized how big and imposing Fenton's is. What if the managers find out I've never worked in a department store? It'll be so embarrassing."

"You're the girl who was voted Miss Congeniality at the Convent and was rushed by three sororities at UCLA. You're born to be a department store queen. Think of yourself as Barbara Hutton."

"Who?"

"Never mind. I'll introduce you to the department managers and then I have to go down to the food emporium. We're expecting a big delivery today."

Cassie and Alexis made the rounds of all four floors and finished on the ground floor next to the display case of Fendi purses. "Come down to the emporium if you need me. You're going to be fabulous."

"Cassie"—Alexis touched the pillbox hat—"you don't think I've overdone it?"

"Have you ever seen my mother not brandishing her cigarette holder?" Cassie grinned. "You could out-dress Wallis Simpson and look perfectly natural."

"I don't know who that is." Alexis shrugged. "But I'm going to make your mother proud."

Cassie took the escalator down to the emporium, feeling the familiar sense of excitement bubble inside her. The emporium was coming to life and it was as breathtaking as James's sketches. The black-and-white floor was polished to perfection. The fridges were installed and the Bridges bottles of organic milk glinted behind glass. The first of Gregory's murals was mounted on one wall and Cassie couldn't take her eyes off it.

"Bad news." James greeted her glumly.

"What's wrong?" Cassie stepped off the escalator, adjusting the hem of her Michael Kors dress.

Cassie had been nervous about seeing James after their trip to Sonoma. She rehearsed telling him she still loved Aidan; he was engaged to Emily. Their relationships were both damaged but that was no reason to risk everything. But Alexis had walked in on her soliloquy and instructed her she was going about it all wrong. "Trust me." She stood at the foot of the Scarlett O'Hara bed. "Ignore the kiss and James will too. Make a big deal of it and your friendship is over. Men are babies, they have too much pride."

Cassie marched into Fenton's the next day and had a two-hour meeting with James about product positioning. By the time the meeting was over, their mutual respect blossomed and the kiss was forgotten. Now they worked side by side and shared milkshakes and French fries from the McDonald's on Market Street.

"The marble pedestals I ordered got stuck in a snow-storm in Utah. They sent them back to the warehouse and a salesperson sold them to a library in Alabama. It will take the supplier two months to make new ones." James took off his glasses and rubbed his eyes. "I really wanted to carry the Roman banquet theme throughout the floor and those pedestals were perfect."

Cassie looked at James. He wore what had become his work uniform: a light blue button-down shirt, khaki trousers, and leather loafers. He shifted from foot to foot like a schoolboy who had failed his science project.

"I'll call Stella Kim, she was Alexis's wedding planner. Alexis and Carter had a *Roman Holiday*—themed wedding and Stella placed marble pedestals all over the ballroom. I bet she could find what you're looking for."

James hesitated. "They have to be the right height, and they have to be Roman columns, not Greek."

"You are picky," Cassie joked. "I'm glad I'm not one of your suppliers."

"I'm sorry." James blushed. "Your mother calls me every day for an update. I dread telling her there's a library in Alabama with her Roman columns."

"I've got Stella's number on my computer. Give me an hour and I'll see what I can do." Cassie walked to the corner of the floor that she had set up as her office.

Cassie called Stella and was told by Stella's assistant to try Axel, her florist. Cassie waited on the phone while Axel's assistant located Axel at the flower mart. Axel shrieked that he remembered Cassie well; she had looked divine in the Roman toga Alexis made her wear as the matron of honor.

"Roman pedestals?" Axel asked loudly. Cassie could hear vendors shouting the price of purple orchids in the background. "Alexis isn't redecorating her monolithic mansion again, is she?"

"No, it's for Fenton's. We're putting in a food emporium in the basement and the pedestals the designer ordered were stranded in Utah."

"A food emporium, how divinely exciting!" Axel cooed. "You should stock my bouquets. I'll hand deliver them daily, fresh from the flower mart."

"That's a great idea." Cassie grabbed a pen and wrote on a big yellow notepad, "Axel signature arrangements available only at Fenton's."

"Darling, I could tell at Alexis's wedding that you had hidden talents. I'd love to help find your pedestals. Let me make a few calls, I'll ring you back."

While Cassie waited she consulted her to-do list. There were always a dozen people to call and she loved the satisfaction of checking off names and numbers. She gazed around at the emporium and imagined it decorated for the grand opening. She had ordered two hundred red balloons imprinted with Fenton's signature. They would cascade from the ceiling while Tony Bennett sang "I Left My Heart in San Francisco."

She and James spent a whole day debating who should perform at the grand opening. She suggested hiring a Bay Area band: Green Day or Train. Finally they agreed no one embodied San Francisco like Tony Bennett. When Cassie called Tony's people and he agreed to participate, she had a smile glued on her face for days.

Cassie crossed Alice Waters's name off the list and put three exclamation marks beside it. She chewed the end of her pen. Which gorgeous young San Francisco socialite would be best to cut the red ribbon? She could call Marissa Mayer: Yahoo! honcho and girl about town, or Gavin Newsom's wife, Jennifer. She flipped through a copy of *San Francisco* magazine. Gavin and Jennifer were such a beautiful couple, they made Brad and Angelina look over the hill. Or there was Vanessa Getty, who always seemed to have a new baby on her hip while maintaining the waist measurements of Posh Spice.

The phone rang at Cassie's elbow.

"I have your Roman columns, darling," Axel cooed. "A friend at the Legion of Honor owed me a favor. Be gentle." Axel's laugh tinkled down the phone line. "They're quite old."

"You're amazing." Cassie beamed. "James will be so relieved."

"I'm creating a new arrangement for Fenton's: red roses, white chrysanthemums, pink tulips. And I'm driving back to the studio to blog about your delicious food emporium!"

"I'll save you a seat at the grand opening. Tony Bennett is going to sing."

"You've made my day," Axel drawled. "I wouldn't miss Tony Bennett for the world."

Cassie hung up and went to find James. He was poring over fabric swatches in different shades of red.

"I found your Roman columns. Axel, Alexis's florist, has a friend at the Legion of Honor. I expect you'll have to return them eventually, but they'll work until the others arrive." Cassie sat down on a stool at the counter.

"You're a lifesaver." James looked up. "Shall we celebrate with two cheeseburgers and a double order of fries?"

"I think I better go back to watercress salads at the café. My skirts are getting tight." Cassie picked up a swatch and held it to the light.

"There's just something about a McDonald's burger when I spend all day staring at linen samples." James smiled.

"It's the grease, it's addictive," Cassie replied. "I should go upstairs and check on Alexis. We had a crisis this morning. Derek injured his back, so I coerced Alexis into being interim store manager."

"Your friend Alexis?" James asked, puzzled.

"She doesn't have any experience, but she has more style than Nicole Kidman, Katie Holmes, and Heidi Klum combined. Plus she grew up in the store with me."

"I'll come with you. I need a break from staring at these swatches. I feel like a bull in the ring."

* * *

Alexis was sitting on a high stool at the Chanel counter next to a woman wearing a Miu Miu dress and thigh-high Prada boots.

Alexis waved for Cassie and James to join them. "Cassie, meet my friend Princess Giselle. She's a real princess from Liechtenstein. It turns out her husband, Prince Günter, and Carter are old friends. Giselle and Günter's castle is getting a new roof and Giselle decided to spend the summer in San Francisco. Carter gave her my phone number and she tracked me down to Fenton's. We were just moaning over the fact she has nothing to wear. Her suitcases were practically empty.

"I loaded her up with a few things from Prada and John Galliano and Caroline Herrera. Giselle can't make her entry into San Francisco society in après-ski clothes from Gstaad." Alexis laughed. "I wish we were in Gstaad, I had the best time there on my honeymoon, but this is California. Now we're finishing up with a teeny makeover." Alexis pointed to a tall pile of cosmetics on the counter. "I told Giselle she is punishing her skin by not using Chanel's skin drencher. And the eye revitalizer is so refreshing, you don't have to sleep."

Princess Giselle kept her mouth closed so the cosmetician could apply lipstick, mascara, and powder. Alexis winked at Cassie and made dollar signs behind her back.

"Just a spritz of Chanel No. 5 and you're on your way." Alexis admired Giselle's complexion. "Kitty will ring you up and I'll have John call a taxi. Let me tap my number into your cell phone in case we missed something. I can always messenger it to your hotel."

"I thought Carter was in Luxembourg," Cassie said after Giselle followed the doorman to a waiting cab.

"One of those little countries starting in L." Alexis shrugged. "Apparently Prince Günter invested the royal fortune in an alternative energy company that was undercapitalized. It was about to go under, but Carter came in and saved the day. He turned the company around and now it is printing money. It paid for a new roof and a summer cottage on the Black Sea. Giselle is so grateful she bought half the second floor, and she's coming back to be fitted for a couture gown for the ballet."

"Your connections are more complex than a black widow's web." Cassie grinned. "James and I are going to get a bite. Come join us."

"It has to be somewhere I can take off my shoes." Alexis moaned, bending down and rubbing her ankles.

They spread out a Burberry picnic blanket and sat cross-legged on the floor of Diana's office. James ducked across the street and returned with three containers of Thai-fusion noodles and a carton of sautéed vegetables. Cassie ran up to the café and got two loaves of bread, a pot of hummus, and three cans of Coke.

"I didn't know the café served Coke." Alexis popped hers open and poured it down her throat.

"It doesn't. The employees keep their own cans in the fridge. I left them five dollars." Cassie giggled.

"Fenton's café has delicious entrées." James ladled noodles and vegetables onto the white china plates Cassie found in her mother's cabinet.

"They've just been serving the same grilled salmon for twenty years." Cassie sighed, stabbing a snow pea.

"I disagree." James sipped his Coke. "My mother would

be dismayed if the café didn't offer petit filet mignon. The emporium will serve samples of the 'hip' foods. We'll keep all our customers happy."

Cassie wound noodles around her fork. She ate them quickly and started choking. James leaned forward and pounded her on the back.

"You just gave me the best idea," Cassie said.

"To chew before you swallow?" Alexis asked.

"I've been trying to line up celebrity chefs to attend the grand opening, but I've only targeted the old guard. We need young chefs that are on the cutting edge of the new cuisine to endorse the emporium."

"That's brilliant!" James's eyes sparkled. "Each chef could give a cooking class using emporium ingredients."

"We can ask Trent Brown." Cassie grabbed a pen and paper from her mother's desk.

"And Roland Ames, the chef at Emerald. He used to be on television. He'd be a natural," James suggested.

"I know the most divine chef in Marin, Andre Blick." Alexis spread hummus on her bread. "He owns a bistro that serves fondue. He is movie-star handsome. The girls in my book club take pictures of him with their iPhones."

"You ask him," Cassie said to Alexis. "No Frenchman could resist your accent."

"I took three years of French at the Convent, followed by a summer in Paris. My accent is flawless." Alexis pouted.

"We could all have dinner there together. Fondue is better shared," James suggested. "What about Saturday night?"

"I have a Skype date with Carter," Alexis said.

"Cassie?" James asked expectantly.

Cassie kept her eyes on the spot of soy sauce that dribbled onto her skirt. "Aidan is taking me out to dinner at Green's."

"Green's." Alexis whistled. "Who did Aidan bribe to get that reservation?"

"I'll go by myself"—James started stacking containers—"but I can't promise Andre will agree to attend the grand opening. I'm not as cute as either of you."

Cassie spent the rest of the afternoon on the phone with suppliers. She was creating a fantasy chocolate section in the front of the store that would feature chocolates she had dreamed of as a child. She finally found a local chocolatier excited to whip up her ideas. She glanced at her watch and realized it was after 5:00 P.M.

"I printed an invitation for Emily, but I don't have her address," Cassie interrupted James, who was bent over yards of red drapery.

James took the envelope and admired the smooth satin finish. "She's expecting a big furniture delivery that day." He took off his glasses and rubbed his eyes. "But I'm sure she'll love to receive an invitation."

"I'm going to see if Alexis has collected any more princesses or movie stars." Cassie grinned. "I'll see you to-morrow."

Cassie took the escalator upstairs and found Alexis surrounded by a group of women wearing leotards and tights.

"Cassie, do you remember Nellie Vincent from the Convent?" Alexis motioned to her to join them. "She's married to Hunter Green now. It's such a small world. Hunter was just in Venice and gave Carter a ride to Berlin on his G4. I said, if those boys are swanning around on their private jets, Nellie deserves to treat herself to a little cashmere."

Nellie slipped on chocolate brown cashmere gloves and made small mewing noises as if she was stroking a kitten.

"And these are the girls from my yoga class: Caitlin, Holly, and Peta. I tweeted them we just got in the most divine pashminas." Alexis consulted her Cartier. "Oh, my goodness, girls, it's almost closing time. We better ring these up and get you home before those pesky husbands start demanding predinner cocktails."

Cassie watched Alexis load the women up with red Fenton's boxes. "And I promise I'll tweet as soon as we get in more of these pillbox hats." Alexis kissed each woman on the cheek.

"Oh, God," Alexis said when the women were gone and the store was quiet. "Wearing Louboutins on a marble floor for eight hours was a mistake. Can we stop and get a pedicure on the way home?"

"I'll text Pia and tell her to run you a hot bath." Cassie grinned.

"Ask her to make a stack of peanut butter and jelly sandwiches," Alexis moaned. "I'm starving."

Cassie swam forty laps and sat for twenty minutes in Alexis's steam room. She wrapped herself in a terry robe and joined Alexis, who was collapsed on the sofa in the living room.

"I'm never going to move again," Alexis groaned when Cassie suggested they eat dinner.

"Pia left us tuna casserole and scalloped potatoes. And I saw a German chocolate cake on the counter. You can't let me into the kitchen alone."

"Did you really tweet those women in your yoga class?" Cassie cut two slices of cake and gave one to Alexis.

"Tweeting is the only way to transfer information." Alexis poured two glasses of milk.

"Fenton's doesn't have a Twitter account or a Facebook page. Someone has to inform your mother about social media."

"My mother thinks tweeting is what birds do." Cassie licked chocolate from her fork.

"He really is cute." Alexis nibbled frosting.

"Who are you talking about?"

"James, our Hugh Grant. Remember how he pounded your back when you were choking? He is such a knight in shining armor. And I love his preppy clothes. He belongs on the set of *Gossip Girl*."

"I'm not interested in anything about James except his ability to match different shades of red." Cassie drank her milk.

"Tell me you don't enjoy working elbow to elbow with a sexy young architect."

"He's engaged and I'm married." Cassie stood up and took her plate to the sink. "I enjoy contributing to something that is going to be a success."

"Men and women work together in offices all over the country, it doesn't mean they jump into bed. They engage in harmless flirtation, then they go home and have sex with their spouses. Marriage doesn't get boring, everyone's happy."

"Thank you, Dr. Ruth, but Aidan acted out the fantasy," Cassie replied glumly.

"Aidan was ambushed," Alexis said slowly, "according to him."

"What are you saying?" Cassie turned to Alexis, her eyes flashing.

"I think it's great that you and Aidan have been talking

on the phone every night. And I'm happy you're going to dinner with him." Alexis inspected the pink polish on her fingernails. "Just be careful, I don't want you to get your heart broken again."

Cassie sat down heavily on the kitchen chair. She pulled Alexis's piece of cake toward her and took a bite. "I've missed Aidan so much." She put the fork down. "I have to trust him, Alexis. I love him."

11.

On Saturday night, Cassie insisted Alexis take Poodles for a walk.

"Please don't come back until I text we are on our way to Green's." Cassie stood at the front door.

"Evicted from my own house," Alexis pouted, buttoning her faux shearling coat. "Are you afraid I'm going to go Simon Cowell on Aidan?"

"I'm not taking any chances." Cassie blew Poodles a kiss and shut the door.

Standing in front of the walk-in closet, she felt like a bride on her wedding day. Aidan had seen her naked more times than her own mother, but she couldn't find the right thing to wear. She pulled on True Religion jeans and a Michael Stars T-shirt. Aidan wouldn't dress up, even if they were eating at Green's. But the waist was loose; thirty laps in the pool followed by time in the steam room had molded her body into a new shape. Even her cheeks looked narrower.

She finally settled on a pale blue silk blouse that made

her eyes look like a winter sky. She paired it with velvet slacks and a pair of Ferragamo loafers from Alexis's collection. It was hard not to develop her own shoe fetish, with Alexis's rows of pumps, boots, and heels just one floor away.

Cassie moved into the bathroom and put eye shadow, blush, and lip gloss on the counter. She studied her face in the mirror, remembering the first time she went to Aidan's house. During dinner Isabel got angry and stormed upstairs, black eyes flashing like a little gypsy.

They had shared a bottle of Pinot Noir and had listened to the Beatles. Cassie had followed Aidan into the bedroom and they had made love quietly so Isabel wouldn't hear. She remembered tucking her body into the curve of Aidan's chest. She pictured all the years of making love: in their bed, on the sofa, in the hot tub in Mexico, under a blanket at Lake Tahoe.

She tried to stop the tears from ruining the mascara she had carefully applied. The excitement of creating the food emporium slipped away. The fun of giggling with Alexis, sharing ice cream and late-night manicures disappeared.

She wanted to rewind time and erase Molly Payne. She remembered sitting under the Christmas tree with Aidan, exchanging gardening gloves and kitchen aprons. Aidan had peeled off her robe and sucked her nipples. She pushed him away, laughing about how the neighbors could see through the window.

She felt her nipples harden and wanted Aidan to climb the three flights of stairs and lift her onto the bathroom counter. She wanted him to tear off her panties and push himself inside her. She wanted him to fuck her until she came, shuddering against his chest.

* * *

Cassie heard the pinging sound three times before she realized it was the doorbell. She spritzed herself with Sarah Jessica Parker's Lovely and walked downstairs.

Aidan wore cream-colored slacks and a shirt so white and crisp it looked like it came from the Chinese laundry. He had replaced his leather jacket with a herringbone blazer and he smelled like Ralph Lauren for Men.

"Hi." He leaned forward and kissed her on the lips. His eyes sparkled and his teeth were white. She remembered every line on his face, the dusting of gray on the top of his head.

"Do you want to come in?" Cassie asked awkwardly.

"We have a seven o'clock reservation." Aidan took her hand and led her down the stone path.

"What's this?" Cassie asked when he stopped in front of a small yellow car.

"I borrowed Isabel's MINI. I didn't want the valet at Green's to frown on us for driving an ancient Toyota."

They climbed in, Aidan's legs barely fitting in the driver's side. She watched him turn down Sacramento Street, concentrating on driving the foreign car. She tried to think of something to say but her mind was blank.

"I didn't tell you"—Aidan stopped the car on the Marina Green—"how beautiful you look, or how much I missed you. I brought you something."

Cassie unwrapped the brown paper and opened the box. Inside was a yellow heirloom tomato sitting on a bed of tissue paper.

"It's from your garden. I've been taking care of the vegetables. The broccoli is flowering and you have a new cauliflower."

Cassie put the tomato in the box and let the tears come. Mascara slid down her cheeks. Tears fell on her velvet pants. She hunched her shoulders, put her head in her hands, and sobbed.

"It's okay," Aidan said when she finally stopped. He put his arm around her and drew her against his chest. "I'm not going anywhere, and neither are you."

She heard his heart pounding. She felt him grow hard inside his pants. She wiped her eyes and sat back in her seat.

"I know I shouldn't have traded cars." Aidan grinned. "I can't fuck you in a MINI."

Cassie blinked, trying to clear her head. She flipped open the mirror and checked the black smudges on her cheeks. She reapplied her lip gloss and tried to smile. "I'd love a big salad and a glass of white wine."

Aidan started the car again and drove the few blocks to Green's. They talked about Isabel and her looming SATs. They discussed Aidan's workload and the lopsided politics of the ethics department. Cassie tried to keep her comments light and funny. She felt like she was trying to grab on to something that would make them a unit again, but it kept slipping away.

"Remember the first time we ate here?" Cassie said as they walked into the restaurant. "You got into an argument with the waiter about Zen philosophy."

"He criticized my choice of wines." Aidan chuckled. "He didn't think it paired well with my entrée. Green's was built by Zen carpenters. It's meant to embody Zen beliefs."

"All the waiters then were Zen students." Cassie nodded, waiting at the hostess desk.

"That waiter obviously didn't get the memo." Aidan massaged the back of her neck.

"I was so embarrassed." Cassie smiled. "I thought they'd never take our reservation again."

The hostess sat them at the window overlooking the bay. Cassie watched car lights twinkling on the Golden Gate Bridge. She saw a couple holding hands at the next table, trading kisses over glasses of champagne.

Aidan ordered a Garden Gulch salad for two and a bottle of Fetzer Chardonnay. He tore open a bread roll and dipped it in olive oil.

"I want you to come home." He reached across the table and squeezed her hand.

"I want to come home," she said.

"Then this is a celebration." He waited while the waiter poured the wine. "I have exciting news."

Cassie tasted the wine. She felt numb. She buttered her roll but left it on her plate.

"My paper was accepted at the conference. We leave April fifteenth. The conference runs from the eighteenth to the twenty-eighth. I booked two days in Venice and an overnight in Verona. And"—his eyes sparkled—"I've been asked to read the paper in Athens. Athens, Cassie! Aristotle's backyard."

"I can't go to Italy in April." Cassie pulled her hand away. "The grand opening is April thirtieth."

"But you're coming home," Aidan replied quietly.

"I'm coming home because I want to stay married. That has nothing to do with Fenton's."

"We talked about this." Aidan drummed his fingers on the table. "You have too many responsibilities at home."

"I enjoy what I'm doing, and I'm good at it."

"Just because I fucked up." Aidan's black eyes flashed. "You want to spend your day kissing up to dowagers wearing ridiculous hats."

"Fenton's has nothing to do with Molly Payne," Cassie

replied. Her heart was beating very fast; she put down her wineglass and placed her hands in her lap.

"Nothing has changed, Cassie. I need you, Isabel needs you."

Cassie took a deep breath. Her stomach did little flips like eggs in a frying pan. "The emporium is coming to life. I can't ditch it two weeks before the opening."

"Remember the pizza we ate in Rome? We counted nine toppings. And the pasta Alfredo at that trattoria next to the Spanish Steps? I can't eat alone. I want to take you to Juliet's Wall in Verona. I want to feed the pigeons in the Piazza San Marco."

"I've been working on the emporium for a month. I can't abandon it before the opening."

The waiter set a large plate heaped with salad between them. He brandished a pepper shaker and sprinkled the plate with ground pepper.

"Your salad consists of De Voto Arkansas Black Apples, Point Reyes Original Blue, and Garden Gulch Red Endive. All grown at our farm in Marin." The waiter bowed. "Enjoy."

Aidan looked at his plate and burst out laughing.

"Just once, I want a waiter in this town to put the plate on the table and walk away."

"Aidan," Cassie whispered.

"They're all unemployed actors. It's a salad, for God's sake, not Shakespeare."

"Aidan." Cassie giggled. "He'll hear you."

"If they want a performance"—he poured another glass of wine—"I could stand on my chair and serenade you."

"Aidan." Cassie glanced around. The couple at the next table smiled at her.

"Or I could undress you and suck your nipples like cherry tomatoes."

"Aidan." Cassie blushed a deep pink. "You have to stop."

"God, I've missed you," he said, heaping salad on his fork. "You keep my feet on the ground."

Aidan refilled her wineglass. Cassie's shoulders relaxed. The tight feeling in her stomach disappeared. Aidan fed Cassie a snow pea, pressing his fingers against her lips. She felt a warmth between her legs, and the stirrings of a luxurious desire.

They didn't discuss Fenton's for the rest of the meal. Cassie went to the bathroom while Aidan paid the check. She looked at herself in the mirror. Her cheeks were flushed and there were mascara smudges under her eyes. She felt suddenly giddy. She was going to have sex with her husband. She was going to have a long, delicious orgasm that she could carry around like a secret.

When she walked out of the bathroom, Aidan was outside waiting for his car. She saw him talking to a woman in a brown suede jacket. The woman had smooth brown hair and wore ankle-high boots. She leaned close to Aidan and laughed, flipping her hair with her hand.

Cassie felt like she'd been slapped. She nodded good-bye to the hostess and walked outside. The air by the bay was freezing. She rubbed her hands together and joined Aidan.

"This lady also drives a MINI. We were laughing about how there should be a height limit. It's okay for you ladies, but my back is going to be permanently bent." Aidan pulled Cassie close to him.

The woman jumped into a red MINI Cooper, waved, and drove away. Aidan put his arm around Cassie, but she still felt chilled. They didn't talk on the way to Alexis's house.

Aidan kept his hand on Cassie's knee and navigated the streets like a race-car driver. He pulled into the driveway and turned off the ignition.

"Let's get your things and go home."

"I'm not going to Italy." Cassie kept her eyes on the dashboard.

Aidan's body twisted in the cramped space. He was silent for a long time. "It's impossible to talk in this hamster mobile. Let's discuss it at home."

"I don't think I should come home until after the grand opening," Cassie said slowly. "You're going to be gone; it's easier if I stay here."

"I applaud your desire to finish something you started," Aidan said finally, "but you're my wife."

"You can survive a month without me," Cassie replied, twisting her wedding ring on her finger.

"I don't want to be without you for a minute." Aidan reached across the seat and unzipped Cassie's pants. He quickly slid down her panties and pushed his fingers deep inside her. Cassie bit her lip, her body suddenly straining. She arched back, feeling the delicious waves grow between her legs. He moved his fingers in slow circles, watching her face, waiting until her body collapsed in a long slow shudder. He pulled his fingers out, leaned over, and kissed her.

"I don't know why you're doing this, Cassie"—his voice was low and gruff—"but the day I get back from Europe, you're coming home."

When Cassie opened the front door, Alexis was sitting in the living room listening to her iPod.

"Why are you giggling?" Alexis asked, removing her head-phones.

"You're sitting in a room designed for Marie Antoinette, plugged into plastic ear buds."

"Maybe it's time to redecorate: something minimal and modern." Alexis eyed Cassie carefully. "Your hair is tangled. You look like you've been fucked."

"We drove in Isabel's MINI." Cassie blushed. "Hardly a teenager's wet dream."

"Something happened." Alexis scooped Poodles from his dog bed and placed him in her lap.

"Aidan's paper was accepted into the conference in Florence. He wants me to go with him, but I would miss the grand opening." Cassie sat by the fireplace. "I said no."

"You said no to Aidan?"

"I can't abandon the emporium, we've all worked so hard."

"You and James have worked so hard," Alexis corrected.

"James didn't come up," Cassie replied angrily. "This is something I started, and I want to finish."

"The grand opening isn't the end, it's the beginning." Alexis stroked Poodles's fur.

"Aidan wants me to come home. He doesn't want me to work at Fenton's."

"What did you say?" Alexis asked.

"I don't know what to do. At first I felt so distant. And then we started laughing at the restaurant. Aidan looked so handsome. He was wearing a blazer and a white shirt." Cassie warmed her hands in front of the fire.

"You're not telling me something." Alexis kissed the tip of Poodles's nose.

"I went to the bathroom while Aidan was getting the car. When I walked out I saw him talking to a woman at the valet stand. They were laughing. She leaned forward and touched his blazer." Cassie paused.

"Cassie, you have to be in the marriage or out of the marriage. You can't get upset if a woman touches his coat."

"I know." Cassie nodded. "I told Aidan I was going to stay with you until he gets back from Europe."

"Is that what you want?" Alexis asked.

"I want Aidan not to have fucked his student. It's still there, Alexis. It sits on my shoulder like the raven."

"There's something you're still not telling me." Alexis frowned.

"He leaned over in the car and he"—Cassie hesitated—"finger fucked me."

"Aah." Alexis nodded like a scientist who had just solved a chemical equation. "Your body wants to run home to him, and your brain wants to stay here."

"What do I do?"

"Beats me." Alexis shrugged. "You get the popcorn, I'll find a rerun of Dr. Ruth."

12.

Cassie got the message her mother wanted to see her at the end of a long day. There was less than three weeks until the grand opening, and she had been working back-to-back twelve-hour shifts. New crises landed on her desk every morning.

The cheese maker in West Marin ran out of chives. The mushroom crop in Inverness was washed away by a spring storm. The handmade chocolate sculptures melted under James's pinpoint lighting.

Alexis also worked tirelessly. Every time Cassie rode the escalator upstairs she ran into an army of women, weighed down by red Fenton's boxes. Alexis introduced Cassie to girls from her book club, the members of her makeup class, the women in her Asian cooking seminar. Alexis was usually leaning on the counter, wearing a form-fitting dress and four-inch heels. She sported a different accessory each week: a stack of gold bangles, a hat from Philip Treacy's new collection, and the items flew out the store.

Alexis created a Facebook page for Fenton's, and a Twitter account, which became her obsession. She flitted from department to department, rapidly texting about new arrivals. By lunchtime twenty women would appear at the counter, fighting over the latest Chanel powder blush or Pucci scarf.

Cassie listened to her mother's message twice, wanting to ignore it until morning. She was looking forward to swimming fifty laps and sitting down to one of Pia's delicious meals. But Diana had broken her toe playing lawn croquet at the Breakers. She was confined to her apartment and frantic to hear about the emporium's progress.

Cassie checked her reflection in the elevator mirror on the way up to Diana's apartment. Her mother couldn't complain about her wardrobe. Alexis was teaching her to dress like the heir to Fenton's. Today she wore a James Perse dress with Chanel ballet slippers. A ruby clip held her hair back, and she carried a Burberry clutch.

She took a deep breath before she knocked on her mother's door. She still hadn't told Diana that Alexis was running Fenton's. In her mother's eyes, Alexis was the sixteen-year-old who persuaded Cassie to skip school to attend Neiman's annual sale. Cassie remembered the fuss when the headmistress found the Neiman's bags stuffed in their lockers.

"Good evening, Maria. How is my mother?"

"Like bull in a china shop," Maria groaned. "She follow me around with her own duster. When she going back to work?"

"Darling, thank God!" Diana appeared in the doorway. She wore flowing silk pajamas and satin slippers. Her hair was brushed smoothly to her chin and she had replaced her cigarette holder with an ivory cane.

"I didn't know you needed a cane." Cassie frowned. "Shouldn't you be lying down?"

"A lovely gentleman in Palm Beach gave me the cane as a

present." Diana hobbled to the conversation pit. "I want to hear everything. I've had James on the phone and he said you're doing a marvelous job."

"Axel is creating a new line of floral arrangements for Fenton's. Miles Cavendish is baking a red velvet cheesecake for the grand opening, and Vanessa Getty is going to cut the red ribbon." Cassie sat on a snow-white love seat.

"Vanessa Getty." Diana nodded approvingly. "The society columnists will love it. James wouldn't tell me the name of your interim store manager. From the numbers I'm seeing, she's doing a fantastic job."

"She's an old school friend," Cassie mumbled.

"Emily Burrows's daughter has all the latest gadgets." Diana sat opposite her, propping her foot on a silk pillow. "Emily says she gets daily tweets announcing new arrivals at Fenton's."

"It's very effective," Cassie replied nervously.

"I told you I'm a big fan of young energy. Emily showed me Fenton's Facebook page: five hundred friends the first week. We should have implemented these ideas months ago." Diana picked up her teacup and sipped the tea thoughtfully. "It's time for a change in leadership."

"What do you mean?" Cassie dropped two sugar cubes in her tea.

"Derek has done a divine job for thirty years, but he's as dated as an avocado refrigerator. We need a new store manager who understands online networking." Diana placed her cup on the white porcelain tray. "I'd like to offer her the job permanently."

"Permanently?" Cassie choked on her tea.

"I'll give Derek a new title, something that keeps him behind the scenes. I can't go to the store quite yet, so please bring her here so I can offer her the job in person." Diana leaned back on the love seat. "Tell me about her, I'm dying to hear."

Cassie studied yellow tulips in the crystal vase on the coffee table. "Alexis is the store manager."

"What did you say?"

"Carter is never here and Alexis was dying of boredom. She has amazing fashion sense. Every woman that comes into Fenton's leaves dressed exactly like her. And she knows everyone. Her cell phone is a Rolodex of San Francisco society."

"Alexis is running my store," Diana repeated slowly.

"I thought it was just temporary. You were going to be back in two weeks." Cassie looked past her mother at the skyline of San Francisco.

"Alexis! The girl who stole my Ferragamos and wore them to her Girl Scout meeting?"

"She was ten years old, and she always admired your taste in shoes."

"She was a dance major in college." Diana shook her head.

"At UCLA. You said she's doing a wonderful job!" Cassie protested.

Diana leaned forward and rearranged the tulips. She tapped her cane on the marble floor and inspected her French manicure.

"Numbers don't lie. The spring collections are being snapped up like hotcakes." Diana plucked a dead petal. "Alexis always had a 'nose' for fashion, but does she have the work ethic?"

"She runs Fenton's like a military academy." Cassie walked to the window. She could see the stone spirals of Grace Cathedral, and the flags flying outside the Mark Hopkins. "The department managers call her the 'colonel.' "

"Good." Diana nodded decisively. "Bring her for tea to-morrow afternoon." Diana eyed Cassie carefully. "You look very well, that dress suits you."

"We're almost ready for the opening." Cassie's eyes sparkled. "James built a wall of green bookshelves. I'm going to showcase cookbooks signed by local authors."

"How does Aidan feel about your long hours?" Diana asked curiously.

"He's going to Italy next week. His paper has been accepted at a conference." Cassie played with the linen napkin.

"You're not going with him?" Diana raised an eyebrow. "I can't see Aidan agreeing to that."

"He wasn't happy," Cassie conceded, "but I've put so much time into the emporium. I couldn't miss the grand opening."

"It's time you developed a little backbone. It can only improve your marriage."

"My marriage is fine." Cassie kept her eyes on her teacup. She hadn't told her mother she was still staying with Alexis.

"If only Dr. Jasper would let me go back to work. I've read *Vogue, W,* and *Town and Country.* I've caught up on my invitations and planned a month of menus." Diana tapped her French nails on the glass.

"Don't worry, Mother." Cassie smiled. "Everyone at Fenton's misses you too."

When Cassie walked into Alexis's kitchen, Alexis was scraping the bottom of a fondue pot. She had been eating like a linebacker: ribs and mashed potatoes, sirloin steak in mushroom gravy, but her body was lean and sinewy as a ballerina.

"Pia made fondue, I was so hungry I ate the whole pot. The women in my dog obedience class stopped by Fenton's. They bought those divine Prada loafers that are comfy as

Keds." Alexis licked the yellow cheese. "We should have a pooch department: sell Burberry dog collars and tiny plaid sweaters."

"Poodles goes to obedience school?" Cassie helped herself to spinach salad and a French baguette.

"It's good for him to socialize with other dogs. I've met so many women," Alexis replied. "Dog training is the new Pilates."

"My mother summoned me to her apartment." Cassie poured a glass of lemonade.

"That sounds ominous. How is she?"

"Fluttering around like a bird with a broken wing." Cassie paused to eat a forkful of salad. "She's very pleased with your numbers."

"*My* numbers?"

"You've created quite a buzz. In fact"——Cassie sprinkled Hawaiian sea salt on the salad——"she wants to offer you the position permanently."

"April Fool's Day is over." Alexis laughed.

"I'm serious, she was very impressed."

"Your mother has never liked me. She's still angry we played dress up with her couture gowns when we were six years old," Alexis replied.

"*You* played dress up," Cassie corrected. "I watered her plants with my plastic watering can."

"They were fake plants." Alexis laughed. "You ruined her wood floor."

"She's going to give Derek a new title and make you store manager." Cassie buttered a baguette. "If you want the job."

"Of course I want the job!" Alexis opened the freezer and took out a carton of ice cream. "I haven't had this much fun since Barbie summer camp."

"Great, we're supposed to have tea with her tomorrow afternoon."

Alexis scooped ice cream into a bowl and drizzled it with chocolate syrup. "What am I going to tell Carter?"

"You found a job that makes you happy and keeps you from running up his credit cards?"

"We've gone over this. Carter *wants* me to run up his credit cards. He'll be satisfied when stores give me royal treatment, like Katie Holmes or Posh Spice."

"Maybe you two should go to couples counseling when he gets back." Cassie ate a spoonful of Alexis's ice cream.

"Says the woman who is living here, instead of with her husband in her own home."

Cassie put the spoon down so it clattered on the tabletop.

"I didn't mean that, Cassie," Alexis apologized. "I can't imagine being in your shoes."

"I keep thinking I should fly to Italy with Aidan." Cassie's eyes filled with tears. "I love working at Fenton's, but when I curl up in bed my whole body misses Aidan. I lie in the dark and picture Molly Payne. It's like attending a séance."

"Being in love is worse than having the common cold." Alexis pushed the bowl away. "You can't avoid it and there's no cure. That's why they invented ice cream."

They moved into the home theater and settled down to a chick-flick marathon: *The Devil Wears Prada, Confessions of a Shopaholic,* and *Breakfast at Tiffany's.*

"I could watch Audrey Hepburn all day." Alexis spun around in her bucket seat. "She's a modern Scarlett O'Hara without the southern accent."

"Did you ever read *Gone with the Wind*?" Cassie giggled.

"She wears those fabulous hats and men fawn all over her." Alexis wound her hair into a ponytail. "I have an idea!" She jumped up, her eyes sparkling. "I'll pretend I'm going shopping. I'll charge a few things to Carter's credit card every day. I'll even run over to Neiman's during lunch and charge things there too, so he won't get suspicious."

"You're going to pretend you're shopping every day." Cassie shook her head. "Wouldn't it be easier to tell Carter the truth?"

"I'll tell him eventually." Alexis paced up and down in front of the screen. "And it'll be good for Fenton's. I'll buy some big-ticket items like the Louis Vuitton spring satchel with the pink and green logos."

"You have to stop lying to your husband." Cassie slipped off her shoes and tucked her feet under the chair. Suddenly she was very tired. Her calves ached and her eyelids drooped.

"The first rule to a happy marriage is tell men what they want to hear," Alexis countered.

"I'm going to bed." Cassie pulled herself up. "I should have become a nun."

13.

The morning of the grand opening, Cassie woke up feeling calm and confident. It was a beautiful spring day. The trees were bursting with cherry blossoms and the bay sparkled like a magic carpet. She decided to swim forty laps before going to Fenton's, so her mind was clear and ready for the evening.

Since Aidan left for Europe, she had devoted herself to the emporium. The murals looked breathtaking. Axel had created a carpet of red roses and carnations that cascaded down the staircase. Guests would be greeted with balls of caviar and flutes of pink champagne.

Cassie checked her phone. Aidan had been sending texts all morning: "eating tiramisu, wish I could spoon-feed you," and "hotel bed too big, need you beside me." Cassie smiled and put the phone on the bedside table.

The day Aidan left for Italy had been a disaster. He had insisted she take the day off and drive him to the airport. Cassie hadn't seen Aidan since the dinner at Green's, and felt the familiar sexual pull that started in the pit of her stomach.

She had dressed in jeans and a low-cut T-shirt. She had climbed into the Prius, and adjusted her Victoria's Secret bra. She had decided it wouldn't hurt to send Aidan off with a groping session in the short-term parking at SFO.

The battery in her Prius had died as she was approaching the Bay Bridge. At first she thought the other cars were driving too fast. Then she had realized she was barely moving and the Prius glided quietly to a stop. Cassie had turned the key in the ignition, helplessly checking Aidan's impatient texts.

Eventually she had called Aidan and told him she was stuck. She heard him yelling over the phone, but cars were honking and she had to hang up to wave down the tow truck. Aidan hadn't texted her again until he was boarding the plane. Cassie had read two terse lines: "Isabel gave me ride. See you when I return."

When she had finally arrived back at Alexis's house, she ran upstairs and climbed into bed. She had closed her eyes and pictured snuggling against Aidan in the airport lounge, sharing a travel-sized Scotch and bag of pretzels. She had tried to think about the red balloons she had ordered for the grand opening. But she couldn't stop her shoulders from shaking. She had buried her face in the pillow and cried.

The next morning Cassie had gone to work wrapped in a deep lethargy. She had moved papers around her desk, she made phone calls to suppliers, she answered James's questions. But all she could see was Aidan arriving at the Rome airport, his leather jacket tossed over his arm, his black hair baking under the Italian sun. She had imagined him sitting at an outdoor café, watching boys and girls zoom by on Vespas.

She was at her desk, placing an order for cage-free eggs, when she received Aidan's first text. He had never been one to text for anything other than utilitarian reasons. Years ago, she had tried sending him fun, flirtatious texts but he told her it distracted him from his lectures.

Cassie had checked her phone, still flinching from her failure to get him to the airport. The text read, "Ciao, bella! Rome cries without you and so do I." Cassie had picked up the phone and read it again. She was about to reply when he sent another: "No Mona Lisa is as beautiful as my glorious Cassie."

Cassie had pushed back her chair and run up the stairs to the first floor. She had found Alexis at the sunglass counter and handed her the phone.

Alexis had put down the Oliver Peoples sunglasses she had been admiring. "Do you have an Italian boyfriend you're not telling me about? Some gigolo that wears a gold cross and black leather pants?"

"James Franco is your fantasy." Cassie took the phone back. "These texts are from Aidan."

"I thought he was furious at you for not providing cab service yesterday." Alexis had grabbed the phone as another text popped up. She had read it quickly and handed the phone to Cassie. "Stop him before it gets X-rated. You'll fry your eyes."

"Aidan has never sent me a text other than 'I'm making pizza, please buy tomatoes.'" Cassie read the text and blushed.

Alexis had tried on a pair of aviator frames and studied her reflection in the mirror. "Either he got drunk on the plane or he's trying to tell you he misses you."

"It's not like him. I don't know how to respond." Cassie had held the phone as if it was an unexploded grenade.

"You've been through hell, this will be good for you." Alexis tried on a pair of tortoiseshell Armanis. "Pretend Aidan's your European lover. Turn the heat up. When he comes home, you can both forget everything else that happened."

Cassie had studied Alexis in the mirror. "How do you have time to watch afternoon TV?" She slipped her phone in her pocket and took the escalator down to the emporium.

Cassie received texts from Aidan every day. Sometimes they were romantic. Often they were so hot she read them in the bathroom so no one would see her blush. She carried her phone in her purse like a pair of silk underwear, and felt a thrill of anticipation each time it rang. She replied with sexy texts that made her giggle when she sent them. The days until the grand opening flew by and Cassie worked with a secret smile on her face, racing the clock to get everything ready.

Cassie pulled into Fenton's parking garage and checked her makeup in the mirror. She wore thick mascara, a sparkly bronzer, and pale pink lipstick. She wanted to look young and sophisticated, serious but with a playful side. She had chosen to wear a Diane von Furstenberg wrap dress and a diamond Tiffany necklace.

In two hours, San Francisco's top tiers of society would gather for the unveiling of Fenton's food emporium. Cassie had signed each invitation and sealed them with red wax. The opening had been tweeted about by the *Chronicle*, *San Francisco* magazine, *7x7,* and *Town & Country*. The mayor was expected to attend and Wolfgang Puck was flying up from Los Angeles.

Cassie walked through the revolving door and stood at

the top of the escalator. She looked down at the basement, feeling like Cinderella arriving at the ball. A sea of red balloons hovered at the ceiling and the walls were draped with red velvet. The murals were lit from behind and made the room look as if it were full of people laughing and mingling.

Cassie walked down the staircase, trying to take it all in. The marble pedestals borrowed from the Legion of Honor were topped with vases of red roses. In the corner the band had set up their instruments. There was a long bar with bottles of wine, champagne, and a dozen different liqueurs.

Every surface was covered with food. Oranges and melons were arranged on one counter; avocados, asparagus, and leeks on another; and brussels sprouts, artichokes, fennel on a third. Fresh apple and rhubarb pies were displayed on ceramic plates. Oysters and jumbo prawns sat in buckets of ice. Cassie could smell fresh bread baking in the oven. She saw glass jars full of coffee beans and smelled the scent of freshly ground coffee.

"You look lovely." James walked up the stairs to greet her. He wore a navy suit with a red tie and red silk suspenders. His hair flopped over one eye and his glasses peeked out of his suit pocket.

Cassie blushed. "I thought you were blind without your glasses."

"I'm wearing my contacts"—he patted his suit—"these are back-up. Are you ready to greet five hundred of San Francisco's elite?"

"I'm so nervous." Cassie walked down the staircase. "I lay awake thinking what catastrophe might happen. Tony Bennett will forget the lyrics or the caterer will serve bad fish and everyone will get food poisoning."

"I doubt Tony Bennett is going to forget the words to 'I Left My Heart in San Francisco,' but we do have a small problem." James followed her down the stairs.

"Oh, God, what did we forget?"

"Miles Cavendish got stung by a bee and is on his way to the emergency room. He's allergic. He said he was swelling up like a watermelon."

"The poor guy; I'm sorry he'll miss the opening." Cassie straightened a line of champagne flutes.

"His neighbor took him to the hospital. Our cake is sitting on his kitchen table." James shifted from foot to foot.

"Our cheesecake isn't here." Cassie froze. The cake was going to be the room's centerpiece. After Tony Bennett sang and the balloons dropped, Cassie and her mother would cut the cake and the archbishop would bless the emporium.

"His back door is open; we're going to have to get it."

"Now?" Cassie checked her watch. "We'll never make it back in time. He lives in the Castro. And the cake is six feet tall! It's not going to fit in my Prius."

"Do we know anyone with a truck?" James asked.

"We'll ask Alexis if we can use her Range Rover." Cassie thought of all the hours she spent designing the cake with Miles. "The cake comes in two sections. We can each hold one and she can drive."

Cassie found Alexis in a dressing room with Princess Giselle. Giselle was draped in yards of silver chiffon and Alexis circled around her, her mouth full of pins.

"Cassie, you remember Princess Giselle? Giselle's social calendar filled up and she needs a dozen new gowns. I explained everyone in San Francisco buys couture. One wouldn't want to wear the same dress as Samantha Traina to the Black and White Ball." Alexis adjusted the chiffon over Giselle's shoulder.

"We have a little situation," Cassie whispered.

Alexis saw the panic in Cassie's eyes and turned calmly to Giselle. "I'll have Kitty bring you champagne and truffles. Try not to move, we don't want to disturb these perfect lines."

"That dress cost twelve thousand dollars," Alexis hissed when they stepped out of the dressing room. "I don't want her to take it off until she's married to it."

"Our cheesecake is stranded on a kitchen table in the Castro. You have to drive us to pick it up," Cassie said desperately.

"I'm not leaving Princess Giselle. She showed me her new black AmEx." Alexis wound her long ponytail into a bun. "You can borrow my car."

"James and I each have to hold a section of the cake," Cassie begged. "Please, guests are arriving soon."

"Can't they just eat caviar and salmon balls?" Alexis secured the bun with a pearl-tipped chopstick.

"The cake is the centerpiece. The whole party revolves around it."

"Fine, but I'm going to promise Giselle front-row seats at the ballet. I told her she has to get her dress before the Traina girls come in." Alexis smiled smugly.

"Throw in an autographed copy of Danielle Steel's new book." Cassie grabbed her arm. "Get your keys. We're running out of time."

"See how handy valet parking is when you have to make a quick getaway?" Alexis grinned when the valet brought up the car.

Cassie climbed in beside Alexis, and James sat in the back. "Since when did you become a seamstress?" Cassie asked as

Alexis turned on Market Street and gunned through a red light.

"I'll be Princess Giselle's personal maid if she shops exclusively at Fenton's. Her palace in Liechtenstein has a hundred and twenty rooms. Imagine the linens she'll need if she buys a house in San Francisco!"

"Do you think you could slow down?" James clutched the headrest on Cassie's seat as Alexis maneuvered around a Muni bus. "I feel like I'm on *Miami Vice*."

"Carter and I attended Porsche's driving school in Alabama last summer. He's having matching roadsters shipped from Germany." Alexis passed a red Ferrari and turned onto a leafy street with small houses stuck together. "I love the Castro." She pulled into a narrow driveway. "Everyone paints their houses and the yards are neat and clean."

The cake was sitting on a long white table in the middle of the kitchen. It was covered in red frosting and the base was littered with rose petals. White chocolate pearls ran down the sides like seams, and a white chocolate bow sat on top.

"I love these Warhol prints." Alexis wandered into the living room. "We should have a modern art department at Fenton's."

"We're all going to be fired if we don't get this cake to the emporium." Cassie slid the top section of the cake off the table and balanced it in her arms.

"You two look like matching bookends." Alexis walked back into the kitchen. "Let me take a picture with my phone." Alexis snapped a picture of Cassie and James standing side by side, holding twin sections of cheesecake.

"Alexis"—Cassie gritted her teeth—"we need to go. And if you pass one car and this cake lands in my lap . . ."

Alexis clicked her tongue. "I'll drive like my grand-mother. Don't blame me if we get stuck at every red light in the city."

Alexis pulled up at Fenton's and slammed on the brakes. "I have to get back to Giselle." She jumped out of the car and tossed the keys to the valet. "I'll join you as soon as I sepa-rate Giselle from her AmEx."

"Alexis has a lot of energy." James laughed as they car-ried the cake into the store.

"In high school she ran half marathons and ate a jar of peanut butter every afternoon. She has the metabolism of a seven-year-old boy." Cassie stepped onto the escalator. "Oh, God, people are starting to arrive. What if the press is al-ready here?"

"You look perfect, Cassie, and so does the cake. Just re-lax." James got off the escalator and placed the cake on a round table. He scattered rose petals on the linen tablecloth and handed Cassie a glass of champagne.

Cassie felt the bubbles drift straight to her toes. She re-membered sitting at Boulevard poring over James's sketches. Now she watched women mingle in little black dresses and wild Pucci designs. They wrapped their French-manicured nails around pots of sea salt, bottles of Chardonnay, bags of chocolate-covered almonds. They nibbled steak tartare and ahi tuna and carried glasses of pink champagne.

A young woman with strawberry blond hair and green eyes framed by thick lashes walked toward them. She wore an antique lace dress and carried an embroidered evening bag. Her mouth was painted pale pink and she had an ivory brooch pinned to her dress.

"James, I've been looking for you everywhere." She smiled, showing pearly white teeth.

"Emily." James's mouth dropped open. "I thought you couldn't make it."

"The furniture shipment arrived early so I hopped on the first plane west. I came straight from the airport." Emily had a whispery voice like Melanie in *Gone with the Wind*. "Who is your friend?"

James looked from Emily to Cassie, a faint blush spreading across his cheeks. "This is Cassie Blake, my boss."

"My mother is our boss." Cassie extended her hand. She noticed Emily had long French nails and wore an emerald and diamond ring on her left hand.

Emily followed her gaze. "It's lovely isn't it? It was my grandmother's ring. James had it reset and gave it to me during a carriage ride through Central Park. He's so romantic. He planned a whole engagement weekend in New York." She patted her hair and glanced around the room. "So this is your emporium."

"Let's get a glass of champagne and I'll show you around." James looked like a little boy whose mother showed up unexpectedly at Open House. He jammed his hands in his pockets and led Emily through the crowd. Cassie stood by herself, suddenly feeling thirsty.

"Darling, there you are." Cassie's mother approached, waving her ivory cane. She wore a white silk pantsuit cinched with a red belt. She had a Gucci scarf draped around her neck and a large ruby ring on her finger. Her lips were painted bright red and her hair was honey blond.

"There are so many people I want you to meet. Ulrica is here from *People* and there's Nikki DeBartolo. I remember when she was a little girl sitting on her father's knee at the 49ers games. Did you see Gina Pell? She writes that wonderful newsletter *Splendora*. And Gavin Newsom is at the bar with his gorgeous wife, Jennifer. So sweet of him to mingle among all these women."

Diana kissed Cassie on both cheeks, enveloping her in a cloud of Chanel No. 5. She pulled Cassie around like a prized pony, telling everyone she was the soul and brains behind the emporium.

"Cassie married a Berkeley professor. It took me a decade to convince her to join me at Fenton's!" She addressed a group of sleek women nibbling foie gras. "I must introduce you to our architect. He's a brilliant young man from Chicago." Diana tapped her cane on the marble. "Where did James run off to?"

"His fiancée arrived from Chicago." Cassie looked around and spotted them across the room, sipping champagne. They stood very close and Emily whispered in his ear, her hand clutching James's sleeve.

"We'll catch up with him later." Diana shrugged. "Ladies, excuse us, I see Willie Brown and Wilkes Bashford and I must say hello. They were practically father figures to Cassie."

Cassie grabbed a glass of champagne from a passing waiter and followed her mother. She scanned the room for James and Emily, but they had disappeared. She realized she was starving, but her mother kept her glued to her like a sidecar. She finally excused herself, pleading she had to use the ladies' room, and attacked a tray of liver pâté and water crackers.

James appeared by her side, holding two glasses of champagne. "Your mother is going to wear you out before you cut the cake." He handed her a glass.

"Where's Emily?" Cassie looked at James carefully. His

eyes were bright and there were lipstick smudges on his cheek.

"On her way back to the airport." James downed his champagne in one gulp. "I'm famished. I'll load up our plates, then let's find a place to sit."

James filled two plates with liver pâté, water crackers, cherry tomatoes, and salmon balls. He guided Cassie through the throng and sat down on the edge of the bookshelf.

"Why did Emily leave?" Cassie asked, skewering a salmon ball with a toothpick.

"I noticed on my credit card statement she flew to Atlanta last weekend." James's eyes narrowed. "I asked how her parents are, but she said they're in Europe."

"Oh," Cassie whispered.

"She finally admitted she went there for a job interview." James rolled tomatoes around his plate. "She got a position in an interior design firm. She starts in August."

"In Atlanta!" Cassie was suddenly confused. "Will you work there too?"

"Apparently I'm not invited." James twisted his paper napkin into a tight ball. "She's going to stay with Percy."

"I'm sorry," Cassie said quietly.

"Her mother will be happy she's marrying a southern boy." James blinked. "At least I found out now and not in ten years."

"You're lucky." Cassie blushed. Suddenly she felt wobbly. Her head ached and her feet hurt. She wished she were tucked up in a chair in Alexis's home theater, watching *Sleepless in Seattle*.

"Oh, God. I didn't mean to say that!" James started. "You're a princess, Cassie. Your husband is lucky to have you."

"He forgot to read the memo," Cassie mumbled.

"He's a professor, he's not stupid." James tried to smile. "I have to stop feeling sorry for myself, we've worked too hard for this. And it's a huge success." He glanced at the jeweled crowd wafting around the room.

"I haven't seen this many women since high school graduation," Cassie agreed, nibbling a cherry tomato.

"We ran through twelve cases of champagne and ten cases of red wine. We're out of oysters and all the chocolate sculptures have been eaten." James grinned. He ate two crackers with goat cheese and washed them down with a glass of champagne.

"You deserve the praise." Cassie was still starving. She popped three cherry tomatoes in her mouth and devoured crackers smothered with pâté. "I feel like Alice in Wonderland. Everything is bigger and more colorful than I imagined. I expect to run into the White Rabbit any minute."

"I'm sad it's over." James played with the tomatoes on his plate. "I'm going to miss San Francisco."

"Are you sorry you came?" Cassie looked up at James.

"You mean about Emily?" James shrugged. "In a way I've been grieving since Thanksgiving. I feel like I was hit by a truck, but I'll recover. I have some interesting jobs lined up this summer, they'll help get my mind off her."

"Are you going to leave right away?" Cassie hadn't thought about anything besides the grand opening. All the work of the past few months led up to this moment.

"I'll stick around until the marble pedestals arrive. It always takes about a month for a new space to settle."

"I don't know if I can handle my mother without you." Cassie sighed suddenly feeling like a little girl on her first day of kindergarten.

"You could spend a summer in Chicago. The humidity is terrible but the food is good." James smiled.

"Aidan will be home in two weeks. I'll be busy being a wife and working woman, if he agrees to me staying at Fenton's." Cassie blushed and put her champagne glass on the floor.

"I told you your husband was lucky," James replied. He slid toward Cassie and she jumped up, knocking over the glass. Glass splintered on the floor and champagne seeped onto her shoes.

"Oh, God. I'm sorry," Cassie said. "I think Vanessa is about to cut the ribbon." She slipped on her shoes and stumbled into the crowd. She saw James snake through the throng toward her, but she ducked behind the dessert counter and slumped onto the floor.

Aidan was five thousand miles away, presenting one of the most important papers of his career without her. Hundreds of people were gathered to celebrate her creation, but she felt like a child crashing her mother's party. She wished she were in her garden, pulling leeks for a chilled gazpacho.

"Cassie," Alexis hissed. "I've been looking for you everywhere." Alexis stood above her like a pink flamingo. She had changed into a long pink evening gown and gold Manolo sandals.

"I think I had too much champagne." Cassie stood up. Her legs felt shaky and her head throbbed.

"Your mother is about to give her speech. Hurry, before she sends out a search party." Alexis slipped between waiters passing out fresh glasses of champagne. "Just stand next to her and smile. I'll get you a shot of bourbon and cranberry juice, it'll cure your head instantly."

"Or it will kill me," Cassie moaned. She smoothed her hair and adjusted the hem on her dress. Her mother stood in front of the cake, tapping her nails on the microphone.

"I look around and see the faces of my oldest and dearest friends." Diana's voice was low and gravelly like Lauren Bacall in an old Humphrey Bogart movie. "And I see young women I've known since they wore pinafore dresses and Mary Janes. It is a very special evening for me because my darling daughter put this together." Diana paused while everyone clapped. "It's also special because it's a new direction for Fenton's. I am thrilled to have the country's top chefs here tonight: Michael Mina, Alice Waters, Thomas Keller." Diana waited while the clapping grew louder. "As well as some of the rising stars of the culinary world." She pointed to Andre Blick and Roland Ames. "I hope you will follow their lead and shop at Fenton's for the ingredients you need to create your own culinary masterpieces." She paused until the clapping subsided. "I would like Cassie to cut the cake and then Mr. Tony Bennett is going to sing a song close to our hearts."

Cassie picked up the sterling silver carving knife and launched it into the cake. Hundreds of red balloons fell from the ceiling and Tony Bennett crooned the opening verse of "I Left My Heart in San Francisco."

James tapped her on the shoulder. "I've always wanted to dance to this song."

"I have a terrible headache." Cassie grimaced, turning away from the music.

"Please, I'd like to dance with you." James took her hand and led her onto the small dance floor. He put his hand on her back and lightly held her other hand. His body was thin compared to Aidan's and he smelled like peppermint. "You're as rigid as a toy soldier. Try to relax."

"I can't," Cassie mumbled, pushing back tears. "It's all so . . ."

"New?" He pulled her closer. "You're going to do great. New isn't bad, sometimes it's a good thing."

Cassie closed her eyes and took a deep breath. She relaxed her shoulders and felt the nervous tension dissipate. She could feel James's fingers pressing into her back, his stiff white shirt rubbing against her cheek.

"Cassie, I need you," Alexis hissed. She stood on the corner of the dance floor holding a shot glass and frantically waving her iPhone. "Carter just called," she whispered when Cassie excused herself. "He got a last-minute seat on Sergey Brin's jet. He'll be here in six hours."

"That's wonderful." Cassie felt dizzy. She took the shot glass and downed it in one gulp.

"I haven't had a bikini wax in months, my roots are showing, and I need a pedicure. What am I going to do?"

"Carter's your husband. You don't have to look like a *Maxim* cover."

"I texted my aesthetician." Alexis ignored her. "She's opening her salon for me. Damien said he'd do my color at his apartment, and Bebe will do my nails at the same time. That just leaves a facial. Where can I get a facial at ten o'clock?" Alexis tapped wildly on her iPhone.

"Alexis, just meet him at the airport. All he wants is to see you." Cassie's head was spinning.

"Oh, God, oysters! I can't meet Carter without oysters. I wonder if Swan's is open at this hour." Alexis slid her phone into her purse. "I'll see you at home, don't wait up."

Cassie turned to the dance floor but the whole room seemed upside down. She saw James walking toward her and heard her mother's voice cooing her name. She backed away from the dance floor, colliding with a waiter carrying thick slices of cake. The plates spun onto the floor, splattering frosting on the black-and-white marble. Cassie bent down to scrape up the frosting, but her stomach leaped into her throat. She straightened up and ran up the staircase and into the street.

Cassie let herself into Alexis's house and turned on the light. She desperately wanted a cup of tea or a fizzy bottle of seltzer but the kitchen seemed too far away. She dragged herself up the staircase, still hearing the band playing in her head, and walked into her bedroom.

Pia had turned the bed down and the lights were on a dimmer, bathing the room in a soft yellow light. Cassie put her purse on the bedside table and draped her Diane von Furstenberg dress over the armoire. She put on a terry robe and sat cross-legged on the bed, waiting for the room to stop spinning.

She wanted to regain the excitement she felt when she saw the emporium decked out for the opening. But she could hear her mother's voice, shrill and demanding. She saw James following her as if they were in a James Bond movie. Even the women in their Pucci cocktail dresses seemed like they were from a foreign country. She grabbed her purse from the bedside table and took out her phone. There were nineteen missed texts from Aidan. She lay down on the comforter and closed her eyes, cradling the phone like a baby.

14.

Cassie's phone rang while she was eating waffles and blueberries with fresh whipped cream. She had started the morning by swimming fifty laps and drinking a tall glass of cranberry juice. Then she wrapped herself in a towel and scrolled through the dozens of e-mails congratulating her on the success of the grand opening. Gradually the strangeness of the evening faded and she grew excited at the thought of women doing their food shopping at Fenton's. She wanted to see them load their baskets with fruits and vegetables, slabs of cheese and loaves of bread, stuffed chickens and jumbo prawns.

"Now I see why you didn't come to Italy," Aidan barked before she could say hello. "So you could dance with that schoolboy dressed like a monkey."

"What are you talking about?" Cassie put her fork down.

"I logged on to Fenton's Facebook page. I saw the photos from the opening. A dozen pictures of you and that faggot in red suspenders dancing cheek-to-cheek."

"Since when do you use Facebook?" Cassie spluttered, a piece of waffle stuck in her throat.

"I'm not a Neanderthal, though I'm not a child like your skinny architect. What's going on, Cassie?"

"Nothing is going on." Cassie paced around the kitchen. "Tony Bennett sang and we had one dance, half a dance actually because Alexis needed me. Then I left. After I collided with a waiter and got cake and frosting everywhere. I was a stunning success."

"There's an idiotic picture of the two of you in someone's kitchen; half a dozen photos of you eating together. I'm not putting up with this, Cassie. If this is your way of retaliating for my indiscretion, it's immature."

"James is a friend." Cassie's throat closed up. Her eyes filled with tears. "I would never do that; I don't want to do that. I can't wait for you to come home."

"I would like to believe you," Aidan said tightly.

"Of course you can believe me," Cassie replied frantically. She looked out the window as if Aidan would walk up the path any moment.

"I leave for Athens tomorrow. I'll call you when I get there. I love you, Cassie." He hung up the phone.

Cassie opened the computer on the kitchen table. She clicked on Fenton's Facebook page and searched the photos of the opening. There were a dozen photos of her dancing with James, his hand curved around her back. There were pictures of them sipping champagne. She clicked through the album and found the photo Alexis took on her iPhone in Miles's kitchen.

Cassie shut the laptop and groaned. "Alexis, what have you done?"

* * *

After Cassie had hung up with Aidan she tried to finish her waffles but they tasted like cardboard. She considered going into Fenton's but black spots danced before her eyes. She poured herself another glass of cranberry juice and took it into the entertainment room. She flipped through Alexis's movie catalog, selected *Dear John,* and collapsed into a bucket seat. Cassie was watching *The Notebook* when Alexis finally arrived home.

"What is this, a Nicholas Sparks marathon?" Alexis flicked on the light and saw the DVD covers on the projector. Her hair was a beautiful ash blond and her nails were ruby red. Her skin glowed and her cheeks were soft and smooth as a baby.

"Where have you been? Your phone's off and you're wearing last night's clothes," Cassie demanded.

Alexis hiked up her pink evening gown and sunk down next to Cassie. "Carter's welcome home turned into a fly-by. He met Rupert Murdoch's son on the plane. He convinced Carter to fly to Australia to check out a new venture: a fuel source involving sheep manure." Alexis slipped off her gold sandals. "We spent the night at the airport Hilton."

"You have that glassy-eyed 'I've been screwing all night' look." Cassie frowned.

"We didn't leave the bed for twelve hours." Alexis stretched her legs in front of her. "I don't know if absence makes the heart grow fonder but it certainly makes the penis harder."

"I don't want to hear." Cassie put her hands over her ears.

"Honestly, it was a fuck marathon. I'm so dehydrated I could swim in a pool of Gatorade. I realized why I put up with Carter's absences and his mid-twentieth century husbanding." Alexis yawned. "He is David Beckham in the bedroom."

"How do you know what David Beckham is like in bed?"

"With those pecs and the way he can kick a ball, how could he not be good?" Alexis shrugged. "I haven't closed my eyes in twenty-four hours. We made love until the car took him to the gate."

"How long will Carter be gone this time?" Cassie rubbed her eyes. She had watched three movies, only getting up to make popcorn and find a box of tissues. Her back hurt and her eyes watered from staring at the screen.

"I don't know. They drive to the outback and stay on some farmstead. Carter says the men eat emu meat and drink Foster's all night. But you know what is great?" Alexis inspected her frosted pink toenails. "For the first time I don't mind Carter being away. I'll miss him terribly, but I'm excited to go to work. Thanks to you, I have a life."

"You have a life, but mine is over," Cassie groaned. "Aidan saw the photos of the opening on Facebook and he's livid."

"Since when does Aidan look at Facebook?"

"That's not really the point. Did you post photos of me dancing and drinking champagne with James?" Cassie demanded.

"I'm sorry, I uploaded them from my phone while I was getting my highlights done." Alexis fished her phone out of her purse and scrolled through her photos.

"Did you look at them before you posted them? They're practically the 'James and Cassie' show, except there is no 'James and Cassie.' Aidan was furious."

"James is engaged, it's all perfectly harmless." Alexis flicked through photos. "I love the one of the two of you holding Miles's cake. You should wear red more often, it suits you."

"Emily showed up at the opening," Cassie said slowly. "She's moving to Atlanta without James. They broke up."

"Maybe not so harmless." Alexis raised her eyebrows. "He does have that 'love-struck teenager' look when he's with you, and you make a lovely couple on the dance floor."

"This isn't funny," Cassie fumed. "I've been sitting here all day, trying to figure out how to calm Aidan down."

"You had one slow dance. Aidan's the one who went full throttle."

"I'm not going to talk about Molly Payne anymore," Cassie said quietly. "You were right, I'm either in the marriage or out of the marriage. I want to be in the marriage." Cassie scooped up popcorn kernels and put them in the glass bowl. "If Aidan and I are going to move forward, we have to trust each other. Which means I have to forget Molly Payne existed."

"Can you do that?" Alexis raised her eyebrow.

"It's like being a little bit pregnant," Cassie replied. "My marriage has no chance if I almost trust him. I just hope Aidan believes me. He thought James is the reason I skipped the conference."

"James is a sweetheart. I loved the red suspenders. I'm going to get a pair for Carter."

"Aidan is going to be home in ten days. I want to move back in with him."

"What about Fenton's?" Alexis asked, grabbing a handful of popcorn.

"I have to show Aidan I can do both." Cassie sighed, picking up a wad of tissues and tossing them in the garbage.

"How often do you and Aidan have sex?" Alexis brushed popcorn kernels from her lap.

Cassie blushed. "None of your business."

"Fuck Aidan every night and make sure he always has clean underwear in his sock drawer. He won't mind if you become a CIA agent."

"You sound as sexist as Carter." Cassie giggled.

"I like to think of men as jungle animals. Sex is the tranquilizing gun." Alexis scooped up another handful of popcorn. "I have an idea! Pick Aidan up from the airport and spend a night at the Ritz or the Four Seasons. A bottle of champagne, a dozen oysters, and he'll be putty. It worked for us. Do you want to see the photos Carter took?"

"That is a good idea." Cassie jumped out of the chair. "No Isabel ruining our first night together."

"No laundry, no dishes, just bubble bath and massage oil. We can go to that sex shop in the Haight this week," Alexis replied.

"I don't need a sex shop." Cassie shook her head.

"We're not in our twenties. Why do you think they invented sex shops?" Alexis stood up and stretched her arms. "I'm sore, I need to get in the Jacuzzi. But first, let's see if there's a pint of Häagen-Dazs in the freezer."

"Carter bought me a present." Alexis scooped caramel crème brûlée ice cream into two bowls.

"If it's a lace teddy I don't want to see it," Cassie groaned.

"It's not underwear, but I almost came when he gave it to me." Alexis walked into the mudroom and returned with an oval hatbox.

"He bought you a hat?"

"Open it."

Cassie took off the lid and peeled off layers of tissue paper. "Oh, my God," she whispered. She stepped back from the table and stared at Alexis.

"Thirty-five centimeters, saltwater crocodile skin, platinum hardware. Look at the stamp on the zipper." Alexis's eyes sparkled.

"Your own Birkin." Cassie breathed. "I can't believe it."

"I started crying like a baby, I ruined Damien's makeup. Carter had to pour me a Scotch and hold me until I stopped shaking." Alexis took the Birkin out of the box.

"I've only seen them in *Us* magazine. I read Victoria Beckham has a hundred Birkins," Cassie murmured.

"She has great taste in bags and men." Alexis handed the bag to Cassie. "Touch it."

Cassie handled the Birkin as if it were an ancient artifact. She snapped open the platinum clasp and ran her fingers over the goatskin lining. She turned it over and admired the mottled crocodile skin.

"And this is the clochette," Alexis explained, "where one keeps the key. Carter bought it in Paris; he ordered it four years ago. Do you know what that means?"

"A Birkin is harder to get than a seat on the space shuttle?" Cassie held it against her thigh.

"I was the one always chasing Carter. I visited him at Stanford every free weekend. I rented an apartment in Cow Hollow on his block. I thought if I backed off, he'd hook up with some Asian dynamo: one of those sexual gymnasts with a mind like Mark Zuckerberg. But he loved me enough *four* years ago to order a Birkin. He knew he wanted to spend the rest of his life with me." Alexis wiped her eyes.

"You have a body like one of Charlie's Angels. Cameron Diaz wishes she had your thighs," Cassie protested. "And you have an amazing mind! You've brought Fenton's into the twenty-first century."

"Even now I think he travels so much because I'm not

enough," Alexis admitted. "Sometimes I want a husband I can curl up in bed with and talk about boring things: who's winning *American Idol,* who got voted off *The Bachelor.*"

"I can't see Carter watching *The Bachelor.*" Cassie giggled.

"Exactly!" Alexis put the bag in the middle of the table. "I realize I have to accept Carter for who he is: a globe-trotting maverick who is trying to save the planet and make a billion dollars at the same time."

"Carter loves you more than the planet." Cassie nodded.

"I'm beginning to believe it." Alexis stroked the bag lovingly. "I'm going to take it upstairs and look at it all day."

"You're going to fill it with your stuff and parade it around Fenton's." Cassie ate a spoonful of ice cream.

"You think I should use it? I thought I might display it on the mantel, like an Oscar."

"Of course you're going to use it. Every customer at Fenton's will want one. We'll open a mini Hermès boutique, it'll be a gold mine."

"I guess you're right." Alexis fiddled with the platinum lock. "But I'm going to order another one, and keep it in the downstairs bathroom like Catherine Zeta-Jones does with her Oscar."

15.

When Cassie arrived at Fenton's the next morning, James was hunched over a stack of papers.

"I'm sorry I didn't come in yesterday." Cassie hopped onto a stool. "I drank too much champagne at the opening."

"I think everyone did." James grinned. "Security found a few iPhones and several orphaned stilettos."

"I caused quite a path of destruction." Cassie grimaced, smoothing her skirt. She had dressed carefully for her first day on the floor. She wore a pink cotton dress with a wide leather belt. She had a diamond clip in her hair and leather sandals on her feet. "I'm going upstairs to apologize to my mother."

"I'd hold off." James flipped through his notes. "We have bigger problems."

"What's wrong?" Cassie asked.

"Look around, what do you see?"

Cassie spun around on the stool. Women milled in the aisles sampling brightly colored vegetables. Employees passed out bite-sized cheesecakes and cups of steaming espresso.

The tables next to the bookshelf were almost full; Cassie heard women exclaiming over jars of marmalade and pots of organic honey.

"It looks like we're really busy. Do we need more help? Is everyone getting their lunch breaks?" Cassie frowned.

"It *looks* like we're busy." James took off his glasses. "Customers are sampling, but they're not *buying*. Do you know how much revenue we made yesterday?"

"How much?" Cassie flinched.

"Two hundred and twenty-seven dollars!" James rubbed his eyes. "We were open for eight hours and rung up two hundred and twenty-seven dollars and ninety-three cents. Do you know what our overhead is?"

"It was the first day, people don't know about us yet." Cassie shrugged nervously.

"That's what I thought, so I've been sitting here all morning. The floor has been full since the minute we opened. People know about the emporium, but they're walking around like it's a garden party."

"Do you think I picked the wrong suppliers?" Cassie asked, fiddling with her hair clip.

"I sampled everything." James shook his head. "It all tastes delicious."

Cassie rested her elbows on the table. In the weeks before the opening, she never doubted the emporium would be a success. Fenton's had been the sought-after shopping destination in San Francisco for decades.

"I thought about rearranging the counters, putting the desserts in the front of the store, but women are entering in droves." James continued glumly. "They're just leaving empty-handed."

Cassie and James sat silently side by side. James wore a

blue button-down shirt and tan slacks. His hair was slicked to one side and he smelt like peppermint soap. He scribbled notes on a yellow pad and rapped his pen on the table.

"I'm going to perform an intervention." Cassie hopped off the stool and strode across the marble floor. She approached a woman wearing an orange Givenchy dress. She carried a straw clutch and wore orange sling-back sandals.

"Have you tried the endive salad?" Cassie asked, grabbing a white porcelain plate from the counter. "It's made with a raspberry vinaigrette."

"This is delicious." The woman blotted her lips with a napkin. "I'm holding a little dinner Friday night. I'd love to serve an endive raspberry salad, maybe paired with a fruity Chardonnay."

"Our endive melts in your mouth, and we have fresh baskets of raspberries." Cassie led her to the produce aisle. "You'll love our heirloom tomatoes." Cassie laid leeks, tomatoes, and red peppers on the counter.

"It looks wonderful." The woman eyed the array of vegetables. "I need to nip up to the third floor. I have a silk scarf on hold, and I promised I'd pick it up by noon."

"Shall I ring this up?" Cassie asked.

"Why don't you wait, I might grab a few things for dessert."

"I'll select some of my favorites." Cassie beamed. "It'll be waiting at the register."

Cassie walked triumphantly over to James. "I just convinced a customer to purchase ingredients for a whole dinner party. She had to run upstairs but she's coming back to ring everything up."

"Congratulations." James rubbed his temples. "I'm sick of

staring at numbers. I'm going to grab a burger and fries. Care to join me?"

"You're addicted to McDonald's." Cassie grinned. "Bring me back a chocolate shake."

Cassie picked out a cherry pie and a pint of cinnamon-flavored ice cream. She selected a Hess Estate Chardonnay and added a lemon pound cake. James returned clutching a McDonald's bag and a chocolate shake.

"How much did she spend?" James asked, swallowing a handful of French fries.

"She hasn't come back." Cassie sighed, sipping the shake unhappily. "Should I go upstairs and find her?"

"You can't stalk the customers." James slumped on the stool. "This is what I mean. They love our merchandise, they're just not buying anything."

Cassie waited all afternoon for the customer to return. The cinnamon ice cream sat at the register, slowly melting. At closing time, Cassie reluctantly put the wine and pound cake back on the shelf. She said good night to James and drove home, trying to squelch the sick feeling in her stomach.

She walked into Alexis's kitchen and picked at the Caesar salad Pia had prepared. She wished she could discuss the emporium with Alexis but she was holed up with Princess Giselle. The Black and White Ball was in two weeks and Alexis had been overseeing late-night dress fittings.

Cassie poured herself a glass of lemonade and buttered a sourdough dinner roll. She remembered her mother's stories of Fenton's fairy-tale success; it had become a San Francisco institution the moment it opened its doors. She thought about the women from Alexis's book clubs who rushed in to buy the latest lipsticks and designer bags. She pushed her plate away and put her head in her hands. She had to figure out what was wrong and find a way to fix it.

On Thursday evening, Andre Blick held a cooking demonstration and women flocked to watch him prepare fondue. Even Alexis pulled herself away from Princess Giselle to see Andre blend chocolate and cream.

"I'll buy two of whatever he's selling." Alexis stood at the back of the crowd next to Cassie. "He's James Franco with a touch of Andrew Garfield. You should bottle him."

"Fingers crossed that's how the other women feel." Cassie scanned the crowd. A dozen hands shot up when Andre asked for a volunteer to test the fondue. He passed out samples and the women oohed and aahed like teenagers at a rock concert.

When the crowd cleared, James added up the sales and showed them to Cassie. Several women had bought Andre's cookbook but only one purchased ingredients to make fondue. Cassie stared at the numbers, trying to keep the pit in her stomach from becoming a crater.

"I don't understand," she moaned to Alexis, putting pitchers of clotted cream in the fridge. "They loved him. It was like a movie premiere."

"Maybe they thought they'd get fat." Alexis scraped cheese from her plate. "Next time have him demonstrate how to make egg white omelets."

"If this keeps up there won't be a next time. "Our numbers are terrible."

"I have to get back to Giselle. She wants me to accessorize her gown. I found a silver Chanel evening bag and a pair of Jimmy Choos that are going to make her come." Alexis patted Cassie's hand. "Tomorrow will be better."

*   *   *

Cassie sat at her desk staring at the week's figures. She looked across at James, wanting him to say something that would stop the panic rising in her chest.

"Your mother is going to want to see the numbers soon." James flipped through the spreadsheets. "I feel like we're waiting for the guillotine."

"It's my head, not yours." Cassie sighed. It was almost five o'clock and the employees were packing away platters of cheese and vegetables. "Your design is perfect, the blogs raved about it. *SF Gate* said: 'James Parrish created a space that inspires the mind and warms the soul.'"

"It hasn't inspired anyone to shop." James put down his pen. "Why don't we go see Diana now? I don't want to spend the weekend worrying whether we'll be open on Monday."

Cassie's mother sat at her desk, sipping black coffee and eating a sliver of cheesecake.

"Darling, it's lovely to see you, and James, our rising star." She got up and kissed Cassie on the cheek. "I'm still receiving e-mails gushing over the opening. You've made quite a splash in our little town. Emerald and now the emporium, everyone wants a James Parrish design."

"I'll miss San Francisco." James gazed out the window at the Bay Bridge. He shifted from foot to foot, gripping his yellow notepad with both hands.

"I hope you're not in a hurry to leave us." Diana sat down in her Louis XIV chair. "Cassie and I will be lost without you. Can I offer you both some coffee? I'm the only person I know who drinks coffee at this hour. In Europe, everyone drinks espresso in the afternoon. It's so civilized." Diana motioned for them to sit on the cream-colored sofa.

Cassie sat awkwardly next to James. She felt any minute she'd be exposed as a failure, and Diana's good mood would evaporate.

"I want to hear all about the emporium." Diana poured two demitasses of coffee and handed them to Cassie and James. "I've been so busy, I haven't had a chance to poke around. I did pick up a scrumptious amaretto cheesecake."

"Andre Blick held a cooking demonstration yesterday." Cassie sipped her coffee. "We had a wonderful turnout."

"I bumped into him at the elevator." Diana dropped a sugar cube in her cup. "He resembles a young Cary Grant. I also met Alexis's Princess Giselle. That woman knows how to use a black card. So tell me"—Diana looked expectantly at Cassie—"how are the sales figures? I've heard a whisper Neiman's is going to open their own food hall. But we did it first, I'm very proud of you."

"It's hard to make projections based on the first week of sales," James interjected. "Buying food at Fenton's is a new experience for our customers. The floor has been full every day. Our produce selection is getting rave reviews."

"Excellent." Diana stood up and walked to the window. She wore Lilly Pulitzer navy slacks with a yellow eyelet sweater. She had a crisp white scarf tied at her neck and white pumps on her feet. She turned and beamed at Cassie.

"I can't tell you how happy I am to see you in charge. And Alexis is turning out very well. That child could sell oil to Sid Bass." Diana plucked a thread from her sweater. "Let me see some figures. I'm dying to show our accountant. He thinks women only buy food at supermarkets."

James placed his yellow pad on Diana's desk. He and Cassie sat like schoolchildren in the principal's office while Diana flipped through the pages.

"This is disastrous." Diana took off her reading glasses and looked at Cassie. "I thought you said the floor was packed."

"It is packed." Cassie twisted her hands nervously. "People just aren't buying. I haven't figured out why, but I will."

"You will!" Diana jumped up and paced around the room. "Do you know what we've spent on the emporium? The fridges alone cost more than you've made in a week. And your suppliers charge a fortune. Label something 'organic' and it's an invitation to triple the price." Diana sat down and tapped her nails on the cherry desk. "I still believe the market is ripe for this type of venture. You must be doing something wrong."

"Maybe I made the walls too red," James volunteered, glancing at Cassie, who was trying to stop her lip from trembling. "Maybe the environment isn't conducive to spending."

"Nonsense." Diana dismissed him. "You have a proven track record. Emerald has a month-long waiting list. It's all about good management. Your employees are your troops, Cassie. You have to train them to win the war."

"It's early." Cassie's voice wobbled. "I thought if I can hold more events, or maybe some two-for-one giveaways."

"It's not a cash and carry," Diana bristled. "We do not give things away at Fenton's. I'm late for the opening of a Russian restaurant. I appreciate you trying to help, James"— Diana stood up and slipped on a white linen jacket—"but this is Cassie's baby."

"I'm going to turn it around." Cassie nodded, blinking so her mother didn't see the tears welling up in her eyes.

"Fenton's can't carry the emporium for long, it will eat up the profits." Diana reapplied red lipstick. "We'll meet again next Friday and I expect to see a very different picture."

* * *

Cassie sat on the sofa, taking deep breaths. She waited until Diana closed the door and then she stood up and placed the coffee cup on the sideboard. Her hands were shaking and she felt like there was a steel band across her forehead.

"Cassie." James put his hand on her shoulder.

"I have to go home." Cassie didn't turn around. She grabbed her purse and ran out the door, down five flights of stairs to the parking garage.

"Cassie," James called as she was about to get into her car.

"My mother's right, James. This isn't your problem."

"We've both worked really hard." James had raced down the stairs and run through the garage to catch up with her. "It just takes a bit of time."

"Maybe I should go back to volunteering with Alice Waters."

"You don't look like a quitter."

"I'm not a quitter, I'm a failure." Cassie turned away so James wouldn't see the tears in her eyes. "I've failed at my marriage, I've failed at Fenton's."

"From where I stand you're the one keeping your marriage together." James put his hand on her shoulder. "And you're going to be brilliant at Fenton's. Your mother is unrealistic; she wants things to happen yesterday."

"Alexis was an immediate success." Cassie moved away. "She's doubled sales."

"Alexis took over something with a sterling reputation. You're starting fresh."

Cassie opened the car door and slumped in the seat. She laid her head on the steering wheel and let tears fall onto her lap.

"Cassie." James got into the passenger seat.

"I'm such a baby. I cry all the time. I didn't used to." She sat forward and wiped her eyes.

"Since Emily and I broke up, I cry whenever I hear Muse on the radio."

"My marriage isn't breaking up," Cassie replied defensively.

"But a grenade landed in the middle of it, that makes you vulnerable."

"The food emporium is so important to me." Cassie put the keys in the ignition. "Aidan didn't want me to do it at all. What will he think if it's a failure?"

"I read somewhere that Simon Cowell couldn't get a gig on television, that's why he produced his own show."

"I'm not Simon Cowell." Cassie tried to smile.

"You're much prettier." James squeezed her hand. "And you don't have his annoying British accent."

"Or his mind for business." Cassie shifted in her seat. "Everything about the emporium is fantastic: the food, the design, the florals. Why isn't anyone spending money?"

"Let's go to Clown Alley, eat greasy fries, and throw around ideas," James suggested.

Cassie turned and glanced at James. He looked so earnest behind his glasses. His legs were spread out in front of him and his yellow notepad was in his lap.

"I should go home." Cassie shook her head. "Aidan will be back in less than a week. I want to figure this out before he gets here."

James leaned forward and kissed her softly on the lips. He tasted like coffee and peppermint. He touched her chin and got out of the car. Cassie watched him walk across the garage. She turned the key in the ignition and drove onto the street, trying to ignore the lump forming in her throat.

Alexis's house was dark when Cassie pulled into the driveway. Alexis was at a gallery opening with Princess Giselle, taking one of her new couture outfits for a "test run." Alexis was obsessed with making Giselle the most blogged about fixture in San Francisco society. She dragged her to restaurant openings, charity functions, ribbon cuttings, anything that would end up on Twitter.

"We are so lucky to have a princess shopping exclusively at Fenton's." Alexis had remarked over whole-wheat pancakes and orange juice that morning. "I'm going to make her this summer's trendsetter. Every woman in the Junior League is going to want to dress like Giselle. She's Princess Kate with a German accent."

"I thought she was from Liechtenstein," Cassie had replied, pushing the pancake around her plate.

"Thank God she has legs like a greyhound." Alexis had finished her orange juice. "She could be one of those royals with thighs like tree trunks."

Cassie stepped out of the car, thinking breakfast was ages ago. She couldn't remember eating lunch and suddenly realized she was starving. She opened the front door and walked to the kitchen. It was Pia's night off and the counters were scrubbed clean. Pia left a note saying there was Swedish casserole in the fridge. Cassie crumpled up the note and threw it in the garbage.

She opened the fridge and stood in front of it. She could make a tuna melt with melted jack cheese and thick slices of yellow tomatoes. Or she could take her time and boil brown rice, chop green onions and mushrooms, and make a pilaf. She grabbed an apron and assembled ingredients. She would forget about the emporium, forget about Aidan coming home, block out James's kiss, and prepare a wonderful dinner. Then she would pour a glass of wine, and eat it by herself at Alexis's kitchen table.

16.

Cassie and Alexis sat in the conservatory drinking iced tea and reading the Sunday newspapers. Cassie wore a sheer cotton robe over her swimsuit. She had risen early and swum fifty laps. Then she sat in the steam room, visualizing women laden with Fenton's bags of sourdough bread, cheese, and juicy green grapes.

Alexis had jogged back from a morning yogalates class and was massaging her thighs with warm jasmine oil. She wore a purple leotard and yellow leggings. Her hair was piled into a high ponytail and tied with a purple ribbon.

"When Carter returns I'm going to borrow his Kindle. We're reading a dozen eucalyptus trees." Alexis surveyed the pile of newspapers on the glass table.

"Aidan thinks reading should be laborious. One should work to turn the pages." Cassie grabbed the Vows section of *The New York Times*. "Have you heard from Carter?"

"He sends texts but he uses words like 'billabong' and 'Woolloomooloo.' I keep having to stop and look them up in an Australian dictionary." Alexis flipped through the *Chronicle*'s pink section. "When is Aidan coming home?"

"Thursday." Cassie took a deep breath. "I reserved a night at the Mark Hopkins with a couples massage and dinner at Top of the Mark."

"Going all out." Alexis whistled. "He'll be in a sexual haze for days."

"I hope I can boost sales this week." Cassie pushed the newspapers away. "I've been brainstorming all weekend and I haven't come up with anything."

"There's nothing like good sex to clear the mind." Alexis got up and stretched her legs. "I'm going to take Poodles to Golden Gate Park. He's in love with a little papillon. Care to join us?"

Cassie shook her head. "I'm going to stay here and worry."

Cassie sat in the conservatory after Alexis left. She hadn't mentioned James's kiss to Alexis. There had been so many things to talk about: the emporium, Aidan, Princess Giselle.

Cassie twisted her wedding ring on her finger, admiring the tiny diamond flanked by two small sapphires. She remembered when Aidan handed her the Fenton's jewelry box and she opened it, startled by the ring's delicate beauty.

"I'm not a big fan of Fenton's but I want you to wear a ring that makes you happy." Aidan pulled her close. They were sitting in the living room, listening to the Beatles and drinking an Oak Knoll Cabernet.

"It's gorgeous." Cassie slipped it on her finger. She had been expecting a plain band or an antique ring from a shop on Telegraph Avenue.

"You're my angel." Aidan pushed back her hair and kissed

her on the mouth. He unbuttoned her shirt and placed his hand on her breast.

"Aidan, Isabel's upstairs," Cassie whispered. Isabel had been seven and often wandered downstairs to get a glass of water or complain she couldn't sleep.

"You're going to be Mrs. Blake soon." He pushed his other hand down her pants, rubbing her underpants with his fingers.

"Aidan, stop," she protested. She remembered hearing Isabel on the stairs, Aidan squeezing her hand like a co-conspirator. After Isabel went back to bed, Aidan led Cassie up to the bedroom and pulled her down on the king-sized bed.

He stripped off his shirt, peeled off his pants, and gently opened her legs. He hovered above her, stroking her with his fingers, covering her cheeks with kisses. When he finally entered her, his hands cradling her head, she thought she would never stop coming.

Cassie looked at her phone. It was almost noon and she had four missed texts. She scrolled through them, jumped up, and called Alexis.

"I just got a text from Aidan. He rescheduled his flight, and he's arriving this evening."

"I can't hear you. There's a rottweiler barking at Poodles," Alexis yelled into the phone.

"Aidan will be here tonight. I'm not ready," Cassie replied, walking into the marble bathroom.

"Of course you're ready. Take a bubble bath, douse your-self in Obsession, and slip on a La Perla teddy."

"We haven't had sex in four months," Cassie moaned. She studied herself in the mirror. Her hair was damp and her cheeks were flushed from the steam room.

"It's like riding a bike," Alexis replied. "I have to go. This rottweiler is trying to turn Poodles into lunch."

Cassie stood at the arrival gate at San Francisco Airport clutching a box of Twizzlers. She wanted to give Aidan a present, something silly that showed she had been thinking of him. Aidan used to go through a whole box of Twizzlers grading papers. She had to buy them in bulk from Costco.

Cassie wore a floral cotton dress with white espadrilles. The fog had come in as she left the city, but she wanted to wear something springlike and sexy. She wanted to sit across from Aidan, sip iced coffee, and pretend last winter never happened.

She saw him walking down the ramp toward her. His skin was tan and he had a day's stubble on his chin. He wore a white shirt and flared pants with a wide leather belt. He swung his leather jacket over his shoulder and carried a jar of green olives.

"I wasn't sure if you'd be here," Aidan said, burying his mouth in her hair.

"I got your text a few hours ago," Cassie replied. She pressed her body against his, feeling his heart beating in his chest.

"I was tired of Athens." He pulled away and took her hand. "Hot and noisy and no taxis. I brought you something." He handed her the jar of olives. "I wanted to bring you Greek yogurt but customs took it away."

"I brought you something too." She blushed and handed him the box of Twizzlers.

"Don't remind me of the papers I have to grade," Aidan groaned. "I missed junk food and American coffee. European coffee is too strong. I couldn't sleep and I had no one to talk to. I missed you, Cassie."

"I missed you too." Cassie held his hand tightly. "I'm glad you're home."

"I can't wait to put on a pair of thick socks and stand in our own kitchen. I walked for hours in Athens." Aidan stood at the baggage claim. "You look beautiful. I'd fuck you right here if there wasn't a couple of hundred people watching."

"Aidan." Cassie blushed. She kept her hand in his while they waited for the luggage. She leaned against him and smelled avocado shampoo and Old Spice aftershave.

"Let's stop on the way home and pick up a couple of steaks. All I ate on the plane was cardboard pizza and shriveled grapes." Aidan retrieved his bag. "Then we're going to bed and I'll have you for dessert."

"Aidan," Cassie hissed, "people can hear you."

"In Italy, couples tell each other they want to make love all the time." He stopped in front of the glass doors and touched her cheek. "Is it a crime to want to have sex with my wife?"

Cassie looked at his black eyes. She remembered his white teeth and the dimple on the side of his mouth. "It's perfect."

"Where did you park?" He bent down and kissed her on the lips. "I'm starving."

"I have a surprise," Cassie said as they drove through San Francisco. The fog swirled around them. Cassie turned on the headlights and rolled up the windows. "We're not going straight home."

"Cassie." Aidan's face turned hard and his lips formed a thin line. "You're coming home with me."

"Of course I am." Cassie felt her cheeks flush. "I thought we could have a special night, without Isabel or laundry or dishes."

"I've been traveling for two weeks." Aidan's voice was tight.

"It will be fun, I promise." Cassie pulled into the driveway of the Mark Hopkins. Uniformed doormen stood at the ornate double doors. Women in long skirts hopped into taxis. Men in suits strolled into the lobby, carrying briefcases and newspapers.

"What are we doing here?" Aidan didn't move.

"I wanted your homecoming to be special," Cassie said, turning off the engine. "I booked a room for the night, with a couples massage and dinner at Top of the Mark."

"The Mark Hopkins, Cassie? Did your mother pay for this?"

"I'm working." Cassie's voice trembled.

Aidan tapped his fingers on the dashboard. He finally looked at Cassie and smiled. "As long as I have you and a king-sized bed I don't care where we are. But I'm not putting on a jacket and tie."

"We could skip Top of the Mark and order room service," Cassie volunteered.

"Deal." Aidan nodded. "Lead the way."

Cassie glanced around the hotel lobby at the giant potted palms and the deep red velvet sofas. She remembered coming to the Mark Hopkins as a child and filling her pockets with peppermints. Every New Year's Eve her mother took her to Top of the Mark and she stood at the window, looking down at the twinkling lights of San Francisco. Sometimes even the fog lay beneath her, and she walked around the restaurant pretending she was in an airplane.

"Nothing changes," Cassie said as they waited at the front desk. "I think the bellman has been here my whole life. The wallpaper is exactly the same."

"Sometimes I forget I married a San Francisco heiress." Aidan rested his elbows on the polished marble counter.

"You'll love it." Cassie blushed. "The rooms have wonderful views, you feel like you're in an airplane."

"I was in an airplane for twenty hours. I want to be in bed."

"We'll be in bed," Cassie promised. "I'll rub your back and massage your feet."

"That sounds better." Aidan put his hand on the small of her back. He rang the bell and tapped his fingers on the counter.

"Miss Fenton, lovely to see you." The desk clerk approached them. "We have a gorgeous room on the eighteenth floor. Please sign here, and give your mother my best. She came in for tea last week, she's never looked better."

"I'll tell her." Cassie signed the slip and took the gold room key.

"Sean will show you to your room. Let me know if I can be of assistance."

"Christ, Cassie. He called you Miss Fenton. I think we should stick to our side of the bay," Aidan said when they were alone in the hotel room.

The bed was covered in a velvet bedspread and there were heavy gold curtains on the window. Cassie put her purse on the bedside table and looked down on the street. She watched cable cars glide down the hill like pieces in a toy train set.

"He's known me since I was in the fifth grade." Cassie had her back to Aidan. She suddenly felt this was a bad idea. They should be home eating soup and brussels sprouts from her garden.

"I'm being grumpy." Aidan pulled her against his chest. "I'm just hungry."

"I can order room service."

"Tell them to bring up a couple of steaks and baked potatoes." Aidan fingered the thin straps of her dress. "But have
them deliver it in an hour. I want to savor you first."

Cassie spent a long time in the bathroom brushing her hair
at the mirror. She unzipped her dress and slipped on the silk
robe hanging in the closet. When she walked into the bedroom, Aidan was already in bed, naked against the satin pillows.

"You are so beautiful," he murmured, tugging the robe
off her shoulder. He untied the belt and let the robe drop to
the floor. She stood at the foot of the bed and he pressed his
mouth against her nipples, rubbing her thighs with his free
hand.

Suddenly Cassie froze. She closed her eyes and saw Molly
Payne as clearly as if she was in the room. She let out a little
gasp and Aidan pressed himself harder against her, clutching
her buttocks with both hands.

Cassie squeezed her eyes tightly and Aidan's hands moved
over her body, touching all the familiar places. He put his
hand between her legs, stroking her with his fingers, and she
felt her knees buckle.

Aidan pulled her down on the bed and kissed her breasts.
He kept his fingers between her thighs, rubbing her with his
thumb until she thought she would explode. She gripped his
shoulders and he climbed on top of her, gently opened her
legs, and plunged himself inside her.

After he came, holding her fiercely and rocking back and
forth, Cassie lay facedown on the pillow. Aidan sleepily
draped his arm over her back and she felt a jolt like an electric current. She closed her eyes, wondering how anything

could feel so good and how she had managed four months without it.

They were awakened by the buzz of the doorbell. Cassie slipped on her robe and opened the door. A uniformed bell-boy rolled in a cart holding dinner plates covered with silver domes, a basket of bread rolls, and a bucket of cold champagne.

"I admit this was a good idea." Aidan sat on the bed, cutting a thick slab of filet mignon.

"Being in bed with you is a good idea." Cassie bit into a soft herb bread roll. She felt light and happy. It was dark outside and the only noise in the room was silverware scraping against porcelain plates. Aidan poured the champagne and she watched bubbles rise to the tops of the crystal flutes.

"Being anywhere with you is perfect." Aidan cut his baked potato, covering each half with a pat of butter.

"Tell me about the conference," Cassie said, taking a sip of her champagne.

"Florence is beautiful, I could spend days at the Palazzo Medici." Aidan ate a large bite of steak. "Verona was charming: laundry hanging out of windows, tiny cars that looked like they belonged in a toy box."

"You went to Verona?" Cassie asked.

"They arranged some day trips." Aidan shrugged. "I was too lonely to enjoy them. Next year we will travel together: Florence, Rome, Venice. They loved the paper, Cassie. I'm going to expand it into a book."

"That's wonderful!" She smiled, then drained her glass. The bubbles seemed to sink straight to her toes.

"I'll be very busy this summer. I'll need your help editing and making sure Isabel stays out of trouble."

"I'm not quitting Fenton's," Cassie replied, putting her champagne flute on the silver tray.

"The grand opening is over," Aidan said quietly. He finished his steak and placed the fork on the plate. "Turn it over to your mother or Alexis or that architect."

"The food emporium is mine, and it's just getting on its feet."

"Are you saying you're going to spend twelve hours a day at Fenton's?" Aidan demanded.

"I'll be home by five o'clock." Cassie tried to keep her voice even. She avoided Aidan's eyes and looked at her plate. "I'll edit at night."

"Cassie." Aidan moved the tray off the bed and took her hands. "Look at your mother. She didn't remarry; she never had time for you. I'm trying to tell you I love you."

"I love you." Cassie gulped. "I can do both. It won't interfere with our lives."

"What about Isabel?"

"Alexis needs an assistant, Isabel would be perfect. She can drive in with me." Cassie fiddled with her robe.

"It would be good for Isabel to have a real job." Aidan nodded thoughtfully. "This can be a pivotal summer in a girl's life. There are so many temptations, she needs something to focus on."

"Isabel has a real fashion sense, I think she'd enjoy it," Cassie agreed. "And Alexis is a drill sergeant, she'd work her hard."

Aidan took a sip of champagne and kissed Cassie on the mouth. He untied her robe and slipped his hand between her thighs.

"I knew I married well." He pulled her down on the bed. "Beautiful and smart. How did I get so lucky?"

* * *

Cassie heard her phone vibrate and stumbled into the bathroom to answer it.

"I have some exciting news," Alexis announced.

"What time is it?" Cassie asked. She glanced at herself in the bathroom mirror. Her hair was tousled and her cheeks were flushed. Her lips were slightly swollen as if she'd been stung by a bee.

"It's ten o'clock. I've been in the store for two hours. Where are you?"

"At the Mark Hopkins with Aidan. The curtains are so heavy I thought it was still nighttime."

"You have that thick, sex-coated voice. I'm guessing it was a successful reunion?"

"Better than riding a bike." Cassie giggled. "We had a wonderful dinner and drank a bottle of champagne. Aidan was so sweet, he really missed me."

"Of course he missed you, you're his angel. Princess Giselle rented the penthouse apartment at the St. Regis. Ten thousand feet of postmodern white furniture, your mother would love it."

"That's wonderful, but I should go. Aidan might wake up any minute."

"That's not the news," Alexis interrupted. "I convinced her to have a house-warming dinner party, something intimate but with the crème of San Francisco society. She's going to buy all the ingredients from Fenton's."

"That is exciting." Cassie closed the bathroom door quietly.

"Vanessa and Billy already said yes. She invited Gina Pell and Allison Speer and the sweet young publisher of 7X7."

"Alexis, that's fantastic. It'll be written up all over the city."

"There's one small thing." Alexis hesitated. "Princess

Giselle's schedule is practically full. The only free night she has for the next few months is tonight."

"She wants to have the dinner party tonight!" Cassie spluttered.

"We sent out evites last night. I'm sure everyone will say yes. Monday nights are deadly quiet. It's such an amazing apartment—360 degrees of the city—it's going to cement Giselle's reputation."

"Then what's the problem?"

"I raved about what a food guru you are," Alexis said guiltily. "Giselle wants you to pick out the ingredients."

"I can't leave Aidan alone in bed," Cassie replied. "He'd never forgive me."

"Grab a cab; you can be here in five minutes. Tell Aidan to catch up on CNN," Alexis pleaded.

"Aidan is fast asleep. He has terrible jet lag."

"Even better!" Alexis exclaimed. "When Carter has jet lag he sleeps for days. You could blast a foghorn in his ear and he'd never wake up. Aidan won't know you're gone."

Cassie opened the bathroom door and looked at Aidan sleeping. He lay on his stomach, his arms splayed across the pillows, his chest rising and falling rhythmically.

"Maybe I could come for an hour," Cassie hesitated.

"Giselle is all booked up after noon: hairdresser, massage, pedicure, and facial."

Cassie glanced at the clock on the bathroom wall. "I'll be there in fifteen minutes. But I can't be gone long. If Aidan wakes up I'm going to turn into a pumpkin."

The taxi pulled in front of Fenton's as Cassie tried to tame her hair into a ponytail. She had applied mascara and blush and rubbed Tiger lip balm on her mouth. She stepped off the escalator and found Alexis and Giselle sampling organic milk at the dairy counter.

"There you are." Alexis kissed her on the cheek. "Giselle loves the organic milk, she says it tastes just like the milk she drank growing up in Liechtenstein. Giselle is in your hands. Remember we want the dinner to be over the top: caviar, oysters, escargot."

Giselle followed Cassie like an obedient puppy. She accepted all of Cassie's suggestions and filled the cart with snails, braised duck, black olives, herb cream cheese, and rounds of fresh baked bread. Every so often she stopped in front of a mirror to check her lipstick and finger the Bulgari diamond necklace around her neck.

Cassie forgot about Aidan asleep at the hotel and began to enjoy herself. She pictured Vanessa Getty and Jennifer Newsom exchanging chitchat over duck pâté and stone-ground wheat crackers. She imagined crystal salad bowls bursting with butter lettuce, cherry tomatoes, cucumbers, and shiitake mushrooms. She saw platters of crudités and pots of mustard and artichoke hummus. She pictured Gina Pell sipping a private label Cabernet and saying she must run home and blog about Fenton's on *Splendora*.

"Oooh." Alexis joined them at the cash register. "It looks like you've been busy. Let me snap a couple of photos of Giselle at the checkout." She took her iPhone out of her purse. "Show those lovely white teeth. Don't you love Giselle's dress?" She turned to Cassie. "It's from Zac Posen's runway collection. Giselle wore it to the Fiske gallery opening and they've flown out of the store. I just had to reorder."

Cassie watched the cashier ring up jars of caviar and bottles of port. Giselle handed him her black card and walked to the full-length mirror, making a full turn and admiring her red spandex minidress and five-inch Bottega Veneta wedges.

"Isn't Giselle the best?" Alexis whispered. "She uses that AmEx like a library card. Darling"—she turned to Giselle—"I'll have Kitty deliver these goodies to the apartment. I picked out a few hostess gowns for the dinner party. I want you to choose your favorite."

Cassie watched them glide up the escalator and exhaled a sigh of relief. She walked over to the coffee bar to grab a quick espresso before she returned to the hotel. She pictured Aidan in bed, his thick chest covered with gray hair, and felt suddenly happy. It felt good to lie next to him, to laugh with him, to feel his arms around her.

Cassie saw the girl as she stirred a sugar cube in her coffee. She was standing at the top of the stairs, clutching a magazine. She had feathery blond hair and wore a red T-shirt. The girl saw Cassie and her eyes narrowed. She waved the magazine and descended the staircase toward her.

"Hi, do you remember me?" The girl stood so close Cassie could smell her spearmint chewing gum.

Cassie recognized the big brown eyes and the smattering of freckles on her cheeks. Her stomach lurched and she spilled coffee on the marble floor. "Molly Payne. What are you doing here?"

"Oh, God," Molly's voice wavered. "I knew it was you." She opened the magazine. "My roommate gets *San Francisco* magazine and she showed me the article about the opening of the emporium. I'm such a bad person. I'm going straight to hell." She started crying.

"Please, not in front of the customers." Cassie pulled Molly's sleeve and led her to a table by the bookshelf.

Molly sat down and put her elbows on the table. She

flipped the pages and looked plaintively at Cassie. "I didn't know Professor Blake was married. I knew he had a daughter, I saw pictures of her in his office, but I thought he was divorced. You have to believe me, I never would have done it if I knew he was married." She wailed like a little girl caught pocketing a tube of lip gloss at a 7-Eleven.

"Aidan told me what happened." Cassie took a deep breath.

"I saw your photo in the article," Molly interrupted, wiping her eyes with her sleeve. " 'Cassie Blake, heiress to Fenton's and wife of ethics professor Aidan Blake.' " She jammed her finger at the page. "I'm worse than those reality stars who sleep with their cousins. I'll never have a happy day in my life, I'm a terrible sinner." She put her head on the table and sobbed uncontrollably.

"Molly." Cassie waited until the sobs subsided into hiccups. "Aidan explained that afternoon. You'd been jilted; Aidan did something nice for you. It was a terrible thing to do, but it was one time. Aidan and I are okay now. He just returned from Greece and we had a wonderful reunion."

Molly lifted her head and looked at Cassie as if she was speaking a foreign language. "It wasn't one time, I loved him. I knew it was wrong, the whole student/professor thing. But he was so sexy. Sort of an older lion in the jungle, beating his chest and calling my name when he came." Molly put her hand over her mouth and stared at Cassie, horrified. "Oh, God, I didn't mean to say that. But I thought he loved me, until he left me with an unused plane ticket and took his TA to Italy instead of me."

Cassie felt a chill pass through her body. Her hands froze and a sharp pain shot through her spine. She looked closely at Molly and tried to keep her voice steady. "What are you talking about?"

"He invited me to this conference in Italy. It sounded so romantic. Riding the gondola in Venice, visiting Verona. I got an evening job to pay for my ticket. I bought some really cute sandals." Molly's shoulders started shaking. "A week before the trip he told me he didn't think it was a good idea. He said he'd be too distracted and everyone would know we were fucking. A couple of days ago I saw pictures of him and his TA on my roommate's Facebook page. They were sharing tongues at a café in Florence. There were dozens of photos: dancing, canoodling, drinking ouzo in Athens. He took her to Athens!" Molly wept harder. "He said Athens was his great love and he wanted to take me there because I was so important to him."

"Are you sure it was him?" Cassie asked. Her brain felt like a pinball machine. Her palms were sweating and she had trouble getting air into her lungs.

"Of course it was him." Molly rolled her eyes. "I'd been screwing him for three months, I knew every inch of his body. Oh, God, I'm sorry, I keep forgetting whom I'm talking to. I've been crying to my roommate for two days. She went to high school with the TA. Her name is Penny; she's really sweet, and has the prettiest blond hair, like Barbie. To give her credit she didn't know anything about me." Molly sighed. "Penny told my roommate she found a text from his *wife,* saying she couldn't wait till he came home. And then yesterday I saw the picture of you in the newsletter and the whole thing fell together like the worst *New York Times* crossword puzzle. You're his wife, you're Cassie Blake, and I am the lowest form of human life." Molly sobbed.

"What did Penny do?" Cassie felt as though she was being strangled, like a rope was pulling at her neck.

"She packed her bag and left in the middle of the night. Didn't even leave a note. He was in for a bit of a surprise when he woke up." Molly started to hiccup. "I never would have fucked him if I knew he was married. I know what it's like to be cheated on. I'm so sorry." Molly dissolved into tears, putting her head on the table and breathing in short gasps like a puppy.

Cassie sat perfectly still. If she moved she would shatter into a million pieces. She examined her diamond and sapphire wedding ring. She looked at her phone, thinking of the hot texts Aidan had sent her. She pictured Aidan burying his mouth in her hair, whispering that she was his angel.

"You're just part of Aidan's harem. I'm the fool. I've been his wife for a decade and I never suspected anything," Cassie said finally, gripping the edge of the table.

"What are you going to do?" Molly asked tentatively.

"Aidan's at the Mark Hopkins, sleeping off jet lag. I couldn't go with him to Italy because I didn't want to miss the grand opening." Cassie glanced around the floor. "I booked a room to celebrate his return. We ate filet mignon and drank a bottle of champagne."

"You're so beautiful and sophisticated, how could he cheat on you?"

"I guess I'll do what Penny did." Cassie continued as if she hadn't heard her. "I'll just leave him there. He'll figure it out eventually."

"If I were you, I'd grab a fork and stab myself in the heart. Then I'd go to the hotel and slice him open like a can of tuna."

"That wouldn't solve anything," Cassie replied weakly. "He admitted he slept with you once, but he said you seduced him and it would never happen again. I've been staying with my friend while I figured out if I could trust him. I finally decided I wanted to stay married, and I was going to move home. We had a really great night. He approved of me working at the emporium; I was even going to bring Isabel to work with me. That's his daughter."

"I'm so sorry," Molly said feebly.

"It's not your fault." Cassie tried to smile. "It's probably happened before, and it would keep happening. Like you said, some men need to be king of the jungle. I'm glad I didn't wait another ten years to find out."

"At least you have this." Molly looked around the room. "It would be so cool to own your own store."

"If I have this." Cassie sighed. "We haven't been open long but sales are terrible. If it doesn't improve we may not make it."

"But there are a ton of women shopping," Molly objected. Since they'd been sitting the emporium had filled up. Dozens of women weaved through the aisles, handling peaches, tasting tangerines, nibbling apple slices.

"Sampling but not buying. I had my first big sale this morning, but it's been pretty dismal."

"Your produce is tastier than what they sell at the co-op." Molly wiped her eyes. "If I had money I'd shop here all the time."

"The grand opening was a huge success. Everyone raves about the design and the merchandise." Cassie glanced around at the women browsing. "They just don't make it to the checkout."

"I guess if you wear Chanel dresses and Prada shoes you don't want to be seen strolling Union Square with a grocery bag."

"We designed special Fenton's bags," Cassie protested.

"But do they still look like shopping bags? My roommate's mother only wears Christian Dior: those wool twinsets you see on old Alfred Hitchcock movies. They did look good on Grace Kelly, I guess anything looked good on Grace Kelly," Molly mused. "And she positively reeks of perfume. I don't know how my roommate could stand it; she must have walked around as a kid with a clothespin on her nose. Even her car reeks. She's got a Jaguar with fancy leather seats; it's like driving around in a living room. I can't imagine her picking up a carton of eggs and a loaf of bread and carrying them to the car in a grocery bag. No offense, but the women who shop here are pretty uptight. They carry themselves as if they've got a ruler stuck up their ass."

"You think they're not buying groceries because of the shopping bag?"

"Sure," Molly said confidently. "Think of that fancy box the pendant came in; red satin with 'Fenton's' written in gold cursive. That's why women shop here. I've seen them walk out weighed down with Fenton's boxes. I'm sure the clothes and shoes are great, but it's all about packaging. I learned that in freshman marketing. My parents wanted me to be a business major." Molly sighed. "But I wanted to study ethics. Maybe you'll give me a job behind the counter when I graduate. I'm really good with people and I love food. I promise I wouldn't eat all the samples if I worked here."

"I don't think that would be such a good idea." Cassie shook her head.

"You hate me, don't you?" Molly hung her head. "I bet the sight of me makes you sick."

"I just think you can do more with your degree," Cassie replied diplomatically. "You're very smart. I never thought the bags could affect sales."

"Of course." Molly smiled, relieved. "Now if you had Fenton's bags like that"—Molly pointed at a woman walking toward them—"people would be lined up at the checkout."

"I'm glad you're still here." Alexis swooped down on the table, clutching her Birkin. "Victoria Traina found out about Giselle's dinner party and she wants to hold her own next Friday. She wants you to pick out the menu." Alexis stopped awkwardly. "Isn't this the girl who returned the pendant, who . . ."

"Molly, this is my friend Alexis. I think you two met. Molly thinks if we provide our customers with Birkins they'd do their food shopping at Fenton's."

"Is that really a Birkin?" Molly turned red. "I've only seen them on a reality show. I don't watch TV but my roommate watches Hulu on her computer. Aren't those like the price of a small house?"

"Not a house in San Francisco," Alexis said dismissively. "What is she doing here?"

"Molly had something she wanted to tell me. We've been chatting, we have a lot in common," Cassie replied calmly.

"I need to talk to you, upstairs." Alexis pulled Cassie up.

"I have to go," Cassie said to Molly. "Thanks for the advice, you've been very helpful."

"Do you want my phone number, in case I have other ideas? Maybe you could sell my pumpkin muffins," Molly said hopefully.

"Not right now." Cassie smiled. "I'm sure I'll see you around."

"What were you doing with the girl who fucked your husband?" Alexis demanded when they were on the escalator. "And why aren't you at the Mark Hopkins servicing Aidan's morning boner?"

Cassie suddenly felt dizzy. Black spots danced before her eyes. "I need to sit down," she said, gripping the side of the escalator. "Let's go to my mother's office."

"Have I missed something?" Alexis demanded, closing the door to Diana's office. "You don't talk to the girl who threw a grenade into your marriage when you're trying to make it work with Aidan."

"I'm divorcing Aidan." Cassie sat on the cream-colored sofa.

"I thought you had a night of fireworks and champagne."

"Apparently Aidan's had a lot of nights of fireworks, just not with me. He and Molly have been having an affair since January. He was going to take her to Italy but at the last minute he took his TA instead; a pretty blonde with hair like a Barbie doll." Cassie felt her temples start to throb. "He cut his trip short because the TA walked out on him when she saw a text from me. She didn't know he was married. Molly didn't know either."

Cassie and Alexis sat silently. Neither knew what to say next. Cassie remembered when her father died and friends arrived to pay their respects. Her mother's living room was full of women spooning egg salad onto white china. Cassie sipped pink lemonade, feeling invisible. No one knew what to say to a little girl who lost her daddy.

"I'm impressed," Alexis said finally. She sat at Diana's desk, running her fingers over the pearl letter opener. "I didn't think Aidan was such a good liar. He's got one hell of a poker face."

"Do you think he's been screwing around for ten years?"

"It doesn't matter, it's over. When are you going to tell him?"

"I can't face him."

"You have to tell him," Alexis insisted. "You've been bleeding long enough. You have to get him out of your life."

"Later." Cassie shrugged. "I can't see him right now."

"I have an idea." Alexis's eyes sparkled. "Wait here, I'll be right back."

Cassie closed her eyes. The pain was like a balloon; when she tried to embrace it, it formed a different shape and escaped her grasp. She had to think about something else. She picked up Alexis's Birkin and admired the platinum hardware. She ran her fingers over the crocodile skin and snapped it open and shut. She held it against her thigh, studying her reflection in the mirror. She thought about what Molly said about designing a shopping bag women would fight over.

"Mission accomplished." Alexis walked into the office. She wore a navy sleeveless dress with a wide belt and Jimmy Choo platform heels. Her hair was piled into an effortless bun and secured with a chopstick. A Tiffany charm bracelet tinkled at her wrist and she wore a strand of freshwater pearls around her neck.

"What did you do?"

"I sent Aidan a Fenton's box of lingerie: thongs, padded bras, a selection of garter belts, lace panties, and teddies. I included a note from you: 'These might be useful in your future conquests.' I signed it 'Cassie Fenton.' I think he'll get the picture."

"You didn't." Cassie's mouth hung open.

"I wanted to add something to the box like a dead chicken, but I resisted the temptation." Alexis started laughing. "You have to forget him. Do you want to go out and get drunk? We can play hooky and spend the afternoon at PlumpJack's. Remember when we'd skip out of last period, change into regular clothes, and see if we'd get carded?"

"I did that once." Cassie cringed. "And I was so terrified we'd get caught I didn't touch my drink."

"That's why you have me riding shotgun," Alexis replied. "We have to do something to get your mind off that prick."

"I have an idea to increase sales at the emporium."

"We can't hand out Birkins, or Birkin knockoffs." Alexis shook her head.

"What if we had someone design a bag that was so gorgeous women *had* to have one? It would have to be big like your Birkin so it could hold groceries, and really original, so women lusted after it. We'd give it an exotic name and make it available only with purchase."

Alexis tapped the letter opener on the desk. She picked up her iPhone and flipped through her photos. "The Princess," she said, looking at Cassie.

"What did you say?"

"We'll call it the Princess and make the first one for Princess Giselle. I can take photos of her carrying it everywhere, stuffed with loaves of bread and broccoli flowers and heads of lettuce."

"The Princess," Cassie repeated. "Bright red, with a clasp shaped liked a tiara. We'll use a cool recyclable fabric and we'll ask Gregory to hand paint each bag with some fantastic design. The bags will be instantly recognizable all over the city." Cassie jumped up, pacing around the room.

"A mini mural on each bag!" Alexis said. "They'll be utterly unique, walking works of art. We just need to find a local supplier."

"Axel! He knows everyone." Cassie fished through her purse for her phone. "I'll call him right now." Cassie stood by the window, waiting for Axel to answer. She watched tourists on Union Square take photos of Gucci and Burberry. She saw squirrels hop across the grass scavenging acorns.

Axel answered the phone. "Cassie, darling, lovely to

hear your voice. I'm creating a spectacular arrangement for Princess Giselle's dinner party. Roses, orchids, tulips, and clouds of baby's breath. That woman knows how to spend money."

"I need your help. Sales at the emporium have been slow. We think women might be embarrassed to walk onto Union Square carrying a grocery shopping bag." Cassie tapped her fingers on the glass. "We need someone to make a bag that is so original, so sexy, women can't live without it. We're going to call it 'The Princess' and it will be available only with purchase."

"I love it," Axel cooed. "*Très Breakfast at Tiffany's*."

"Do you know anyone that can make them fast? We have an idea for the design and the fabric."

"Let me think," Axel demurred. "I have a friend, Thom Paik, in the Sunset. He can whip up a batch quickly."

Cassie hesitated. "I don't want them made in a sweatshop."

"Do you think I'd send you to someone who employs twelve-year-old girls?" Axel huffed. "I'll call him and tell him you're coming. He'll take care of you."

"That would be fantastic." Cassie's eyes sparkled. "How can I thank you?"

"I heard Vanessa and Billy are attending Giselle's dinner party. If you can convince Vanessa to use me instead of Stanlee Gatti for her florals, I'll be your slave."

"Done." Cassie grabbed a pen. "What's his address?"

17.

Cassie sat at her desk flipping through the sales figures. She wore a sleeveless cotton dress and white sandals. Her hair was tied in a low ponytail and she had a bright red Princess bag slung over her chair.

It was unseasonably warm for early June in San Francisco. The fog failed to make its afternoon appearance and tourists sweltered in light wool coats. They filtered into the emporium and left with cartons of organic ice cream and bottles of fizzy lemonade. The women who lived on Nob Hill were grateful they could nip into Fenton's, pile fresh fruits and vegetables into their Princess bags, and avoid the sweaty crowds at Safeway.

The popularity of the Princess bags had grown slowly, but now it was at a frenzy. Princess Giselle carried hers everywhere: to lunch at Emerald, to charity teas at the Zoo and at MOMA, even to dinner at Michael Mina's with a bright red Valentino dress.

Alexis photographed her wherever she went and made sure the photos ended up on every blog from *W* to *Instyle*.

Women grew curious about the Princess. There were rumors it was made exclusively for Princess Giselle by Louis Vuitton with original artwork by Julian Schnabel. Women Googled it, asked their Facebook friends, whispered about it during yoga and Pilates. No one knew where to get one.

"We need to create a sense of mystery," Alexis had counseled. "We can't just hand the Princess out at the cash register and expect everyone to want one. Think about the Birkin. It takes four years to get off the waiting list."

"In another four weeks we might be out of business," Cassie had replied miserably. The prototype Princess sat in front of her, bright red spandex-like fabric illustrated with a fabulous scene of a farmers market. She wanted to get them into women's hands as fast as possible.

"Trust me," Alexis replied. "I have a plan."

Alexis unveiled her plan at the Asian Art Museum's annual fashion show. It was the red carpet event of the season. Invitations were so coveted they were traded for insider information about Apple's latest iPhone release and Facebook's IPO. Women ordered their couture outfits months ahead, wanting to outshine the models strutting down the runway in Zac Posen, Stella McCartney, and Versace.

Alexis had insisted Cassie dress up for the event, and pamper herself with a blowout and facial. Her days passed in a blur. She got up and swam fifty laps, then put in eight hours at Fenton's. In the evenings she picked at Pia's casseroles, watched Alexis devour ice cream, and climbed into bed with a cup of hot milk and a box of tissues.

Aidan appeared at Alexis's front door one morning after Cassie finished her morning swim. Alexis was at a sunrise yoga class and Cassie was spooning brown sugar into a bowl of oatmeal. She threw a robe over her bathing suit and ran barefoot to the foyer.

When she saw Aidan she froze. He was wearing a white V-neck shirt and jogging shorts. She could see the gray hair curling on his chest, the thick muscles on his upper arms, the hands that had held and stroked her. She took a deep breath, trying to shut down her heart as if it had a switch with an off button.

"What are you doing here?" Cassie opened the door a crack.

"I brought you fruit from the co-op: green grapes, peaches, pomegranates." Aidan held up a paper bag. "They're all in season."

"I don't want organic fruit, or vegetables from the garden, or sexy texts. I want you to leave me alone," Cassie replied tightly.

"Let me come in, Cassie." Aidan wedged his knee in the door. "I need to explain."

"Molly explained everything in graphic detail." Cassie held on to the door handle. "I'll be late for work. I have to go."

"Cassie." Aidan's voice was harsh and commanding. "You can give me five minutes."

Cassie wavered. She wanted to slam the door and run upstairs but she knew he would just come back. She pulled the robe tightly around her.

"Five minutes." She opened the door.

"I've missed you." Aidan stood in the foyer. He had a day's stubble on his chin and dark circles under his eyes, and his hair was damp as if he'd come from the gym. He still had the tan he got in Greece and his teeth were bright against his brown skin.

Cassie led him into the conservatory and sat gingerly at the glass table. "I've contacted my attorney and started the divorce proceedings."

"Cassie, listen to me." Aidan grabbed her hands across the table. "I've never loved you more. It was all madness. You don't know what it's like to be pushing fifty, to be surrounded by young people who have their whole lives in front of them."

"I don't want to hear it." Cassie pulled her hands away and hugged her chest.

"The department got a new hire this year: Randy Lipton. He had a Ph.D. from Stanford and walked around campus in surfer shorts and Rainbow sandals. Coeds lined up outside his office the first day of classes. When I told them professors don't hold office hours the first week of school, they just giggled. They were like groupies, waiting for a rock star to appear backstage. I know how juvenile I sound." Aidan rubbed his temples. "But when Molly made a play for me I couldn't resist. I needed to feel like a man."

"Aidan, I'm not your therapist. I promised to love you in sickness and in health but that wasn't enough. I don't love you anymore, I can't love you." Cassie kept her eyes on the table.

"You can love me." Aidan latched on to her words. "We can see a therapist together."

"You fucked Molly, you fucked your TA. You lied to everyone and cheated." Cassie shook her head.

"Everywhere I went, Randy was the rising star. He came to the gym one night and asked me to play a game of squash. He trounced me, Cassie. I couldn't walk after the game! I hobbled off the court like the fucking Hunchback of Notre Dame."

"Being jealous of a young stud is no excuse for screwing your way across campus and through Europe." Cassie lifted her eyes to meet Aidan's.

"I was crazed." Aidan pulled his hair. "But the madness has passed. I woke up one morning in Athens and knew I had to be home with you. I got the first plane out." Aidan leaned across the table. "And our sex was so good, Cassie."

Cassie jumped back as if she'd been shot. She felt like she was looking at Aidan through a kaleidoscope. Every time she turned it, it formed a different pattern.

"You caught the first plane out because Penny left you! You don't know how to stop lying. What's going to happen when your hair turns white and your back goes out? Are you going to bed the whole junior faculty? Good-bye, Aidan." She stood up and walked toward the foyer.

"Cassie." Aidan followed her. "Give me one more chance."

"I'm not a magic genie." Cassie walked to the front door. "I can't fix you. Let me know when you get the divorce papers."

Aidan grabbed her arm and grazed her cheek with his lips. Cassie could smell his aftershave and his avocado shampoo. She wriggled out of his grasp and opened the front door.

"Please leave," she whispered.

"Have you thought about what this is going to do to Isabel?" Aidan stood in the middle of the tall double doors.

Cassie tried to keep her breathing steady. She dropped her hands to her sides and waited for them to stop shaking.

"Isabel can still work at Fenton's this summer. Good-bye, Aidan." She slammed the door and ran upstairs.

When she reached her room, she walked straight to the

closet and leaned against the full-length mirror. She closed her eyes, trying to erase the feel of Aidan's mouth on her skin. The cold glass against her cheek soothed her. Slowly she opened her eyes, slipped off her robe, and searched for the perfect outfit to wear to work.

Since then she tried to throw herself into working at Fenton's, dressing in breezy summer dresses, spending extra time on her hair and makeup, but she couldn't regain her earlier passion. She told herself it was like learning to walk again, one baby step at a time. Sometimes crawling seemed impossible.

On the morning of the Asian Art Museum fashion show, Cassie went to Joseph Cozza's on Maiden Lane and came out with skin that had been scrubbed, buffed, and plastered with seaweed. Joseph convinced her to get the Brazilian blowout and her hair lay smoothly on her shoulders like a silk cap. Even her hands had been coated with almond butter, placed in mittens, and buffed with an exfoliating brush. She felt almost happy as she walked into Fenton's to pick up the dress Alexis had selected for the fashion show.

"Hi, stranger." James grinned as she got on the escalator. He wore navy slacks and a white button-down shirt. His hair was brushed to the side and he carried a stack of papers under his arm.

"You're wearing your glasses. Have you been staring at figures all day?" Cassie smiled. She hadn't been avoiding James but she kept their conversations short. She found her eyes still filled unexpectedly with tears, and she had to slip on sunglasses and bite her lips to stop them from trembling.

"Closing out some final deliveries." He took off his glasses and rubbed his eyes. "Are sales improving?"

"Not yet." Cassie grimaced. "Giselle has been parading the Princess around but Alexis is keeping its origin under wraps. She has some big plan to launch it at the Asian Art Museum today. If she doesn't launch it soon, our ship will sink."

"Who knew they taught marketing to dance majors?" James laughed.

"She's like a tornado," Cassie agreed. "Giselle's dinner party was such a success we've been inundated with requests to plan menus for her friends."

"That must be boosting sales a bit." James nodded as they got off the escalator. "I had lunch with your mother yesterday. She didn't seem quite ready to throw in the towel."

"Alexis filled her in on the Princess, so I think we've gained a temporary stay of execution." Cassie headed toward the dress department.

"Cassie." James put his hand on her wrist. "Your mother told me what happened between you and Aidan."

"Aaah." Cassie exhaled like a tire puncturing. "I'm sure she enjoyed that. She's always been Aidan's biggest fan."

"She was concerned about you. I'm sorry you had to go through that, he doesn't know what he's giving up."

"He has lots of distractions." Cassie blinked away the tears. "I better go. If I'm late for the fashion show, Alexis will skin my hide and sell it to make shoes."

"I wanted to know if you'd like to have dinner. We could go to Boulevard and I'll walk you through the menu." He smiled like a schoolboy, sticking his hands in his pant pockets.

Cassie hesitated. James was so easy to be around and he made her laugh. "I don't have time." She shook her head. "I need to concentrate on the emporium if it's going to pull through. Aren't you going back to Chicago soon?"

"Third week of June. I get a couple of weeks off. Then I'm gutting a steak house and turning it into a raw food restaurant."

"Maybe I'll see you before you leave." Cassie pulled her hand away.

"I'll bring in some McDonald's." James smiled awkwardly. "Knock 'em dead this afternoon."

Cassie stood in the dressing room, admiring herself in the mirror. The dress Alexis had selected was a delicious raw silk the color of cherries, slit up the sides and with a plunging neckline. She slipped on a delicate gold belt and three gold bangles and examined the shoes Alexis left in a Bottega Veneta box: red stiletto heels with gold buckles and a dusting of diamonds. She put them on and turned in front of the mirror. She wished Aidan could see her, then she pushed the thought away, grabbed her purse, and hurried down the escalator.

"I feel like one of Charlie's Angels," she said to Alexis, who was waiting in front of a stretch limousine.

"Then the first part of my plan is working." Alexis grinned. She wore an almost identical dress the color of raspberries, with a silver belt and an armful of silver bangles. "What do you think of our princess?"

Giselle strutted toward them in a dress so tight it looked like it was sprayed on. Her legs seemed to go on forever and her hair fell to her waist like spun gold. She wore a ruby and diamond choker and a diamond tiara on her head.

"I think she's going to cause an accident." Cassie giggled at the construction workers and tourists who stopped and stared.

"We each get one of these." Alexis handed Cassie a Princess bag. "But don't open it until I say so. Let's go." She opened the door of the limousine. "It's time to put Operation Princess in motion."

The Asian Art Museum was packed by the time they arrived. Women stepped out of Mercedes and Jaguars carrying Louis Vuitton bags with solid gold buckles.

"Why are we circling? We're almost late." Cassie glanced at her watch.

"Haven't you learned anything from watching E!? We can't make an entrance unless everyone's here." Alexis signaled the driver to stop. "You go first," she said to Cassie. "Remember, Giselle's the princess, we're the ladies in waiting."

Cassie, Alexis, and Giselle walked into the museum, Princess bags draped over their shoulders. Alexis grabbed them each a glass of champagne and circled the room twice, blowing kisses and waving to the women in floppy hats and Gucci shoes. Then she crossed the runway and led Cassie and Giselle to their front-row seats.

Cassie saw the Traina girls with their mother, Danielle Steel. She spotted Annette Bening, who she knew was performing a play at the ACT. She saw the girls from Yahoo!: Marissa Mayer and her pack of wealthy dot-commers. She spotted Allison Speer, public relations queen, sitting next to Kendall Wilkinson.

"Ladies." The emcee tapped his microphone. "We are thrilled you could join us for this star-studded event. We are lucky to have the designers with us this afternoon and if you behave, they might be taking special orders." The emcee winked and the women chuckled appreciatively. "Please join us in the east wing for a delicious buffet after the show. Let me introduce our fabulous models."

The women clapped and waited for the models to appear on the runway. There was a loud rustling behind the curtains and the emcee appeared again, red-faced and clutching his microphone. "My apology for the delay. There's been a small wardrobe malfunction. Feel free to refill your champagne glasses. The show will begin shortly."

Everyone waited expectantly but nothing happened. The women started squirming, fanning themselves with their programs. They made small coughing noises as if that would prompt the show to begin. Alexis positioned her bag on her lap and said to her neighbor: "I hope the show begins soon. I did back-to-back Pilates classes this morning. I'm starving."

"A few more minutes, please." The emcee came back on stage, wiping sweat from his forehead. "We're fixing the problem as quickly as possible."

"I don't know about you," Alexis whispered loudly to her neighbor so the first few rows could hear. "If I don't eat something, I'm going to faint." She unbuckled her bag and took out a bunch of green grapes, a jar of sun-dried tomato hummus, a round of olive bread, and a basket of cherry tomatoes.

Cassie saw women crane their necks as Alexis handed her neighbor a crust of bread spread with hummus. Alexis turned to the second row and passed around the basket of tomatoes. She nudged Cassie and Cassie obediently opened her bag and shared its contents with the women near her. Soon the first three rows were eating duck pâté, asparagus tips, tangerine slices, and sweet radishes.

Giselle opened hers last. She leaned down to retrieve her bag so her breasts brushed against her dress like two ripe melons. She opened the clasp and extracted a cream-filled éclair wrapped in silver paper. She put the éclair in her mouth, licking the sides like it was a long, thick penis, and wiped the cream off her lips with a silk napkin. Then she let out a long sigh like a protracted orgasm, and muttered something in German.

The lights dimmed and music blared from hidden loudspeakers. The models strutted down the runway, six-foot amazons wearing layers of makeup and very little clothes, and everyone applauded in relief. Alexis packed the food back in her bag and stashed it neatly under her seat, winking at Cassie to do the same.

"Where did you get that bag?" A thin woman wearing a floppy hat accosted Cassie. "I'm always starving but I can't tote a Caesar salad around in a Fendi clutch."

"It's an exclusive," Alexis interrupted. The women stood in small groups in the east wing, nibbling hors d'oeuvres and dissecting the fashion show.

"I must have one." The woman stroked Cassie's bag. "I love the fabric, it's so supple. And the artwork reminds me of van Gogh. I've never seen anything like it."

"Fenton's food emporium," Cassie replied, moving the bag to her other shoulder.

"Don't tell anyone," Alexis whispered, standing between them. "They're only available with purchase, and supplies are extremely limited."

The limousine dropped Giselle off at her St. Regis penthouse and Alexis stretched her legs in front of her. "I'd say that was a success." She grinned.

Dozens of women approached them during the reception begging to know where they could get a Princess bag. Alexis whispered in their ears and the women floated back to their friends, eyes sparkling with their secret.

"I hope we have enough bags." Cassie giggled. "I may have to call Mr. Paik and rush order some more."

"Did you see Giselle swallow that éclair?" Alexis laughed. "She should moonlight as a porn star."

"I have one small question." Cassie slipped off her Bottega Venetas and wiggled her toes. "Did you have anything to do with the 'small wardrobe malfunction'?"

"Convent girls never tell." Alexis smiled like the Cheshire cat. "We deserve a treat. Let's go home and watch *Breakfast at Tiffany's*. Driver"—she tapped the glass partition—"could you stop at the market? We need to pick up a carton of Ben and Jerry's ice cream."

The day after the fashion show women lined up at Fenton's before the doors were open. They made a beeline to the emporium, filling their carts with fruits and vegetables, fish and poultry, wine and cheese. They handed their gold cards to the cashier and claimed their prizes: their own Princess bags stuffed with their purchases.

Cassie saw women carrying Princess bags all over the city. Thom Paik had to hire a night shift to keep up with production. Cassie kept Gregory supplied with cases of wine and baskets of Fenton's pâtés and soft cheeses. Sales of merchandise were going through the roof. Cassie's mother came down to the emporium several times a day to bask in the success.

"Darling, there you are," Diana cooed. She was dressed in what she forecasted to be the summer color: bright yellow that belonged on a rain slicker. She wore a white silk scarf and white sandals accessorized with colored gems.

"You look very stylish." Cassie smiled.

"I have an important lunch date with Hermès. They finally are considering opening a Hermès boutique in Fenton's." She tapped her cigarette holder on Cassie's desk. "I actually have two lunch dates, I need your help."

"My help?" Cassie asked dubiously.

"I was supposed to have lunch today with Grant Landers. Do you remember him? You used to take dancing lessons together. He sold his start-up to Google and started a line of swimsuits. All the profits go to charity. I promised we'd discuss carrying them at Fenton's." Diana plucked a lily from the vase on Cassie's desk. "Could you do me a huge favor and have lunch with him? I can't put off the people from Hermès."

"Why don't you reschedule with Grant?" Cassie frowned.

"He's already driven up from Palo Alto. Please, Cassie. His mother and I go way back."

"Fine." Cassie stacked the papers on her desk. "But I have three appointments this afternoon to look at apartments."

"I respect your desire not to stay at Alexis's indefinitely," Cassie's mother said carefully. "But do you really want to be alone right now? You could stay with me."

Cassie's face softened. "I've lived with someone my whole life. I think being alone is exactly what I need. I'm going to find a one bedroom with lots of light and get a cat."

"Cats aren't very good company." Diana shook her head. "They can be quite self-centered. Grant is waiting in my office. I'll tell him you'll meet him on the first floor."

Grant stood in the swimsuit section, examining fabric. Cassie remembered him as a skinny redhead who held her too tight when they danced. Now his hair was more strawberry blond. He wore a white T-shirt, tight jeans, and leather sandals.

"Cassie Fenton, you still look like you're twelve years old." His smile revealed bright white teeth.

"It's nice to see you." Cassie blushed. "My mother tells me you're doing wonderful things for charity."

"It's hard when you make so much money so young." Grant shrugged. "You really have to search for meaning in life. Besides the obvious things, like money, women, and fame." He laughed. "Why don't we talk about it over lunch? I have reservations at Emerald."

Cassie and Grant sat at a table by the window and Grant ordered a Loire Valley Chardonnay.

"If I only drink wine at dinner, I'll never be able to sample all the fine wines in the world." He broke a breadstick and dipped it in olive oil. "I try a different region every month, it's very educational."

"Tell me about your swimsuit line," Cassie said politely.

"I was sitting on the beach in Fiji a couple of years ago and I saw these native girls playing in the sand. Here I was, staying in a thousand-dollar-a-day resort, and they probably didn't have a decent education. I started a foundation to build schools in tropical countries where the natives live on the poverty line."

"That's really admirable." Cassie nodded.

"Swimsuits seemed a natural fit." Grant sipped his wine. "Plus the perks are great. I pick out the models and I'm present for the fashion shoots. Next week I leave for Antigua."

Cassie ordered a grilled vegetable plate and moved the food around on her plate. She still didn't have much of an appetite, and usually nibbled nuts and dried fruit at her desk. She listened to Grant's plans to get his swimsuits into Fenton's and Neiman's and tried to smile enthusiastically.

"I have to go." She placed her napkin on her plate. "I'm apartment hunting this afternoon."

Grant put his hand over hers. "Your mother told me about your marriage. I'm sorry."

"I'm fine, thank you."

"You're very pretty. I just don't want a serious relationship right now." He squeezed her hand harder.

"Excuse me," Cassie spluttered.

"All this money, this freedom, it's life-changing. I don't feel like settling down for a while. If you want to come to my place I can show you my latest swimsuit designs. I just want to be up front." Grant leaned forward, his chest puffing up like a peacock.

"Up front?" Cassie felt like she was choking.

"Expectations." He put his other hand over hers. "Women your age, a failed marriage, biological clock ticking. I'm sure you're great in bed, I just wouldn't want to go there under false pretenses."

Cassie felt like every nerve in her body was about to snap. She stood up slowly so Grant wouldn't see her shaking. "I thought this was a business lunch."

"Your mother called and told me what you've been through." Grant didn't release her hand. "And she's right, you're a looker. I just didn't want to lead you on."

"Good-bye, Grant."

"We haven't had dessert." He pushed his chair back.

"I'm sure there are a few swimsuit models in the restaurant, there always are." Cassie grabbed her purse. "I'll tell my mother we had a delightful time."

Cassie stormed into Diana's office. "You sent me on a blind date with a soft porn addict and pretended it was a business lunch."

"Cassie"——her mother stood up from her desk——"Grant is a very motivated young man."

"Motivated to get models into the sack! How dare you!" Cassie was shaking. "I don't want to date, and if I did, I'd like to know it was a date ahead of time."

"I thought it would be less pressure this way." Diana shrugged. "The men in San Francisco are either married or gay. Internet companies are producing lovely young men who are intelligent and have money."

"Mother." Cassie's face was bright red. "I'm not even divorced. I don't want a man."

"I know I didn't marry again," Diana said delicately, "but I always had romantic interests. I already had a child. For you, it's different."

"I'm thirty-two, I have plenty of time to have a child. It's too soon to think about dating." Cassie suddenly felt tired. The half glass of wine she drank made her head throb. She pictured Grant sitting across the table, sniffing his wineglass, and shuddered.

"It's never too soon to be happy," her mother replied, inspecting her manicure. "In today's world you have to go out and look for it. Think of all the people who do Internet dating."

"If you sign me up for Match.com, I quit," Cassie threatened.

"I'm sorry Grant wasn't a gentleman." Diana tapped her nails on the desk. "But you need to keep your eyes open. You have beautiful skin, Cassie, but it doesn't stay soft forever."

"I'm taking the rest of the day off." Cassie threw open the door. "I'll see you in the morning."

The first apartment the real estate agent showed Cassie was a studio in the Marina. She had always loved the Marina

Green. She imagined taking long walks by the bay, watching boats sail under the Golden Gate Bridge.

"It has a lovely exposure. You said sun is important to you." The real estate agent lifted the blinds to reveal a sliver of the bay hidden behind taller apartment buildings.

"It's a little cramped." Cassie turned around in the living room/bedroom. "I think I'd feel more comfortable up the hill."

"No one in the Marina worries about earthquakes anymore." The agent shrugged dismissively. She was a small blond woman with thin ankles and muscled upper arms. "But I'll show you a couple of places in Cow Hollow."

Cassie trudged through a one bedroom in Cow Hollow feeling her spirits fall. After she had stormed out of her mother's office she was more determined to get her own apartment. She pictured herself tossing salads in her kitchen, and eating them in a sun-filled garden. Maybe she would make a friend or two in the building and have potlucks like when she was in college.

The apartments she saw weren't big enough to have people over and they had that impermanent feel of a rental. The walls were beige and the floors were chipped hardwood. The closets were bare and smelled of mothballs.

"I want something with a little more character." Cassie sighed. "With a fireplace or a garden."

"June is a difficult time of year for rentals." The agent consulted her book. "I have one that will be available in about a week. It has very nice bay windows, not a lot of closet space."

"I need a view more than clothes." Cassie smiled. "I'd like to take a look."

* * *

The apartment was on the second floor of a duplex on Steiner Street. The lobby had velvet wallpaper and big potted palms and there was a gilt mirror on the wall. Cassie climbed the wooden staircase and smelled lasagna and garlic.

"The back apartment is leased by an old couple, but the front apartment is a sublet. If you don't mind the smell of Italian cooking, it might work. It gets nice light, especially in the evenings." The real estate agent sorted through her keys and opened the door.

"What beautiful floors!" Cassie exclaimed. The floors were polished maple and the walls were painted pale blue. There was a fireplace in one corner and tall bay windows covered by sheer curtains.

"I think the rugs belong to the tenant." The agent opened the curtains. "But you could ask him if they can stay with the apartment. The bedroom also gets lovely light and the closet has been converted into an office." She showed Cassie the next room. "If you stand by the window you can see Coit Tower. There's a bakery on the corner that bakes delicious croissants."

"It's quite spacious." Cassie surveyed the bedroom. A queen-sized bed stood in the middle of the room flanked by two wood bedside tables. A sketch of the Bay Bridge hung on the wall and a chest of drawers stood in the corner. Cassie peeked in on a windowless bathroom and a small closet with a built-in desk and folding chair.

"The lease has another six months." The agent trailed Cassie. "But I could probably negotiate something longer."

Cassie returned to the living room and stood by the window. The street was full of trees and there was a boy zipping up and down the sidewalk on a scooter.

"I like the feel of the neighborhood." Cassie hesitated. "I'd definitely want a longer lease."

"I have a meeting." The agent glanced at her watch. "But I can draw up a lease and present it to the landlord in the morning."

Cassie sat on the window seat and looked down on the street. The afternoon sun streamed in, creating spidery shafts of light. "Do you mind if I sit here for a few minutes? I'm going to live here alone and I just want to see how it feels."

"The divorce apartment." The agent nodded knowingly. "You want to know if the four walls are going to close in on you. I really have to run but you look pretty safe. I'll leave the key and you can slip it in the mailbox on your way out." She fiddled with her key chain and handed the key to Cassie.

"Thank you." Cassie blushed. "I won't stay long."

"Don't worry." The agent opened the door. "Eventually you'll love living alone. You can eat whatever you want and leave your makeup on the bathroom sink."

Cassie reclined on the window seat looking out at the bay. She saw boats rocking in the distance and the outline of the Marin hills. Two women pushed strollers across the street and an old lady carried a sack of groceries.

The apartment was brutally quiet. She missed the sound of vegetables being sliced on the kitchen counter. She missed hearing the shower running and the dryer tossing Aidan's socks.

Cassie wondered if she should move to her mother's Nob Hill penthouse for a while. It was convenient to Fenton's and she'd never be lonely with Diana to spar with in the evenings. She imagined the parade of suitors that might arrive at the door, picked by Diana for their breeding and prospects, and shuddered.

"Cassie, what are you doing here?"

"James!" She turned to the front door. "What are you doing here?"

"I live here." He closed the front door. He was carrying two bags of Chinese takeout and a pile of magazines. "At least until the end of next week. Did you come to say good-bye?"

"My real estate agent showed me the apartment and I just wanted to sit and admire the view." Cassie jumped up from the window seat. "I had no idea it was yours!"

James put his bags down and walked over to Cassie. "Please stay and have dinner."

"I can't." Cassie blushed. "I have to be . . ."

"Nowhere." James put his hand on her wrist. "I have too much for one person to eat. You're doing me a favor. Without you, I'll be eating Kung Pao chicken for a week."

"Now you see the exciting life of a bachelor." James ladled wontons into a soup bowl. "I did go a little crazy tonight. I got fortune cookies and ice cream for dessert."

"I thought you were a foodie." Cassie ate a forkful of Chinese coleslaw. They sat at a round table in the kitchen. James had covered it with a blue tablecloth and dragged an extra folding chair from the closet.

"I love everything about food," James admitted, "except cooking it. I have two left thumbs in the kitchen."

"That explains the McDonald's addiction," Cassie joked. She had felt nervous about staying for dinner, but James was so easy to talk to. She felt like a kid hanging out at a friend's house after school.

"Luckily this neighborhood has some wonderful takeout places. There's a Russian restaurant on the corner that makes the best borscht with sour cream." James sprinkled seasoning on his teriyaki noodles. "Are you going to take the apartment?"

"Carter is coming home soon. Alexis will have enough problems without me being around."

"He still doesn't want Alexis working at Fenton's?" James frowned. "Alexis is the department store queen. She has her own fan page on Facebook."

"He doesn't know she's working at Fenton's." Cassie laughed. "He's been on a kangaroo farm for weeks. My mother suggested I move in with her but we'd claw each other's eyes out."

"Diana can be a challenge," James agreed diplomatically. "She's thrilled with the success of the emporium."

"I'm happy it's doing well," Cassie replied hesitantly. She put her fork down and fiddled with her napkin.

"Does Fenton's make you happy?" James heaped noodles on Cassie's plate.

"I feel like a child who begged for a puppy and then wanted to return it," Cassie admitted. "I love talking with the suppliers and I enjoy being around food, but there's just something about the clientele."

"They dress like movie queens and behave like spoiled children at a birthday party?" James grinned.

"I feel so guilty." Cassie breathed. "In a way Aidan was right. I'm not cut out for San Francisco society. I'm more comfortable around vegetables."

"You could try something different."

"I don't think I'm up for different right now. Maybe I just need to settle in." Cassie shrugged. She picked at a forkful of chicken.

"You need to do what you love, Cassie."

"I haven't been very successful in the love department." Cassie put her napkin on the table and pushed back her chair. "Dinner was delicious, but I better go."

"You can't go before we open our fortune cookies." James stood up. "You'll never know what you missed."

"I don't have much luck with fortune cookies." Cassie grimaced. "Mine usually say things like 'Beware man carrying sticks. He will break your back.' That's why I eat Japanese food."

"I'll open your fortune and you open mine. If it's terrible, I'll throw it away and you'll never know. Why don't we eat them in the living room? You carry the cookies and I'll grab the ice cream," James suggested, clearing away plates and containers of noodles.

Cassie sat on the window seat and tucked her feet underneath her. She looked down on the street. The streetlights were on and the sidewalk was bathed in a yellow light. She saw a couple walking arm in arm, leaning into each other and laughing.

James carried a TV dinner tray with a carton of vanilla ice cream.

"The TV dinner tray is one of my favorite inventions." James handed Cassie a bowl and spoon. "You can eat alone and never get lonely. Jon Stewart is always there to keep you company. You go first; what does my fortune cookie say?"

" 'You can never be too kind,' " Cassie read the thin white paper. " 'Your kindness will be returned in gold.' "

"Very wise." James sat on the window seat next to her. "My turn. 'Plant happiness like a small seed. Soon it will flower.' "

James put his glasses on the TV tray and leaned toward

Cassie. He tucked her hair behind her ears and kissed her softly on the mouth. He leaned against the window and kissed her harder, his lips wet and sweet.

Cassie felt the pressure of his mouth on hers, of his hand on the small of her back. She kissed him back. His body was thin and hard and smelled like peppermint soap. She leaned against the window and the bowl of ice cream turned over in her lap and clattered to the floor.

"I'm sorry." She pulled away and hunched down on the rug. "I've ruined your rug. I'll get a paper towel." She ran to the kitchen and returned with a roll of paper towels. She mopped up the ice cream, keeping her eyes on the floor so James wouldn't see her blush. "I really should go," she said when the puddle of ice cream had disappeared.

"You can't go." James sat on the rug next to her. "Your skirt is wet, it's see-through."

"James, I don't think . . ." She stumbled.

"Don't think." He pulled her up and led her to the bedroom. "I'll think for both of us."

James closed the curtains and put his arms around Cassie. He kissed her tentatively, like a boy on a prom date, until she started to kiss him back. Cassie waited while he unzipped her dress, feeling his cold fingers on her naked back.

He pulled the dress over her head and unsnapped her bra. He touched her breasts, drawing circles around her nipples, and then he pulled off her panties and let them drop to the floor.

"I knew you were beautiful." James unzipped his pants, took off his shirt, and pulled her onto the bed. His body was thin and hard like a cross-country runner. He ran his fingers over her stomach, kissing her mouth, her neck, her breasts.

He pushed her back and studied her face, tracing her nose and mouth with her finger.

Cassie's legs opened by themselves, her body straining to reach him. James turned away and fumbled in the bedside drawer. Then he turned back, found her hands, and held them tightly. He covered her body with his and pushed deep inside her.

Cassie came first, a long orgasm that crept up on her, not allowing her to back away. James waited till she stopped shaking and then he pushed harder, gasping, falling on her breasts, and shattered against her.

James turned on his side and pulled her close to him. Cassie lay with her eyes open, hearing his breathing rise and fall. She felt the pieces of her heart rearrange themselves like a Rubik's cube. She tucked herself against his chest, closed her eyes, and slept.

18.

Cassie lay on her stomach and opened her eyes. The sun streamed in the bay window, making a pattern on the rug. Her body felt thick and sleepy, like she had spent the night in a warm bath. She turned over and leaned against the pillows, listening to sounds in the kitchen.

She heard the fridge open and close, and the toaster pop. She heard glasses clinking and a drawer opening. She closed her eyes and pictured James on top of her, his body hard and narrow. She remembered the way he held her hands when he entered her, as if he was afraid she would leap off the bed, and felt a tiny flicker of desire.

"I don't have a lot of breakfast foods." James put a TV dinner tray on the bed. It held a glass of orange juice, a slice of wheat toast, and a bowl of Froot Loops.

"You eat Froot Loops?" Cassie giggled.

"My grandmother used to feed them to the cows as a treat." James poured milk in the bowl. "Smart cows, they're delicious. And they make the milk turn colors."

"All these years I've been missing out." Cassie ate a spoonful of Froot Loops.

"I'm the one who's been missing out." James sat on the bed and kissed her softly on the mouth.

"I should go." Cassie pulled away. "I'll be late for work."

"Take the day off." James put the tray on the floor. "Let's pull a Ferris Bueller."

"A what?"

"When I was a kid we watched that movie *Ferris Bueller's Day Off* a hundred times. It was filmed in Chicago. Ferris calls in sick to the principal's office and spends the day with his girlfriend and his best friend exploring the city. The movie was the director's love letter to Chicago."

"Alexis was brilliant at finding excuses for us to leave school early. She had four straight years of orthodontist appointments. We used to sit at Fisherman's Wharf and eat ice cream with the tourists."

"Please, Cassie. I want to spend the day with you." He lay down and ran his hands up and down her back.

"Last night was wonderful." She felt his fingers play on her spine. "But you're leaving in a week."

"Think of it as my good-bye present." James pulled himself on his elbow. "We'll ride the cable cars and climb to the top of Coit Tower. We'll stuff ourselves with sourdough bread and Ghirardelli chocolate."

"My mother did behave atrociously yesterday." Cassie leaned back against the pillow.

"You're doing a good deed. You're showing a midwestern boy the delights of San Francisco." James circled her breast with his thumb.

"I've always wanted to go to the aquarium on a weekday." Cassie closed her eyes. "I used to have a mad crush on the penguins."

"Call your mother, but first we have a little unfinished business." He climbed on top of her and covered her mouth with his.

"I thought we finished it pretty well last night." Cassie giggled, feeling him hard against her stomach.

"Last night was the hors d'oeuvres," he whispered in her ear. "This morning we're having the main course."

"I told my mother I had a terrible cold." Cassie laughed as they walked into the sunlight. The morning was warm and the sky was a bright, cloudless blue. They had written out an itinerary, brainstorming their favorite places and foods. James wanted to climb Lombard Street, "the world's crookedest street," and see *The Thinker* at the Palace Legion of Honor. Cassie wanted to visit the Botanical Garden at Golden Gate Park and eat fried calamari in Chinatown.

"She said I sounded awful, and I should stay in bed."

"We could stay in bed." James laced his fingers through hers. "Or we could build up an appetite walking the city and go back to bed for dessert."

"You are a foodie," Cassie teased. "I'm going to cure your fast food addiction."

"You could show me how to cook dinner." James pulled her close as they waited to cross the street. "And we could have another sleepover."

"We're having one blowout day of fun." Cassie shook her head. "Then I have to go back to work and you have to get ready for Chicago."

"One day of fun. Ready?" He took her hand.

"Ready." Cassie nodded.

* * *

They rode the cable car to the top of Lombard Street, leaning out of the car and pulling the bell at each stop. The cable
car driver rolled his eyes and muttered something about
young people not obeying the rules. James slipped him a
ten-dollar bill and stood at the front of the cable car, singing
"I Left My Heart in San Francisco" for the tourists.

"I didn't know you could sing." Cassie laughed after they
jumped off.

"No one asked for my autograph, or an encore." James
grinned. "But I've always wanted to sing on a cable car. Like
Gene Kelly in *Singin' in the Rain*."

"My mother used to watch old movies at night after I
went to bed," Cassie said. "She was crazy about Jimmy Stewart and Cary Grant. We ate at Ernie's so she could see the
photographs of movie stars on the wall."

"My mother took me to Ernie's every time we visited
San Francisco. She made me wear a shirt and tie and taught
me how to eat escargots. I fell in love with the little girls
who came to dinner with their parents. They had their hair
in pigtails and wore white socks and shiny leather shoes. Even
as a kid I knew California girls were beautiful, so tan and
freckled from the sun."

"I thought boys were icky as snails," Cassie replied as
they reached the top of Lombard Street. "I was only interested in Cabbage Patch Kids. I believed they were born in
real gardens."

"The tourist guide says you have to run all the way down
Lombard Street without stopping." James stood looking out
at the bay. The street rolled out crazily below them, small
clumps of grass growing between the cobblestones.

"It's pretty steep," Cassie replied nervously.

"It's Ferris Bueller Day, we have to take chances." James grabbed her hand. "Pretend we're seventeen."

"No bad knees, sore ankles, or cheating husbands?" Cassie giggled.

"You need to laugh more often." James kissed her on the forehead. "First one to the bottom gets to choose where we have lunch."

"I'm going to win." Cassie tightened her sandal straps. "Because we are not eating at McDonald's."

They ran side by side down the cobblestones. Cassie almost tripped and had to stop and adjust her shoes. She watched carloads of tourists climb the hill. She saw James ahead of her, waving his arms like a schoolboy, and felt almost happy. She started running again and reached the bottom breathing hard, her hair flying behind her.

"I won." James grinned.

"I had a wardrobe malfunction." Cassie frowned. "It's impossible to run in Tory Burch sandals."

"No excuses." James grabbed her hand. "Let's go to Pier 39 and eat candy floss and ride the bumper cars, then we'll have lunch."

They milled around Fisherman's Wharf, feeding each other cotton candy, buying souvenir key chains with pictures of the Golden Gate Bridge. They took pictures in the photo booth and rammed into each other with bumper cars. They listened to a musician play the guitar and watched a juggler on stilts keep a dozen balls in the air.

"Do you miss Emily?" Cassie asked. They sat on the balcony at McCormick & Kuletto's, eating bowls of clam chowder and crusts of sourdough bread. The fog crept in and Cassie felt suddenly cold. She was still wearing the thin cotton dress she put on yesterday morning.

James put his spoon down and looked at her earnestly. "I miss having someone to share things with. I miss the way Emily fixed a daiquiri. But I can't miss someone who lied to me. Marriage is about two people against the world. I'm lucky I got out early."

"I wish I could forget Aidan." Cassie gulped down the hot soup. She immediately regretted saying his name; it tainted the air like spoiled fish. But he was always hovering before her. She felt like she acted to win his approval, to show him she could survive without him.

"You don't need to forget." James shook his head. "You need to be loved."

"That's why I shouldn't go out in public." Cassie wiped her eyes, trying to smile. "I still get emotional, like someone who's pregnant and sees a kitten."

"Excuse me, please." An old Japanese woman wearing a bright red shirt and wide-brimmed hat approached their table. "Can you take picture, please?" She pointed to the adjoining table. A man wearing a Giants baseball cap put down his spoon and nodded shyly.

James hopped up and snapped photos of the couple. The old man put his arm around his wife and they showed yellowed teeth for the camera.

"Anniversary, forty years." The woman took back her camera. "I take one of you to say thank you." She motioned for Cassie and James to sit together. James handed her his iPhone and the woman clicked and studied the picture. "Very pretty girlfriend." She handed the phone back to James. "You ask her and she say yes. You lucky, you get forty years."

"I think we should leave," Cassie said awkwardly when the woman returned to her table. Suddenly she wondered what she was doing, having sex with James, holding hands, and running around the city like a schoolgirl.

"Cassie." James reached across the table and squeezed her hand. "You can't chicken out. It's Ferris Bueller Day and we have half a day left."

"Maybe I should go home. I haven't even changed my clothes." Cassie stood up.

"You pick the next place we go, your favorite spot in the city." James brushed her hair from her face.

Cassie turned to leave. The old couple bowed and waved cheerfully. "Okay," she said. "But first I need to buy a sweatshirt. I'm freezing."

They caught the bus to Golden Gate Park. Cassie leaned against James, trying to regain her sense of happiness. She closed her eyes and tried to erase the images of Aidan that floated in her head: Aidan wearing socks and an apron in the kitchen; Aidan standing in a towel, shaking his hair after a shower; Aidan sitting by the fireplace sorting through CDs.

Cassie imagined eating ice cream with Alexis and sharing Chinese takeout with James. She pictured Gregory's giant murals on the wall of the emporium and Axel's gorgeous bouquets that greeted her when she went to work. If she could fill her brain with things that made her happy, the pictures of Aidan might fade.

"My mother and I used to come here every Sunday," Cassie said as they entered the Botanical Garden. It was like walking into a Matisse painting. Flowers and plants created a kaleidoscope of colors. A white pagoda had a line of tourists waiting to get in, and green signs explained the names and origins of flowers.

"Fenton's was closed on Sundays and my mother thought outdoor exercise was very important. I think this is where I fell in love with gardens. I was like Alice in Wonderland after she fell down the rabbit hole. I used to talk to the flowers."

James took her hand and they walked around the park, trying to pronounce the Latin names of their favorite plants. They bought a box of caramel corn from a street vendor and sat on a wooden bench.

"It's hard being an only child," James said out of the blue. "Your parents' expectations land squarely on your shoulders."

"What do you mean?" Cassie ate a handful of caramel corn.

"I only had two career choices that made my parents happy: architect or attorney. You only had one."

"I like working at Fenton's," Cassie said coldly. "The emporium is important to me."

"Your eyes light up when you talk about gardens. You're like a child on Christmas morning."

"My mother has spent her life building Fenton's," Cassie mumbled.

"It doesn't mean you have to make it your life."

"That's what Aidan used to say." Cassie pulled away from James.

"I just think you should give it some thought." James put his arm around Cassie. "Like your fortune cookie said: plant a small seed of happiness and it will grow."

"I can't live my life based on a fortune cookie," Cassie retorted, grabbing another handful of caramel corn.

"You can't run away from happiness, it will find you," James replied.

"More fortune cookies, or the back of *Mad* magazine?"

"That's an original." James turned and touched her cheek. "It's my way of saying I'm falling in love with you."

"James." Cassie blushed, spilling the caramel corn on the ground.

"I'm a sucker for love, but this isn't new, Cassie." James tucked her hair behind her ear. "I thought you were gorgeous the night you walked into Boulevard. You're like a fawn, you just seem untouched."

"You're leaving for Chicago." Cassie stumbled on her words. "It's too soon. I'm not even divorced."

"I've been thinking a lot about this," James said seriously, lacing his fingers through hers. "Why don't you come to Chicago with me? I have a nice one bedroom downtown. You could figure out what you want to do. Maybe open an organic food store, nothing over the top, just a corner store with produce from your own garden."

"James." Cassie shook her head.

"We could stay on my grandparents' farm for a while. You could plant a vegetable garden. I want to be together, Cassie."

"We've been together one day!" Cassie objected. "We don't know each other."

"You're beautiful and smart and care about other people more than yourself. You eat peas with a fork, and you put salt on French fries." James put his hand under her dress. "And I know how to make you come."

Cassie felt his fingers rub against her panties. She closed her eyes and tried to surrender to the luxurious warmth of his touch. She heard tourists walk by; a boy asked his mother for ice cream. She opened her eyes and pushed his hand away.

"Not here," she whispered.

"Let's go home." James pulled her up and led her out of the park.

Cassie and James took the bus to James's apartment and ran upstairs. They took their clothes off standing up and he entered her as they hit the bed. Cassie came so quickly she had to catch her breath. She hung on to him, panting, waiting for the shudders to subside. James pulled her arms over her head and pushed harder, clasping her hands tightly, until they came together and rolled on the bed, soaked in sweat.

James rose naked and walked to the kitchen to get glasses of ice water. He came back into the bedroom and stood by the window.

"People in the street can probably see you." Cassie sat against the pillows. Her cheeks were flushed and her hair was tangled.

"Cassie." James sat on the bed and handed Cassie a glass of water. He traced the outline of her nipples with his fingers. "Come with me."

Cassie drank her water and watched the sky turn pink outside the window. The fog had gone out past the Golden Gate Bridge and the sunset was a muted palette of colors.

"I can't abandon my mother or the emporium." Cassie shook her head. "I promised I'd watch over Isabel this summer."

"I told you I know you." He placed his glass on the bedside table. "You put others first."

"We could try long distance?" Cassie looked at James's damp hair curling over his forehead. She studied the lean muscles on his arms and the blond hair on his legs.

"Long distance didn't work for me." James shrugged. "I

want to grow with someone. I want to design a house in the suburbs and have four kids and a golden retriever."

"I should go." Cassie got up and grabbed her dress from the floor.

"You could stay the night. Go to work from here in the morning."

Cassie slipped on her dress and zipped up the back. Her neck was still damp and she smelled like sex. "It's street cleaning tonight. I'd have to move my car anyway. It's better if I leave now."

James followed her to the front door. They stood on the landing, listening to the sounds of people coming home from work. James brushed her hair behind her ears and kissed her slowly on the mouth.

"The invitation stands."

Cassie ran down the stairs, crossed the street, and got into her car.

19.

W here have you been?" Alexis demanded as Cassie crept into the house. "I got two texts in twenty-four hours. Did you have to sleep with the landlord to get an apartment?" Alexis sat in the living room brushing Poodles with a small wooden brush. She had a pile of magazines beside her and a leather album on the floor. She flipped through the magazines and tore out pages.

"What are you doing?" Cassie tried to change the subject. She felt like Alexis could see through her cotton dress. Sex hung around her like a curtain. Every nerve in her body was charged with sexual frisson.

"I'm creating an album for Princess Giselle of her magazine clippings. She's concerned Victoria Beckham has more Twitter followers than she does." Alexis put Poodles in his dog basket and looked closely at Cassie. "You did sleep with someone, you're a walking George Michael song."

"I had fun." Cassie blushed. "I'm going to bed."

"I've listened to you moaning about Aidan for four months and you're not going to tell me the good stuff?" Alexis jumped up. She wore a light pink robe and pink satin slippers. Her face was scrubbed clean and her hair lay in a ponytail down her back.

"Okay, but I need a cup of coffee." Cassie walked toward the kitchen.

"You look like you need a cold shower." Alexis followed her. "I'll make the coffee. Start from the beginning. No censoring, I want to hear everything."

"I slept with James," Cassie said after Alexis handed her a porcelain coffee cup.

"James?" Alexis looked up from the peanut butter and jelly sandwich she was making. "You didn't tell me you were seeing him."

"I ran into him by accident." Cassie stirred sugar into her coffee. "My real estate agent was showing me apartments and she showed me his apartment. It's in Cow Hollow, with a lovely view of the bay."

"You fucked him to get his apartment?" Alexis bit into the sandwich, jelly oozing out of the crusts. "I told you, you could stay here. Carter likes a house full of guests. It makes him feel like one of those British lords on a BBC miniseries."

"I stayed in the apartment to get a feel for the light and James just walked in." Cassie grinned, remembering his face when he saw her. "Carrying Chinese takeout and a stack of *Mad* magazines."

"Not exactly caviar and roses." Alexis poured herself a glass of milk.

"He didn't know I was there," Cassie protested. "He's a take-out junkie. He can't cook."

"Every guy has an Achilles' heel, you can live with that. What happened next?"

"We ate in his kitchen and then we took our fortune

cookies and ice cream into the living room. He read mine and I read his." Cassie sipped her coffee. "I spilled ice cream on the floor and while I was cleaning it up we sort of . . ."

"Sort of what? This is better than *The Bachelorette*." Alexis spread peanut butter on another slice of bread.

"Sort of ended up in the bedroom, in bed, making love."

"Was he good?"

"Alexis!" Cassie's cheeks turned red.

"You're thirty-two and you've been out of the dating market for ten years. Performance counts," Alexis said matter-of-factly. "You don't want to date a dud."

"We're not dating," Cassie replied.

"So he was a dud. Pity, I still think he looks like Hugh Grant. If he had a British accent I couldn't resist him."

"He was wonderful. He's sweet and funny and we had so much fun. We pulled a Ferris Bueller today."

Alexis stared at Cassie as if she was brain damaged. "*Ferris Bueller* as in the movie with Matthew Broderick and Charlie Sheen when they were seventeen?"

"I called in sick and we spent the day exploring the city. We rode cable cars and walked through Golden Gate Park and ate clam chowder at Fisherman's Wharf. Then we went back to his apartment and made love again."

Alexis put her sandwich on her plate and looked at Cassie carefully. "You have that 'that was the best sex I ever had and I'm reliving it as I tell you' look. What's the problem?"

"James said he's falling in love with me. He asked me to move to Chicago with him."

"There are some good songs about Chicago, it must be a great town."

"Very funny." Cassie stood up and walked to the fridge.

Her muscles ached and her throat felt dry. She took out a pitcher of lemonade and filled a glass with ice.

"I knew he was in love with you." Alexis nodded wisely. "He was practically carrying a sign."

"I said no." Cassie poured a glass of lemonade.

"Did you take time to think about it?" Alexis dunked her sandwich in a glass of milk.

"There's nothing to think about." Cassie sat at the table. "I can't just pick up and move."

"You were about to move," Alexis replied. "You were apartment hunting."

"In San Francisco! I can't abandon the emporium even if I wanted to be with James."

"Do you want to be with him?" Alexis clasped her hands together and leaned her elbows on the table.

"You're not Dr. Phil." Cassie frowned. "He's lovely to be around. But I can't leave my mother and the emporium. I promised to keep an eye on Isabel this summer."

"If you didn't have those commitments, would you go?" Alexis prodded.

"I do have them!" Cassie stood up and paced around the room. "I can't add quitter to my résumé."

"Cassie, no one would call you a quitter. You've launched the emporium. It's wonderfully stocked; you've created great relationships with the suppliers. Someone could take it over."

"My mother has been waiting for me to join Fenton's since I was six years old."

"Your mother wants you to be happy," Alexis said.

"She tried to set me up with a millionaire playboy." Cassie grinned. "She doesn't want me to be an old maid. It would be bad for her image."

"Then she'd approve." Alexis nodded. "She loves James. I think she has a secret crush on him."

"It's too soon." Cassie shook her head. "I don't know how I really feel about him. I'm not going to pick up and move cross-country. What if he sings in the shower, or puts Tabasco on his eggs?"

"Carter sings in the shower," Alexis mused. "He actually sounds a lot like Sting."

"I think I should spend some time alone. Get my own apartment, work at Fenton's, keep my feet on the ground."

Alexis drummed her nails on the table. "You don't want to end up a member of the Spinsters. They are the cattiest women at social functions."

"I'm not going to be a Spinster." Cassie giggled. "Maybe I'll join one of your book clubs or take cooking classes at night. I've always wanted to learn how to make a soufflé."

"You can't make love with a soufflé." Alexis ate the last bite of bread and washed it down with milk.

"Life isn't sex and shopping," Cassie retorted.

"It is about trying to be happy," Alexis said slowly.

"I don't need a man to make me happy. Aidan made me unhappy. Aidan broke my heart." Cassie drained her glass. Suddenly she felt tired. She wanted to climb in bed, pull the comforter over her head, and sleep.

"Don't run away from the possibility of happiness." Alexis swept breadcrumbs from her lap.

"You and the fortune cookies!" Cassie pushed her chair back. "I don't need any more advice, I'm going to bed."

When Cassie came down to breakfast the next morning, Alexis was already at work. She left an invitation to a cocktail party Princess Giselle was hosting to save the baby whales.

"Since when has Princess Giselle had an interest in whales?" Cassie called Alexis on the phone. She propped the phone under her ear and stirred a pot of oatmeal on the stove.

Cassie woke up feeling guilty for snapping at Alexis. She remembered how Alexis took her in when she appeared at her door, sopping wet and burning up with fever. Alexis allowed her to stay for months, encouraged her to swim in her pool and sit in her steam room. She listened to Cassie and never criticized Aidan until the marriage was truly over.

Cassie spooned the oatmeal into a bowl and thought about James. She missed his smile, and the easy way he carried himself. She pictured him leaning out of the cable car, crooning a verse of "I Left My Heart in San Francisco," and giggled. He seemed to enjoy himself and it was contagious. She felt lighter when she was with him, like a college coed.

"Whales swim under the Golden Gate Bridge and they get stuck in the bay," Alexis explained. "Boats have to turn them around and lead them back out to sea. It's a real problem."

"It sounds like a noble cause." Cassie looked out the window. She knew she should go to work. She had dressed in her favorite Pucci dress and sling-back sandals and brushed her hair back with an enamel clip. She wanted to be excited about going into Fenton's, about driving through the city on a warm summer day. But sitting by herself in Alexis's kitchen, thinking about Aidan and James and her mother, she was tempted to lock herself in Alexis's entertainment room and watch *The Wedding Planner* and *The Proposal*.

"Giselle has cultivated some of the city's more eligible bachelors," Alexis replied. "You should come."

"I don't want to meet men." Cassie sighed.

"If you're not going to Chicago with James, it doesn't hurt

to show your face. Fenton's is catering it. You'll be supporting your own store."

"I'll think about it, if I don't have to wash my hair that night." Cassie added milk to the oatmeal. She poured in brown sugar and added sliced strawberries.

"Where are you? I've been here for hours. Karen Caulfield just bought out the Chanel boutique. Her husband is the venture capital king. Carter used to have his poster on the wall in college. We should have lunch and celebrate."

"I'll be in soon." Cassie stirred the oatmeal. It smelled delicious, like vanilla and berries, but she couldn't make herself take a bite.

"You can't sit at home and watch old movies," Alexis admonished her.

"How did you know?" Cassie laughed.

"I've known you since kindergarten," Alexis replied. "Come to work and I'll buy you a vanilla custard, with whipped cream."

"Okay." Cassie put the milk in the fridge and took the bowl to the sink. "I'm coming."

"Good girl." Alexis smiled. "I'll be waiting."

Cassie discovered a huge bouquet of flowers on her desk at the emporium. There were a dozen pink roses, puffs of baby's breath, several graceful water lilies, and clusters of pink and white chrysanthemums in one of Axel's signature crystal vases. The card read simply: "Keep talking to the flowers."

"Wow, you must be good in bed." Alexis whistled. "I only get arrangements like that if I perform certain acts I studied in *The Tao of Sex*."

"They smell lovely." Cassie walked around the desk.

"You look as pale as one of those actors in the *Twilight*

movies." Alexis studied her critically. "Are you sure you don't want to race to the airport, meet James at the gate, and fly off into the sunset?"

"No." Cassie giggled.

"I've always wanted to do that." Alexis picked a rosebud and slipped it in her hair. "It looks so cool in movies. Let's have lunch and I'll distract you with details about Giselle's party. It's Friday night and it's going to have an ocean theme. There are going to be goldfish in goldfish bowls on the tables and women are asked to wear blue."

"I hope you're not serving salmon." Cassie laughed, following Alexis onto the escalator.

"A gorgeous Valentino just came in that would fit you perfectly: turquoise silk with a lace slip. I'll bring it down so you can see it."

"I didn't say I was coming." Cassie shook her head.

"You didn't say you weren't." Alexis got off the escalator and waited at the café to be seated.

After lunch, Cassie began to feel better. The emporium was busy and customers stopped her to tell her how delighted they were with the produce selection.

"I can't get such sweet heirloom tomatoes anywhere else in the city," a perfectly coiffed brunette cooed, carrying her Princess bag to the escalator. "You've made shopping fun. And I love the cooking demonstrations. I wanted to take Andre Blick home." Her laugh tinkled like a dinner bell. "But my husband wouldn't approve."

Cassie worked straight through until five o'clock, talking to suppliers, making sure every counter was stocked with fresh merchandise. She spent an hour creating a display of picnic foods: bunches of grapes, pots of Brie, stone wheat crackers, and loaves of French bread. She arranged them on a round table with a picnic basket and a checkered table-cloth. She found herself glancing at the escalator, half expecting to see James, his hands shoved in his pockets, coming to see her.

Her cell phone rang as she was studying projections for June and July. The graphs were rising steadily higher. A selection of pre-made entrées packaged in Fenton's signature red boxes was flying out the door. Cassie had begun a home delivery service that was popular with women who couldn't fit food shopping into their social calendars. She and Alexis invented a smoothie made of organic blueberries, raspberries, and vanilla milk and named it the Fenton's Fizz.

"Did you get my flowers?"

Cassie smiled at the sound of James's voice. "They take up half the desk, but they are beautiful."

"I had a great time, Cassie."

"So did I." Cassie plucked a sprig of baby's breath.

"I'm leaving on Saturday. I wanted to see if you changed your mind about my invitation?"

Cassie looked around the room teeming with shoppers. "I'm sorry, James. I've had too much change. If we could take it slowly . . ."

"I'm sorry, Cassie. I can't do long distance." He paused. "I talked to my landlord. If you want the apartment, it's yours. I'll leave the rugs and the sketch of the Bay Bridge."

Cassie smiled. "I think I will take it, it gets beautiful light."

"Would you like to go to dinner Friday?" James asked.

Cassie took out a long-stemmed rose and laid it on the desk next to the baby's breath.

"I don't think that would be a good idea."

"I don't want you to remember me eating Chinese and McDonald's. I want to take you somewhere fantastic: Michael Mina's or Fleur de Lys. We can go dancing in the Starlight Room. It's my last night."

Cassie saw Alexis getting off the escalator carrying a blue silk dress. "I have plans Friday night, James. I'm sorry."

20.

Cassie rode the glass elevator to Princess Giselle's penthouse, nervously clutching her evening bag. She hadn't wanted to go to the cocktail party but Alexis had insisted earlier that evening.

"Carter is coming home next week and you're moving to your apartment, where you'll spend the rest of your life drinking hot cocoa and talking to your cat." Alexis knocked on Cassie's door on Friday evening.

"I don't have a cat." Cassie sat by the window flipping through an issue of *Architectural Digest*.

"Since when did you become interested in interior design?" Alexis picked up the magazine suspiciously.

"There's an article about Emerald." Cassie blushed.

"You need distraction!" Alexis threw the magazine on the bed. "It will be our last girls' night. I hung the Valentino in your closet. Come look at it, Cassie, it's orgasmic."

The Valentino was Italian silk with a cutout back and antique ivory buttons. Alexis had paired it with delicate Miu Miu sandals and a matching turquoise evening bag.

"It is gorgeous." Cassie touched the silky fabric.

"You can't be in the same room as that dress and not want to show it off. It's *un*-American. Let's go Cinderella, I promise I'll get you home by midnight."

Princess Giselle's apartment took up the entire fortieth floor of the St. Regis. Cassie had read about it in magazines. It had 360-degree views of the city and two thousand square feet of patios. The floor-to-ceiling windows made you feel as if you were standing in the clouds. The bay glittered in the distance and the whole city lay at your feet like a board game.

"Whatever you've read, be prepared for something better," Alexis said as they waited for the elevator doors to open. Alexis wore an aquamarine lamé minidress and gold sandals. Her hair was curled into a bun and secured with a diamond chopstick. Her lips were painted pale pink and she wore no jewelry except for diamond earrings. "Giselle has added her personal touch to the furnishings. It's a cross between Louis XIV and Andy Warhol. You're going to love it."

The living room was buzzing with women wearing silk cocktail dresses and metallic sandals. Men sporting Italian blazers and suede loafers gathered at the bar that stretched across one wall. The floors were polished wood and the ceilings were so high Cassie had to crane her neck to admire the chandeliers. Signed Andy Warhol prints of Marilyn Monroe hung on the walls, and a twelve-foot gilt mirror stood by the window.

"I didn't know people lived like this." Cassie didn't know where to turn. There were leather conversation pits and clusters of sofas covered in ivory velvet. Giant palm trees divided the room and bookshelves were lined with first editions. A glass coffee table held gold chess pieces and there was an original Rodin statue in the corner.

"Giselle says the whole apartment could fit into a wing of her palace in Liechtenstein. But the interior is nothing compared to the view." Alexis walked to the sliding glass doors.

Cassie followed her outside and caught her breath. The sun was setting and the sky looked like it had been sprinkled with confetti. The hills were pieces on a game of Chutes and Ladders. The mansions in Presidio Heights were figures on a Monopoly board.

Cassie could see the dome of Grace Cathedral and the narrow streets of North Beach. They were so high up, it was as if someone had pushed the mute button. The honking cars, the people chattering on cell phones were silent.

"This is why the rest of the country hates us." Alexis stood at the railing. "San Francisco has the most amazing view and California weather. You don't get this in Chicago."

"I'm fine, Alexis." Cassie smiled. She leaned on the balcony, watching the lights turn on below her. She could see the flags waving at the Mark Hopkins and the department stores clustered around Union Square.

"There are a few people I'd like you to meet. Greg Pruitt is here. He was *San Francisco* magazine's May cover boy. He's a partner in a venture capital firm and gives half what he earns to charity."

"I'll stay away from young philanthropists for now." Cassie shook her head. "But I am hungry." She realized she hadn't eaten since lunch and the view was suddenly making her dizzy.

"Let's go inside." Alexis walked across the patio. "Giselle ordered the jumbo prawns and the steak tartare. I don't know where you get the cherry tomatoes but they are sweet as candy. And the avocado salad is to die for."

As they entered the living room, a woman wearing a

pale blue dress fitted like a Grecian column called to Alexis. "I must introduce you to my cousin, Chantal. She just arrived from Paris and is all alone. I told her you speak perfect French and know the city."

Alexis squeezed Cassie's hand. "I smell an American Express card, I'll be right back."

Cassie stood alone at the bar, picking at a bowl of pistachios. Her dress felt too tight and her feet hurt. She debated ordering a glass of champagne but she was afraid it would give her a headache.

"Can I get you a drink?" A man stood beside her. He had dark curly hair and green eyes. He wore a white shirt, dark brown slacks, and a thick gold chain around his neck.

"I don't think so, I haven't eaten yet."

"A beautiful woman should not be without a drink in her hand." He flagged down the bartender. "It is like looking at an unfinished Renoir."

Cassie accepted the glass of champagne and took a sip.

"My name is Jorge. I am a friend of Giselle's from Marbella." The man extended his hand. His hands were tan and he had a gold ring on his little finger.

"I thought Giselle was from Liechtenstein." Cassie frowned.

"Europe is a small place, we all know each other." Jorge shrugged. "And we get bored of the same faces. Giselle was smart to come to America. I like California very much, especially the women." He moved closer to Cassie.

"I'm happy to hear that," Cassie replied uncomfortably. She moved along the bar but Jorge followed her.

"Perhaps you can show me the rest of the apartment? The living room is so exquisite, I can only imagine the bedroom." He put his hand on Cassie's.

"I'm sorry." Cassie blushed and took her hand away. "I'm waiting for someone."

"I'm sure whoever it is will wait for such a beautiful woman." He draped his arm over her shoulder. "We won't be too long."

Cassie pulled away and hurried across the room. She tried to catch Alexis's eye, but she was talking animatedly with two elegantly dressed women. Cassie sat down in one of the conversation pits and lay back against the cushions.

"Can I get you a drink?"

Cassie jumped, thinking Jorge had followed her. She turned and saw James, wearing a blue linen shirt and white pants. His hair was brushed over his forehead and his cheeks were smooth as if he had just shaved.

"What are you doing here?" Cassie stood up.

"Alexis invited me. Don't throw me out; this place is the Taj Mahal. They should charge admission." James grinned.

"I was thinking of leaving myself, but Alexis is wooing international clients." Cassie sat down on the leather love seat.

"You look gorgeous." James sat on the armchair opposite her.

"I was just propositioned by a Spanish playboy. He wanted me to show him the bedroom. He didn't think it would take long." Cassie tried to laugh. "Not a very promising pick-up line."

"I hope you said no." James smiled like a schoolboy.

"I ran away. If he looks for me, you'll have to hide me."

"Actually, I have something to tell you." James ran his hands through his hair. "Why don't I get a couple of drinks and we go outside?"

* * *

Cassie followed James onto the balcony. It was dark and the sky was lit up with stars. Cassie felt a breeze blow up from the bay and stood under one of the outdoor heat lamps.

"I've missed you." James handed her a glass of white wine.

"I missed you too." Cassie blushed. She turned away and sat on one of the long white sofas that littered the patio.

"You can't run away from me." James sat next to her. "Unless you jump. It's a long way down."

"We said good-bye." Cassie studied her wineglass. "I don't want to make it harder for either of us."

"I'm glad you're taking the apartment," James said slowly. "It already feels like you're there. It's not as lonely."

"What did you want to tell me?" Cassie felt James's thigh against hers. She smelled his aftershave and saw his heart beat in his chest.

"I got a really exciting offer." James put his wineglass on the coffee table. "A consortium bought an old castle outside of Florence and turned it into a boutique hotel. It's in the hills overlooking the Arno, surrounded by gardens. They want to turn part of it into a cooking school. They would invite chefs from all over the world and attract a high-end clientele." James paused and turned to Cassie. "They want me to design it."

Cassie froze. She tried to make her mouth form a smile. She imagined James in Tuscany, surrounded by vineyards and olive orchards. She pictured him working in a castle, his sleeves rolled up, his glasses perched on his nose.

"I've seen pictures of the castle." James's eyes sparkled. "All the guest rooms face the river and there is a weeping willow in the garden. The interior has been painstakingly refurbished. The salons have stone fireplaces and original molding. The cooking school will open onto a brick patio and guests will be able to sit and enjoy what they cooked."

"What about your projects in Chicago?" Cassie asked finally.

"The firm will assign them to another junior partner. This is a big deal, Cassie. It will be written up in magazines. It means other international jobs." He squeezed her hand.

"It sounds very exciting." Cassie nodded, gulping her wine. "When do you leave?"

"They want me to start in two weeks. The project will probably take four months." James grinned. "I'm still pinching myself, I feel like Michelangelo."

"You deserve it." Cassie tried to stop the tears that welled up in her eyes. "Your designs are fantastic."

"There's one more thing." James held her hand tightly. "They want to grow an organic vegetable garden on the property. The cooking school will use only their own fruits and vegetables, like Alice Waters and her Edible Schoolyard."

"That's interesting."

"Somehow they heard your name and they want you to develop it."

"They want me to do what?" Cassie replied stupidly.

"They want you to oversee the vegetable garden."

"Did you give them my name?" Cassie jumped up and walked over to the heat lamp. She felt chilled and couldn't stop shivering.

"Of course not." James shook his head. "They were going to call and discuss the position but I wanted to talk to you first. Fenton's has a tremendous reputation. It could have been one of your clients or Alice Waters." James shrugged. "They are keen to have you."

"That's flattering." Cassie warmed her hands, trying to stop shaking.

"Will you come? It's only for four months." James stood close to her.

"I can't leave the store." Cassie shook her head.

"Your mother would love it!" James protested. "Think of the exposure for Fenton's. You'd build an international reputation."

"I just signed the lease on your apartment." Cassie could feel James's breath on her neck.

"My mother has been dying to rent a little pied-à-terre in San Francisco." James put his hand on her back. "She'd jump at it."

Cassie walked over to the railing. She watched the lights of Oakland and Berkeley twinkling on the other side of the bay. She saw an airplane drift in and out of the clouds. She felt James put his arm around her. He turned her face to his and kissed her softly on the mouth.

"I'm going to kiss you until you run out of excuses." He grinned, releasing her.

"Italy has terrible Chinese food and hardly any McDonald's." Cassie rested her head on his shoulder.

"Then you're going to have to teach me how to cook," James replied.

"I speak very little Italian." Cassie frowned.

"We'll learn together. I learned my first words already: *ti amo*."

"What does that mean?" Cassie giggled.

James kissed her again, pushing her hair behind her ears. "It means 'I love you.'"

21.

Cassie sat at a window table at Fenton's café, sipping an espresso. She picked up a pack of sugar and then put it back on the table. Italian coffee was so bitter; she had to learn how to drink it black. She glanced at her watch. Alexis was joining her for afternoon tea but she was late.

Cassie checked her list to see if she had taken care of all her last-minute errands. She had her passport, she sent her attorney her contact information in Florence, and she left a whole notepad of instructions for the assistant manager taking over the emporium.

"I'm sorry I'm late." Alexis swooped into the café wearing a bright yellow linen dress and gold espadrilles. She kissed Cassie on the cheek and sat down opposite her, keeping on her Oliver Peoples sunglasses.

"I love the dress and the sunglasses. You look like Katharine Hepburn in *Philadelphia Story*." Cassie put down the espresso cup and blotted her lips with a napkin.

"Haven't seen that one." Alexis put her napkin in her lap. "Your mother was right. Yellow is *the* color of the summer.

I'm seeing it everywhere." Alexis took off her sunglasses and studied Cassie. "You already look European. I love your hair and that dress is perfect on you."

Cassie blushed. She had moved out of Alexis's house and was staying with her mother until her departure. Diana insisted Cassie visit her stylist and get a more continental hairstyle. Her hair fell to her neck in long smooth layers, and she had wispy bangs covering her forehead. Diana also brought home Fenton's boxes of dresses and skirts, sweaters, cigarette pants, and short bolero jackets.

"Mother, I don't need shoes." Cassie had opened a box of suede Tod's loafers, Gucci pumps, and Manolo sandals. "I'm going to Italy."

"You're representing Fenton's." Diana walked in circles around the pile of boxes in the guest bedroom. "You need to dress like a young sophisticate, not an American schoolgirl."

"I have more clothes than Grace Kelly when she departed for Monaco to marry Prince Rainier." Cassie fingered a black cocktail dress and a lace sundress with spaghetti straps.

"I'm very proud of you." Diana tapped her cigarette holder on the mahogany desk. She wore a yellow silk top and harem pants cinched with a red ostrich belt. "This is a huge undertaking. Alice was tickled when I told her. She credits your success with the years you spent volunteering in her garden."

"I still feel bad about leaving the emporium," Cassie replied nervously.

"Nonsense." Diana clicked her tongue. "It hums like a machine. Vanessa Getty was on the cover of *W* this month, eating a Fenton's heirloom tomato and holding a Princess bag."

"Maybe you can visit us." Cassie studied her mother's

face. Her skin looked pale in the afternoon light and there were new spidery wrinkles around her mouth.

"Italy in the fall?" Diana mused. "It would be wonderful to visit the Vatican and meet some designers in Milan. If Fenton's isn't too busy, I'll think about it."

"James would love to see you." Cassie smiled. "He's afraid he won't work fast enough without you whipping him into shape."

"James is a fine young man." Diana walked over to the door. "He reminds me of your father; that thin athletic build. I'm going to have Maria prepare some dishes you can take with you. You don't want to eat in restaurants every night."

"I know how to cook, Mother." Cassie grinned. "And I'm going to teach James."

"I suppose it would be tricky to get them through customs." Diana frowned. "I'll have her write up the recipes."

"Your mother is going to miss you." Alexis signaled to the waiter. "It's her way of showing you. I have something to tell you." She smiled like a Cheshire cat and covered her face with the menu.

"You're having a baby?" Cassie leaned forward.

"Carter's only been home a week." Alexis shrugged after she placed her order. "Hermès approved the mini boutique in Fenton's. I'm going to be surrounded by Birkins!"

"What a coup." Cassie smiled. "My mother has wanted a Hermès boutique for decades. She'll be thrilled."

"I was just in her office. We're going to Emerald to celebrate. We'll probably sit around talking about you." Alexis grinned.

"Have you told Carter about Fenton's?" Cassie nibbled a slice of German chocolate cake.

"I told him the day he landed." Alexis scooped whipped cream with her fork. "I decided you can't have lies in a marriage, even if they're lily white."

"How did he take it?" Cassie ate another bite of cake.

"At first he was furious, but he started reading blogs that said I am one of San Francisco's most powerful women under forty. He saw my Facebook fan page and how many followers I have on Twitter. *San Francisco* magazine is doing its cover story on us next month: San Francisco's new *it* couple. He's so happy he can't get enough of me. We have sex all night; I can hardly walk in the morning. He promised me a baby."

"Really!" Cassie's eyes sparkled.

"A baby Birkin. The latest model: twenty-five-inch, ostrich skin, twenty-four-karat gold hardware. He's going to pull some strings so we jump ahead on the wait list."

"Who said a girl can't have everything?" Cassie sipped her espresso.

"Have you talked to Aidan?" Alexis took a bite of chocolate cake.

"I called him and told him I would be out of the country for four months." Cassie shrugged. "The divorce should be final when I get back. He thanked me for letting Isabel work at Fenton's."

"Isabel has amazing fashion sense for a teenager." Alexis nodded. "I'm thinking of adding some lines by young designers, like Ashley Olsen. And she's a very hard worker. I'm going to offer her the position part-time in the fall."

"I did a little research on the consortium that owns the castle," Cassie said slowly, looking directly at Alexis. "A familiar name appeared: Princess Giselle."

"Giselle may have suggested your name for the position

but the board had to vote." Alexis didn't blink. "You've put Fenton's on the map in the food world." She paused and finished her coffee. "You're not angry, are you?"

"Angry that I get paid to spend four months in Tuscany creating a vegetable garden and living in a castle with James?" Cassie grinned. "But what happened to being completely honest?"

"Not telling you something doesn't constitute as lying," Alexis replied innocently.

"I'm going to miss you." Cassie smiled, looking out the window at the tourists milling around Union Square.

"While you're zipping through the hills of Tuscany on the back of a Vespa? You'll be back before you know it." Alexis pushed the chocolate cake away and fiddled with the pearl choker around her neck. "You know what would be great?"

"What?" Cassie asked.

"If in a year from now we are sitting here pregnant. We could wear Gwyneth Paltrow's new line of maternity dresses and shop for Bugaboos and those darling onesies by Petit Bateau."

"James and I aren't even married," Cassie protested.

"He'll pop the question the minute you're free." Alexis shrugged. "He's like the prince in the fairy tales we read when we were children. He finally found his fair maiden."

Cassie put down her fork and looked out the window. She saw couples walking arm in arm, peering into department store windows. She watched women pushing strollers and balancing cups of coffee. She saw a mother hold a little boy's hand as they crossed the street.

She turned to Alexis and smiled. "Yes, it would be great."

Acknowledgments

I am thrilled and grateful to work with such a stellar team. Melissa Flashman is the smartest agent any author could wish for. My brilliant editor at St. Martin's Press, Hilary Teeman, her assistant, Sarah Jae-Jones, and Audrey Campbell, my wonderful publicist, have made getting this novel out there a dream. Thank you also to Jennifer Weis and Mollie Traver, and to Elsie Lyons for her beautiful cover design.

A special thank-you to my dear friends who share the Southern California sunshine: Kristina and Larry Dodge, Jerry Rubenstein, Karla DeLovio, Toni Stein, Jessica Edward, Cathie Lawler, and Darla Magana.

And a huge thank-you to my amazing family: my husband, Thomas, and my children Alex, Andrew, Heather, Madeleine, and Thomas.

1. After Aidan tells Cassie that Molly seduced him, Cassie decides to give their marriage another chance. Do you agree with her decision? Is a one-night stand different from an affair, or would you react the same in both situations?

2. Alexis defends her love of sex and shopping by saying that girls need to have fun. Do you agree with her, or do you think she is compensating for things missing in her marriage?

3. Alexis seems to have it all—money, a beautiful house, a successful husband—but she is still searching for something that fulfills her. Should she be happy with her life as it is, or do you understand her need to work outside of the home?

4. Cassie is hesitant to manage the food emporium at Fenton's because she doesn't think Aidan would approve. Do you think she puts too much value on Aidan's feelings, or is compromise an important aspect of a marriage?

5. While Cassie is staying with Alexis, Aidan comes to visit and Cassie realizes she can't trust him. Is that attitude self-defeating? If she is going to give the marriage another chance, should she trust him or is she correct to have reservations?

6. Do you think Alexis and Carter's marriage is kept fresh and exciting because he is constantly traveling, or do you think it creates a distance between them? Would you consider marrying a man who travels all the time?

7. Do you think Cassie is too dependent on praise from her mother? Do you think it stems from being neglected as a child, or is it just a healthy respect for a woman who has had much success creating a fabulous department store?

8. Do you think Cassie and James belong together? How would you characterize their relationship?

9. Describe the friendship between Alexis and Cassie. Does one support the other more, or are they equal?

St. Martin's
Griffin

10. Do you have any sympathy for Aidan, who is getting older and working in a field where he is surrounded by bright young people? Or is what he's done completely reprehensible?

11. How big a part does San Francisco play in the novel? Can you imagine the novel being set in any other city?

12. Alexis believes it is all right to tell little white lies in her marriage. Do you agree or disagree?

13. How do you feel about James' refusal to start another long-distance relationship? Does it make sense given his experience with Emily, or should he love Cassie enough to endure anything to be together?

TURN THE PAGE FOR A SNEAK PEEK AT
ANITA HUGHES'S NEXT NOVEL!

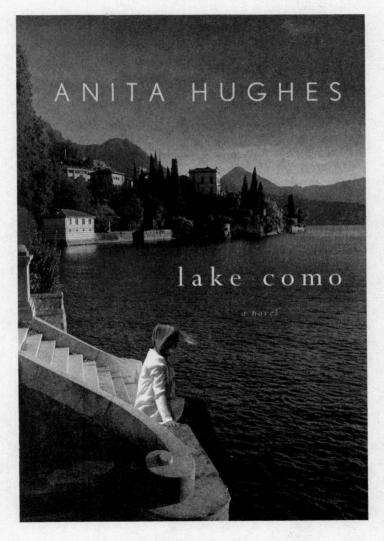

A N I T A   H U G H E S

lake como

a novel

Available Summer 2013

Hallie stood in the arrivals terminal of Milan's airport, waiting for her luggage. It seemed like days since she boarded the plane in San Francisco. Francesca had driven her to the airport, ladening her with pastries for Portia and Sophia and a selection of baby clothes for Marcus's wife, Angelica.

"Tell Marcus to call the minute the baby arrives," Francesca had said as she hugged Hallie at the security check-in. "And give Angelica lots of hugs. At least I have one child whose life isn't full of drama."

"I can't believe Marcus is going to be a father," Hallie agreed, picturing a dark-haired baby with round fists and feet. Marcus managed the Tesoro business interests in Milan, and his wife was newly pregnant.

"Tell Angelica to save the clothes for you." Francesca squeezed Hallie's hand. "In a couple of years you'll need them."

"I hope so," Hallie said, blinking away tears. She refused to let Peter take her to the airport, and he barely glanced up from his laptop when she lugged her suitcase to the door. She put her bag in her mother's Volkswagen and hugged the cake box against her chest.

Hallie watched her bag come off the carousel. Portia wanted to meet her in Milan but Hallie insisted she could get to Lake Como by herself. Suddenly she felt tired and alone. The Italian men and women resembled film stars with their glossy black hair and smooth olive skin.

Until Hallie landed in Rome, she had felt chic and sophisticated. She wore yellow Kate Spade capris with a matching hoodie and flat Tory Burch sandals. She carried a cavernous Michael Kors tote and wore white Oliver Peoples sunglasses.

But stepping off the plane in Rome, Hallie felt like a teenager crashing her first adult cocktail party. The women wore pencil-thin skirts and carried Gucci clutches. Their skin glowed as if they had emerged from a spa instead of an international flight.

Milan was worse. Hallie saw bright silk dresses that belonged on a runway and four-inch stilettos encrusted with jewels. The men wore shirts open to the waist and leather loafers without socks.

"Potrebbe aivatani con le valige?" a man asked, pointing to her suitcase.

Hallie jumped. No one had spoken to her since the flight attendant announced their arrival in Milan.

"My Italian is rusty," she apologized, shrugging her shoulders.

"Would you like help with your luggage?" the man asked in accented English. "You are too pretty to handle such a big suitcase."

Hallie blushed. The man was tall, with curly black hair

and black eyes. He had a dimple on his chin and carried a suit bag over his shoulder.

"No, thank you. I'm taking the shuttle bus to the train station."

"I will take you to the train station." The man rolled her bag toward the exit. "A shuttle bus is no place for a beautiful American."

"Really, I've done it before." Hallie ran after him. "I'm going to Lake Como to visit my half sister."

"Ah, Como," the man sighed. "A playground of miraculous beauty."

"My grandmother has a villa there," Hallie replied. "Sophia Tesoro."

"I do business with Marcus Tesoro! I manufacture silk," he said. He unzipped his bag and extracted a silk scarf with a floral design. "You must have this, it brings out the blue in your eyes."

"I can't take it." Hallie pushed the scarf into his hands.

"I insist." The man draped it around her neck. "Here is my card. I am Alfonso Diamante. I will check you are wearing it the next time I am in Como."

Hallie sat on the bus, the fine silk caressing her shoulders. She felt grimy from the long flight and unsettled by the encounter at the airport. She wasn't used to talking to dark, handsome strangers. She tore up the card and stuffed the scarf into her suitcase. She closed her eyes, wishing Peter were in the seat next to her and that she was wearing his oval diamond on her finger.

Sitting on the express train to Como, Hallie remembered why she wanted to travel alone to the villa. The scenery was so spectacular: the villages with tall church spires, the fields of brightly colored flowers, the green mountains capped with snow. Hallie didn't want to miss a minute of it by conversing with Portia.

By the time Hallie arrived in Como, her jet lag was replaced by the excitement of being on holiday. Tourists chatted in German and French. They pointed out landmarks, craning their heads as the train pulled into the station.

Hallie jumped off the train and breathed the perfumed air. She could smell jasmine and roses and oleander. The cobblestoned streets baked under the noon sun and the lake glittered like a sheet of new pennies. Hallie rolled her suitcase toward the ferry, passing cafés and gelato stands.

The black-and-white boats sat in the harbor, waiting to take passengers to villages around the lake. Hallie was going to Bellagio, one of the most popular destinations. The line was full of families licking ice-cream cones, young lovers holding hands, nannies trying to round up their charges while the parents sipped a last aperitif in the bar next to the dock.

A red speedboat pulled up to the dock and a man jumped out. He had curly black hair peppered with gray and a sharp, angular chin. His eyes were pale blue and his profile belonged on a Roman statue. He wore silk shorts and a navy shirt, and a gold cross hung around his neck. He took off his sunglasses and searched the terminal, suddenly waving at Hallie.

"Pliny?" Hallie squinted in the sun. She dragged her suitcase to the side to get a closer look. The speedboat was built like a bullet, sharp and snub nosed, and it had the Tesoro crest painted on the side.

"Sophia sent me to pick you up." Pliny made a little bow. "No guest of the Tesoros arrives in Bellagio by passenger ferry."

"You didn't have to," Hallie said, and slipped out of the line. "I like playing tourist."

"Sophia is pleased you are here." Pliny grabbed Hallie's suitcase. "She thinks you will talk some sense into Portia."

"Me?" Hallie let Pliny help her into the speedboat. Pliny started the motor and Hallie sat back against the soft leather upholstery.

"Constance told Sophia you have a good head on your shoulders," Pliny said in careful English. "I am glad you are here, too; you have grown into a beautiful woman."

"Thank you," Hallie mumbled, letting her hair cover her cheeks so Pliny wouldn't see her blush.

She glanced at Pliny curiously, trying to imagine Pliny and Francesca together. There were fines lines around his eyes and mouth, but Hallie could imagine him as the young man on the ski slope. She pictured Francesca falling in fresh powder and looking up to see an Italian prince offering her his hand.

"It is very difficult for Sophia," Pliny explained over the roar of the engine. "They are about to erect a statue of my great-grandfather in the Piazza San Giacomo. Sophia has worked on this for many years, the bishop and the cardinal have given it their blessing."

"How wonderful!" Hallie exclaimed.

"A scandal involving Portia and Riccardo could ruin everything." Pliny's eyebrows knotted together.

"It's not Portia's fault Riccardo left her," Hallie said doubtfully. She wasn't used to talking to Pliny. At Portia's wedding he had been busy toasting the bride, and on her previous visit she and Portia had been teenagers trying to stay beneath his radar.

"Italy is different from America," Pliny replied. "Men are never at fault."

"That's Victorian!" Hallie bristled.

"That is the way it is," Pliny said, and shrugged. "Sophia hopes you will convince Portia to take Riccardo back."

"Don't you want Portia to be happy?" Hallie asked.

"There are many ways to be happy," Pliny said. He guided the boat between two sailboats with bright billowing sails. "I was devastated when your mother left. But my children made me happy: my home, Bellagio, Italy."

"I'm sure Portia will make the right decision," Hallie murmured.

"It must be the right decision for the Tesoro name," Pliny insisted, guiding the boat into a small harbor.

Hallie shivered under the hot sun. She couldn't understand how Sophia and Pliny cared more about the Tesoro name than about the members of the family. She remembered how Sophia refused to allow Portia and Marcus to go with their mother. She pictured Marcus, a small boy with his father's blue eyes, and Portia, practically a baby, forced to stay when Francesca returned to America.

"I want you to enjoy your holiday." Pliny smiled. "Lake Como in August is for lovers and dreamers. Sophia is holding a feast tonight in your honor."

Hallie watched the village of Bellagio appear beyond the curve of the lake. The promenade was lined with olive trees and the villas were surrounded by gardens as large as parks. Hallie saw the Hotel Metropole perched above the dock, and a string of cafés where smartly dressed tourists ate shrimp and paella.

Hallie turned to Pliny. "I'd be happy with a plate of antipasto and a bowl of fresh berries."

"There will be antipasto and prosciutto and every kind of fruit. The cooks have been preparing for days and Sophia sent Lea to the market twice this morning." Pliny steered the boat into a small cove.

The chatter of tourists and the *put-put* of motors were replaced by silence. A fish poked its head above the water and dove back under the surface. Hallie glanced up at the Tesoro villa and saw grand balconies with wrought-iron railings, stone walls covered in ivy, and glimpses of marble through open windows.

"Sophia has invited Riccardo and all their friends." Pliny tied the boat up at the private dock. "He wouldn't dream of refusing the invitation. Sophia is hoping for a reconciliation."

"Hallie!" A young woman with raven black hair and large brown eyes ran down to the dock. She wore an orange chiffon skirt and a white halter top. She had gold hoop earrings in her ears and leather sandals with colored ribbons on her feet.

"Portia," Hallie said, and hugged her sister. Hallie felt sharp bones through the halter top and could see the outline of Portia's rib cage.

"Infidelity is wonderful for the diet," Portia said, laughing. "I look like a prison camp survivor."

"You're gorgeous," Hallie replied. Even with the skin pulled tight on her cheeks and the sharp angles of her hips, Portia was strikingly beautiful. Her hair was glossy as paint and her mouth was an invitation to be kissed.

"Sophia hired a hairdresser and a masseuse," Portia said, and grimaced. "She wants me to look my best tonight. I'm like a can of meat trying to push back its sell-by date."

"In America you'd be a supermodel." Hallie followed Portia up the winding path to the house.

"Apparently Riccardo likes more buxom women." Portia shrugged. "His mistress has the hips of a Venetian courtesan."

"Pliny told me that Sophia wants you to take Riccardo

back," Hallie said. She put her hand on Portia's arm. "You don't have to settle, you can have any man."

Portia was about to speak, but looked up and saw her grandmother appear on the balcony. Sophia was dressed in black silk and her white hair framed her face like a helmet. She stood with her arms on the railing, a diamond-and-ruby bracelet glinting in the sun.

Hallie saw a flicker in Portia's brown eyes, like a flame trying to ignite. Portia slipped her arm through Hallie's and skipped toward the house.

"I feel better already," Portia whispered as they approached the stairs. "After lunch we'll go to the garden. I'll show you my new archery set."

"Sounds dangerous," Hallie said, giggling. "I wonder who's the target."

Hallie and Portia climbed the stone steps to the balcony, where Sophia waited to greet them. Sophia was petite like Portia, with a tiny waist and small hands and feet. Her face was lined and blue veins covered her wrists, but her eyes belonged on a Siamese cat. She looked at Hallie closely, as if inspecting a new couture gown.

"You are a true beauty," Sophia said finally. "I see little resemblance to your mother."

Hallie bit back a reply and smiled graciously. "Francesca says I take after my grandmother."

"Constance is a formidable foe but a fine woman," Sophia said, and nodded. "I haven't seen her since she and her husband stayed at the villa years ago. Theodore liked to play cards, and Constance was fond of a glass of Drambuie after dinner."

Hallie tried to keep her face expressionless. She knew Constance had visited Lake Como when Portia and Marcus were young, but she never said she stayed at the villa. Hallie imagined Constance and Theodore dining with Sophia and Pliny and shivered.

"I gather Constance never told Francesca she was our guest." Sophia smiled as if she could read Hallie's mind.

"Hallie's been on a plane for hours," Portia interrupted. "Let her shower and change."

"Lea has prepared brunch." Sophia moved toward the house. "We will eat and then you can take a siesta before the evening's celebration."

Hallie followed Sophia through the double glass doors into the foyer. She had forgotten the scope of the house, the sweeping marble staircase, the intricate murals painted on the ceiling. Every chair, love seat, and ottoman was covered in thick gold brocade. It was like standing inside a jewelry box.

"Portia tells me you have taken up interior design," Sophia said.

"I work for one of the premier designers in San Francisco," Hallie said, nodding.

"Maybe you can teach Portia." Sophia walked through double oak doors into the family dining room. "If she had an interest she wouldn't concern herself with Riccardo's peccadilloes."

"Veronica is not a peccadillo. She's a twenty-two-year-old actress with breasts like hot air balloons and the hair of Medusa," Portia muttered, putting a celery stick and a baby carrot on a dessert plate.

"Riccardo will tire of her." Sophia shrugged. "They always do."

The table was covered with a burgundy tablecloth and set with inlaid china. Crystal pitchers held fresh juice and stone platters overflowed with fruits and vegetables. There were eggs simmering under silver domes, whipped mashed potatoes in warming trays, grilled mushrooms and tomatoes.

"It is healthy to eat a large midday meal," Sophia said, and handed Hallie a plate. "Tonight you will dance it off."

Hallie felt the jet lag return, crushing her like a boulder. She filled the plate with melon balls, strips of ham, and green olives. She poured a glass of cranberry juice and sat in one of the ornate brocade chairs. She tried to bring the fork to her mouth but suddenly she grew dizzy.

"I'm sorry." Hallie gulped, trying to stop the room from spinning. "The jet lag caught up with me."

"Are you feeling ill?" Pliny appeared from the foyer. He walked over to the table and touched Hallie's arm. "My mother has never been on an airplane, she doesn't understand how travel can affect you."

"I could use a glass of water," Hallie murmured.

"You need to put something solid in your stomach," Pliny insisted. "I will fix you a plate."

Portia ran to the kitchen to get a glass of water. Pliny strode quickly around the table and set a full plate in front of Hallie.

"Eat, you will feel better," he prompted.

Hallie's head tipped forward and she knocked the plate on the floor. Eggs and prosciutto spilled onto the ceramic tile and the plate shattered into pieces. She slumped in the chair and the stained-glass windows, the plastered walls, the gold drapes disappeared. She let the cool blackness swallow her up like Alice falling down the rabbit hole.

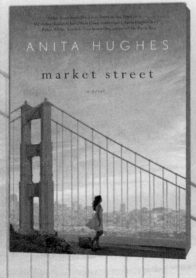

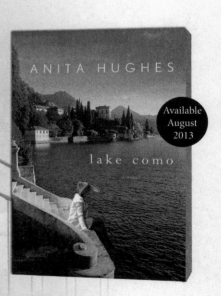

"If Candace Bushnell has a West Coast counterpart, Anita Hughes is it!"

—Karen White, *New York Times* bestselling author of *Sea Change*